Ellen the Bride

Book 3 of the Ellen the Harpist Series

Diane Michaels

MiddleRun Press
New York

MiddleRun Press
New York, NY
info@middlerunpress.com

First edition: June 2018

ISBN 978-0-9977107-7-9

TO KEVIN

CONTENTS

"WHY DO WE NEED an effing swear jar?" My eyes darted between the scowl on Chloe's face and the Mason jar on steroids she had shoved in front of me.

Her chest rising and falling with an exasperated sigh, she said, "It's not a swear jar. I'm making you pay a dollar each time you begin a conversation with, 'I was thinking about my wedding' or turn any conversation we're having into a wedding planning session."

My face crumpled into a mirror image of her grimace. "Geez, Chloe! Josh proposed to me less than forty-eight hours ago. You can't ban me from talking about my wedding, especially since you will be my best woman. It's your job to help me with the preparations. If you're going to penalize me rather than help, I'm changing your title back to *maid of honor.*" I spun my engagement ring in angry circles around my ring finger.

My housemate's cheeks inflated in an effort to slow the outward flow of air through her pursed lips. "I'm thrilled for you and Josh. And I can't wait to help you put together a gorgeous and festive celebration. Before your wedding takes over our lives, though, we need to establish guidelines. Isn't it better for you to toss a dollar bill into the jar every once in a while rather than to let the wedding become a sore spot between us?"

"It sounds overly harsh to me. Not to mention expensive. I will have to talk about my wedding with you. A lot. Planning it will be a big part of my life from now until my wedding day. And I value your input." I cocked my head. "Will you allow me to discuss the wedding with you after I've put money into the jar? And what happens to the money at the end?"

"Each dollar buys you a session of uninterrupted wedding discussion. The money will be mine, however. A consolation prize for enduring your endless chatter. I promise you can talk about the wedding as often as you like so long as you faithfully contribute to the jar."

At least she wasn't prohibiting me from ever mentioning the wedding. It still didn't sound fair, though. "What are you going to buy with my money?"

"Noise canceling headphones." Chloe plunked the jar on the coffee table with a thud. The sound of one hard object meeting another resonated with finality. I trumped her last word on the subject with the squeal of my sneakers grinding against the wood floor as I pivoted away from her. Chloe halted my emphatic exit. Extending her arms, she reeled me into her chest for a bear hug. "Come here, you! I am so freaking excited for the two of you. I really am. Who knows? Perhaps I'll never shut up about your wedding, and you'll never have to put money into the jar. I have so many ideas to make your wedding perfect! Have you guys set a date?"

Josh floored me with his proposal two nights ago. It wasn't that I hadn't thought about us getting married. Before he left to play the violin on a Broadway tour, before I embarked on my cruise adventure, I had imagined having a discussion with him about us getting hitched at some point in the future. The wrenching afternoon we spent together in Port Canaveral three and a half months ago threatened to rob us of any future together.

Life had been perfect since we repaired our rift two months ago. I hadn't yet allowed myself to consider the next phase of our relationship. Being a couple, being in love was enough. A glance at the glittering reminder on my ring finger of how much Josh loved me erased the frustrations Chloe had raised in me. I grew warm and still. As oversized as my happiness was, the smile acknowledging it required only a slight upturn from my lips. Two yellow-green stones formerly employed as a pair of eyes on the owl locket he had given to me for my birthday sat on either side of a round half-carat diamond perched atop a gold band. I resisted the urge to hold up my hand to the light, a new habit I had developed. I didn't want Chloe to start charging me whenever she caught me admiring the setting. Her muffled cough hinted that she might.

"The ironic thing is, considering your new penalty system, we've agreed to delay the start of making plans for the wedding." I had yet told anyone — even Josh after I had arrived at this decision on Friday night — the reason I had insisted we hold off on the preparations. Riding the wave of excitement over our engagement kept leading me to an imaginary precipice. When I peered over the edge, the thrill of being engaged morphed into a sensation similar to walking onto a stage to play a concert for which I hadn't prepared.

Spending the rest of my life with Josh hadn't triggered my dread. I loved him with every fiber of my being. Planning a big shindig wasn't responsible for making me nervous, either. I knew way more about the inner workings of weddings than most brides-to-be, having played the harp at nearly two hundred of them.

Besides my own expertise, I'd have my friend Amber's help when she was home on shore leave. It had been over a year and a half since I had played on one of the spectacular weddings she used to coordinate. Thanks to a disgruntled former assistant, our last wedding together in New York had been a near disaster, not to mention a career-ender for her. She had escaped the humiliation by becoming the activities director aboard a cruise ship.

Amber was the fourth person I had called on Friday night. My mother was the first, and calls to my other college BFF Gwen and my brother Nathan had followed. My mother responded to my news as if I had fired a starting pistol. Who knew she was such a fan of weddings? If the thirteen emails and seven phone calls I'd received from her over the last two days offered any indication of her obsession, I didn't know the half of it.

My mom and I didn't have the ideal mother-daughter relationship thing going for us. Spending time with her always set me on edge. I shuddered at the thought of planning a wedding together. One of us may have to apply for a restraining order. Maybe I should borrow Chloe's idea and introduce her to her own swear jar for overzealous wedding planners.

With Amber's help, I hoped to hold my mother in check. Putting off making any plans was less likely. Nearing the end of her vacation, Amber would join up with the Orpheus again in three weeks, not to return home until early November. The smart thing would be to create the framework for our wedding with her before she left and start fleshing it out on our own later in the summer. I was sure I'd be over my inexplicable fears by then.

Was I supposed to fill a scrapbook with ideas for the big day? It seemed way too Pinterest-y, and I didn't do Pinterest. Closing my eyes, I scanned the wedding tableau forming in my mind. Me, smiling. Josh doing the same. I was in white, holding a bouquet. What did the dress look like? Or the flowers? The image was too fuzzy. Chloe and Gwen were beside me. OK, I'd invite my mom. Boom. Now she was in the picture, standing with Nathan and his partner Derrick. Everyone had this knowing, insipid smile on their face. Great. I was taking part in a cult wedding. Pass the poisoned Kool-Aid, please.

It was just a wedding. All we needed were two people in love and someone to make it legal. And a wedding venue, some tasty food, fancy clothes, and music to underscore the whole thing. Throw in flowers, photographers, a cake, and we'd be done. Well, we'd have to choose our wedding date and decide whom to invite. But still. How hard could planning a wedding be?

"What about having our wedding at the Central Park Boathouse? Or ooh! Oheka Castle. How about Oheka?" I nibbled a French fry, waiting for Amber's reply.

"Are you kidding me? Do you think I can ever set foot in the Boathouse again after the last nightmare of a wedding? Even if they haven't banned me, the venue is beyond the range of your budget. As is Oheka. Tell me why you like each of the sites. Your descriptions will help me put together a list of alternatives."

I ticked off ideas with my fingertips, counting each against my palm. "I want to be the only bride at the venue on my wedding day. I prefer spaces with natural light streaming through windows. The Boathouse has a quiet, woodsy feel, which appeals to me. On the other hand, Oheka's opulence holds a certain appeal. I love how, for a single day, you can pretend the mansion is your own home. And playing the harp at the top of the main staircase is the best! Those acoustics are amazing. Oh, but of course I'm not going to play at my own wedding. Now, where was I?"

Amber snickered. "I have a good sense of which qualities appeal to you. Should we search for a site in New York City or on Long Island? We can probably stretch your budget further in New Jersey."

"Let's start with New Jersey. But if you know of a great venue on the Island, I'll consider it."

"Give me a few days to brainstorm. When do you and Josh want to tie the knot?"

I bobbled my head, undecided. "Can we plan a wedding in only six or seven months? Mid-January to the end of March would be the perfect timeframe for us. Our work schedules will be at their lightest then."

"So, what you're saying is you want to hold your wedding aboard the Orpheus?" Amber squawked with amusement.

"No! Don't torture me!" It still bothered me that my gig aboard the Orpheus had ended in such an ignoble manner. While I doubted I would have agreed to sign on for a second contract had everything worked according to plan, I hated having a black mark on my employment record. "Why would you even suggest such a thing?"

"Didn't I tell you? I've decided to spend one more winter on the ship before calling it quits. I'll be back in New York for good next May ready to launch wedding career 2.0. Yours can be my first. You could be a June bride. How perfect would that be?"

The second Amber said *June bride*, I freaked out. Trust me, I was clueless about my reaction. I hooked my pointer over the edge of the neckline of my t-shirt, fanning myself with the cloth. The increased airflow couldn't slow my beating heart. Chugging the remains of my water, I waved to our server with my empty glass.

"Are you OK there, Ellen? You look a bit flushed. Usually, a less than committed groom or a parent reluctant to have to pay for the affair has the first panic attack. I wouldn't have pegged you as the jittery sort."

I silently tried to determine the cause of my panic attack. Given my mother's obsession with planning our wedding, I knew we could count on her to help foot the bills. Why was I quaking in my shoes?

Right after my mother congratulated us the night I had called her to tell her Josh had proposed, she mentioned what a shame it was my father wouldn't be walking me down the aisle. As soon as the words were out of her mouth, she brushed the thought away. Could that be my problem? While the sadness of not sharing the day with him lurked in the back of my mind, I knew I could celebrate my marriage without him. I'd never stop missing him, but I had contained the ache of his absence since his death nearly two years ago.

Because I had spent much of my career serenading couples during their wedding ceremonies, I had a unique perspective on what it meant to be a bride. Some brides naturally possessed the regal bearing of Kate Middleton. Others came across like girls playing princess for the day. An annoying few behaved like characters on the worst kind of reality TV show. I wasn't the princess type. I feared bridal conventions and expectations would drive me to become someone I was not. Could this be the source of my anxiety?

"Promise me you won't let me become a Bridezilla?" I begged Amber.

"Ha! You're the last person I'd expect to become a Bridezilla. Planning a wedding is about making good decisions and sticking with them, something Bridezillas are terrible at doing. Figure out what you want, and if what you want suits Josh, your families, and your budget. I'll guide you through the trickier decisions. Don't try to control everything. You don't have to arrange the flowers, bake the cake, or even play the music at your wedding. Choose wedding vendors with whom you can communicate well and trust them to take care of you on your wedding day. Your job will be to say, 'I do.' The vendors and I will manage the rest. Everything will be perfect."

I freed my neck from its rigid pose. "You're right. Planning my wedding is too grown up an activity, though. I've had my fill of adulting for the day. I'm going to order the clown ice-cream cone, and you can't stop me."

"Would you order it to go? I have a doctor's appointment to get to."

A few minutes later, I stopped in front of a garbage can in the subway station into which we had entered to lick the remains of ice cream drippings from my hand. A noise not dissimilar to a colony of penguins screeching out the song *Clocks* during mating season distracted me. Bending to pick up the napkin I had dropped, I twisted my head over my shoulder to seek the source of the cacophony. It came from a young woman coaxing the offending wails out of a violin. A tip bucket sat empty in front of her. As Amber and I walked by her, I held my hands over my ears.

She stopped playing when she noticed me. "Yo! You! Yeah, you with your ears covered. Do you have any idea how hard it is to be a musician? I'd like to see you try!" With a glare that may well have put a curse on me, she resumed her efforts to scare away the other subway riders.

With mock sincerity, Amber said, "Ah, New York! I will miss this place when I leave next month!"

"You should consider taking her with you. Should I ask if she has a CD for sale?" With a laugh, we hugged before running off to catch our trains.

I RAN OUT OF FINGERS long before Josh ran out of names to rattle off to me. "Oh, I forgot my cousin Gus. His was the first wedding I was in if you don't count the time I was a ring bearer for my babysitter."

"Are you going to ask your babysitter to be in our wedding party, too?" I had no control over the flow of sarcasm oozing from my mouth. Something had to fill the hollow in my gut. Josh's unending litany of best buds had emptied me of my self-worth.

Chloe and Gwen had agreed to be my best women. (Can I tell you how incensed Chloe was when I dared to ask her to be my maid of honor? No insult could be greater than calling her a maid, I'd since learned.) My best friend from high school, Sheila, also accepted my invitation to be in our wedding party. Josh had asked his two brothers to be his best men (they rejected my suggestion of being called dudes of honor, however). Now he planned to add a dozen of the friends he had collected since birth to the party. Oh, and Cousin Gus. It worked out to five guys for every woman.

A panicked expression contorted my face. Josh responded with confused guilt. "How many guys are normally in a wedding party?"

"Not fifteen. My minuscule line of attendants will disappear next to your unending assemblage of friends." I spread my arms apart to signify his army of buddies. To illustrate the contrast, I drew my pointer fingers five inches apart from each other to represent my depleted troops.

He ruffled my hair with a laugh. "So have more than three bridesmaids."

Swatting away his hand, I said, "Brideswomen, Josh. You heard Chloe go off on this topic the night you proposed. I suppose I could ask Amber. And my best friend from elementary school, Amy. My mom has already put her parents on the guest list. But I don't have tons of friends like you. Besides, if I did wrangle enough friends to match the number of groomsmen you've chosen, there would be thirty people in the wedding party, sixty if they each brought a plus one. My mom would freak if the wedding party comprised half the guest list."

"I don't have to invite everyone I've mentioned to be in the wedding party. Or even to come to the wedding. I could pare my list down to six or seven. Eight, tops." He snuck a peek at his phone, eager to avoid getting sucked into our first wedding-related tiff.

While he detached himself from the conversation, anxieties slithered around inside me, turning my brain into a martial arts training center. There was no way I could let him leave the ninjas he had recruited unsupervised. "I still have only five attendants."

"Ask Nathan. Derrick, too. He'd be the perfect guy to have in a wedding party. Hmm. Maybe I'll ask him."

"Don't you dare! He's mine." We hadn't even begun to plan our wedding in earnest and already my blood pressure rose with each conversation I had about it. Basic things took on significant meaning when you attached the word *wedding* to them. Chloe, Gwen, and I had long ago planned to be in each other's bridal parties. I couldn't wait to share my wedding day with my BFFs. Our casual discussions hadn't factored in the sorts of complications I'd encountered in planning a real wedding. Now, even the simple task of populating the altar had become a competitive sport, *Ellen v. Josh*. "Sorry. Getting hitched is supposed to be fun. Let's agree to find the most laid-back solution to every potential problem we encounter. Why don't you choose just seven groomsmen? I'll ask Amber, Amy, Nathan, and Derrick. If one of your guys gets his nose out of joint for not being included in the wedding party, have him give a reading."

"Works for me. Let's pick a code word. Shout it out whenever you need me to dial it back."

"Chloe." I tilted my head toward the door to my apartment.

"Chloe? Kind of an odd choice, but OK."

"No. I don't mean *Chloe* is the code word. I mean I hear the jingle of her keys in the hallway. She and I had our own wedding frictions to avoid. If she heard us talking about the wedding, it would cost me yet another dollar. I'd already lost seven to the Censorship Jar. She promised she'd join the wedding conversation whenever I threw money into the jar, but she never paid attention to me when I did. My discussions about the wedding had become an excuse for her to drift off in thought or to grumble to herself."

Chloe had gone through a rough patch aboard the cruise ship this past winter. While it pained me to admit it, initially, I had been a bit of a pill about taking the four-month gig on the Orpheus. I had spent most of the first week complaining. Chloe, on the other hand, couldn't have been more enthusiastic about embarking on our adventure. A month into the contract, I began to have fun (except for the part about missing Josh while he was away on his Broadway tour). She, meanwhile, underwent a change of heart. She didn't own up to the source of her unhappiness until the day we were thrown off the ship following an environmental protest she had staged. Even in offering her explanation about the cause of her breakdown, she left part of it unspoken. Two and a half months later, I was still clueless, and she showed no signs of having made a full recovery.

Minus the two years she had spent at the San Francisco Conservatory pursuing her master's degree, Chloe and I had lived together for nearly eleven years, since orientation week of our freshman year of college at Indiana University. She and Gwen became my best friends right from the start of college. Gwen was warmth and optimism embodied. Chloe's warmth radiated at a different temperature than Gwen's, but it, too, blanketed me with love, comfort, and support. Quick to share advice and clothes, she gave freely, often before I knew what it was I even needed. And no one was more adept at guiding me through my personal crises.

Chloe was confident, outgoing, determined, and a born leader. I'd never known her to flounder on her path in life until we were aboard the ship. With a temporary surge of energy generated by her anger at falling ill with the norovirus in March, she focused her attention on making her stand against cruise ship buffets, an unworthy enemy if you ask me. Her plan involved us gluing place settings to the deck. Needless to say, things ended badly. Since being fired, Chloe had slipped into a passive, less in-control state of being.

It would be self-centered of me to suppose my engagement impacted her mood. She had been down on marriage for the past couple of years, but she had never resented my relationship with Josh. Exempting her fixation on the wedding jar, I knew she was happy for us.

Maybe her extended celibacy streak had eroded her confidence. She stopped hooking up with guys before we boarded the ship in January. And she hadn't been in a committed relationship since she broke up with Elliott nearly two years ago. Whatever was keeping her from finding her groove, Chloe would probably do what she always did: avoid talking about it until she could no longer contain her emotional response to the problem. I wished I could help her, but I've learned the hard way interfering only makes things worse for both of us.

Chloe returned home from teaching in time to hear the tail end of my conversation with Josh about the size of our wedding party. She twisted her lips to the side, eying the jar on the coffee table. I made a lip-zipping gesture with my hand. With a shrug, she set her bag on the dining table.

"Good day at the office, honey?" I tossed a friendly smile at her.

"Yeah. I'm loving being a flute teacher. I didn't expect to miss teaching my students during winter, but I did. It's so cool when something I've been telling them to do all along suddenly makes sense to them. One kid had a huge breakthrough today. You should have seen the grin on his face. I'm so proud of him!"

"It makes you an awesome teacher to be able to draw the best out of your students and to share their joy."

She scrunched her face. "If I were such a great teacher, he wouldn't have struggled in the first place. I'm just glad he overcame his hurdle."

"Students have to be ready to move forward. We can offer motivation along with our expertise, but the students will do with it what they will."

"Tons of teachers I know have studios filled with students who are constantly improving. It's got to be something I'm doing wrong."

I reached for her shoulder. "Uneven progress is normal. I wouldn't believe any teacher who told me otherwise. You shouldn't be so hard on yourself."

Josh hugged Chloe. "Like she said. Hey, I have to head back to Clifton to meet a friend. I'll call you later."

"Just don't offer him a gig in our wedding party." With a kiss and a laugh, Josh headed home.

I fished a dollar from my wallet, waving it in Chloe's face. She snatched it from my fingers and deposited it into the jar. I said, "I don't have much wedding nonsense to spew, I promise. Josh had a brilliant idea: I may ask Nathan and Derrick to be bridesdudes. Should I?"

"Great idea! But weren't you going to ask Nathan to walk you down the aisle?"

"Eh. I'm backing away from having him process with me. If my dad were alive, I'd definitely do the traditional thing because it would have been special, me being his little girl. But why should one man walk me down the aisle in order to hand me off to another man? I'm a grown-ass adult — quit snickering. I am! I'm not anyone's to give away. Even without the celebrant asking, 'Who gives this woman to be married to this man?' having an escort implies that if a man has to lead me to my future groom, I'm not doing so of my free will."

"You make a really good point. You and Josh could process together."

I furrowed my brow in thought. "Hmm. Food for thought. I don't want to ditch every tradition, though. I have an image in my mind of seeing each other for the first time on our wedding day from opposite ends of the aisle. It will be perfect, in a simple, heartfelt kind of way. But just by staging it, I'll end up turning it into some diva-like huge entrance." My throat tightened, and my shoulders crept toward my ears. "Now I'm second guessing everything I've decided about the processional. I swear! I have no control over anything. Planning a wedding doesn't follow a logical path. Each detail opens a new vein of indecision. Even if I can figure out what I want to do, I'm still going to have to run every decision I make by my mother. I guarantee she'll challenge me on things like having men as my attendants or for not having a man walk me down the aisle. What do they say about spicy food? It burns twice?"

"Tee hee! You may very well be the first bride to liken planning a wedding to sitting on the can the morning after having indulged in some particularly hot Thai food. Don't assume you and your mother are going to clash over every detail. You're guaranteeing you will fight by expecting the worst from her. The smartest thing you can do is to choose your battles. Figure out which parts of the day matter the most to you. Be ready to acquiesce to her on certain things. Even if she makes some suggestion you absolutely hate, let her know you listened to her rather than show her you're mad at her for making suggestions."

"You really are the best woman! To show my undying gratitude, I'll call it quits on wedding talk for the day. Is it wine o'clock now?" I asked, ready to move on from talking about my wedding.

"Is it ever! I thought you'd never ask."

I DEVELOPED an obsession the day I agreed to sign a contract to take a gig aboard the Orpheus. Each time I had driven into Manhattan via the Lincoln Tunnel before I signed on, I craned my neck to glance across the Hudson River at the cruise ship terminal in hopes a ship or two would be in port. Upon spying the gleaming mass of a ship in its berth, I had imagined the excitement bubbling inside each passenger boarding the vessel. I wondered where the crew members would be spending their precious hours of free time away from the ship.

With three months of cruising under my belt, I had retained my fascination with seeing the cruise ships in the harbor despite my lack of interest in working aboard one again. Spotting an unfamiliar ship, I'd momentarily yearn to be aboard before I shook off the impulse. Twice since I disembarked in disgrace, my gaze fell unexpectedly upon the Orpheus, an experience akin to running into an ex. My stomach tied itself into a tight knot, and my lungs forgot to expel my last breath. *How can the ship's presence surprise me?* I'd asked myself. The Orpheus docked in New York City every Sunday. I cursed myself for being foolish enough to have forgotten I would see her when the Hudson came into view.

I wasn't heading to Manhattan this morning. I took the last exit before the tunnel. The road descended toward sea level underneath the helix. The voice on my GPS app chirped a series of turns. Obediently, I followed her. One last left turn put the Hudson River, flowing past me on the right, nearly even with the road. The butt end of the Orpheus saluted me from her berth.

I had spent the first two weeks aboard the ship under the tutelage of a pianist named Sheldon. I had no say in the matter. He ingratiated himself into my life, spewing harsh critiques at me with the intention of developing me into a master, like him, of the art of playing background music. I would have been an idiot to shun him and his expert advice, demoralizing though it was. After he disembarked, I unpacked the information dump he had left behind. It took some time, but I've since acknowledged the best part of working aboard the Orpheus was becoming a better entertainer, thanks to Sheldon.

And thanks to Sheldon, I was on my way to a gig. A friend of his managed a restaurant in Weehawken. She asked him for his advice about adding live music to their Sunday brunch. He sold both her and the owners on the idea of hiring a harpist. Me. They agreed to bring me in for one day to see if I was a good fit for the restaurant. Maybe playing brunch at the Vista today would turn into a steady gig, the Holy Grail for a freelance musician.

With wedding research dominating my screen time, I hadn't bothered to google the venue. Half a mile before I reached my destination, it dawned on me my gig would come with a view of the Hudson River. And the Orpheus. My stomach eschewed the simpler slipknot I had tied it in earlier in favor of a clove hitch.

The Vista sul Mare restaurant jutted out over the Hudson. Seagulls dotted its blue roof and the tops of the wooden piles piercing the gray-green waves of the river. While the restaurant's view of my former performance space hadn't won me over, a parking spot within feet of the building did. The sky was overcast. With rain in this afternoon's forecast, the shorter my harp's trip to my car at four o'clock, the better.

It wouldn't have been the hardest trip I had ever made from my car to a venue had I chosen to bring my harp, bench, and amplifier inside all at once. I opted to walk through the front door on my first trip like a civilized being rather than a pack mule. I had over an hour to make a second trip with my harp and amplifier before the start of the gig.

A brick path led me to a door on the side of the building. Always thinking like a harpist, I tested the door to check if it would stay open on its own. No such luck. I've wheeled my harp through tricky doors before. On the occasions when holding a door open while wheeling the harp through it required acrobatic moves, I've considered my circus-like entrance to be my warm-up act before the main event.

My bench in my left hand, I shrugged my gig bag higher onto my right shoulder, scanning inside the dining room for a person who appeared to be in charge. The room was quiet. I measured my steps across the blue and gray wave-like patterned carpet. Around each square table, wooden chairs with navy seat cushions waited to welcome guests. Glassware sparkled atop white tablecloths. Napkins in a simple fold rested on plates. The decor knew better than to compete with the view of the New York skyline and the river shimmering beyond the walls of windows.

"Are you Ellen?" a chic, middle-aged woman called out to me. She wore a gray pencil skirt, a white blouse, and a buttonless gray and black jacket whose bottom edge hung below the hem of her skirt. She had tucked her wavy, dark hair into a low bun. A ribbon of white hair wove its way along the right border of her face.

"Yes, I am." I extended my hand to shake hers.

"Welcome! Sheldon has said such nice things about you. I'm Helena, the manager. Let me show you where to set up."

I followed her to the far corner of the dining room, setting my bench in front of the corner formed by the meeting of two walls of windows. The Orpheus hunkered down in the harbor opposite us. I gave her a stern glare, warning her to keep to her side of the river.

Helena lingered next to me without speaking, giving me the impression I had to start a conversation with her. "So, you and Sheldon know each other?" Duh. I knew they did. No other topic had come to mind, though.

"I just love Sheldon! Claude and Lily, the owners here, have another successful restaurant on the Upper East Side. It's where I began my career years ago, first as a hostess and then as a manager. Sheldon was a regular fixture behind the piano. The food always was good, but Claude and Lily owe much of their early success to him. Obviously, the location here is the star. But the restaurant needs more than a view and a skilled chef to make it special. We came to the conclusion live music was the way to go. Sheldon wasn't interested in the job, but he sang your praises. I can't wait to hear you play!"

"Sheldon sets the bar very high. I believe I learned more from him in the two weeks we worked together aboard a ship — that ship, in fact — than I have over four years in music school and my career thus far. I'm super excited to have the opportunity to play here today. The setting is gorgeous!"

"It is, isn't it? I'm sure you'll be a perfect fit for the Vista. I have to get back to work. Let me know if you need anything!"

I returned to my car to retrieve my harp and amplifier. My instrument took to its new home in front of the view like a diva chewing the scenery at the Metropolitan Opera. The medium brown-stained wood was a shade darker than the chairs in the room. The harp cast a muted reflection onto the windows behind me, mimicking the skyscrapers of the New York skyline.

Aboard the Orpheus, I rarely saw daylight, land, or even the sea while I played. At the Vista, I would trade the rocking ship for a richer sense of being on the water, one I knew would inspire my music.

A steady, once-a-week brunch would bring welcome stability to my income in the leaner months. I built my performance schedule around a sparsely populated weekly teaching schedule. On one given day, I might perform with a symphony in a fancy concert hall; the next, I'd be playing Disney tunes at a baby shower in someone's living room. During the busy holiday season, I stuffed gigs into every minute of every day, knowing full well the first two or three months of the year would be a bust, workwise.

At noon, guests streamed into the room. In tribute to my mentor, I began my first set with Sheldon's favorite medley of songs from *The Sound of Music*. I itched to show off a touch of my personality with a few current tunes, but I used Sheldon's tips for reading the room. Until the mimosas and Bloody Mary's flowed readily, the mood in the room remained staid. I matched the tone, alternating between light classical repertoire, Broadway favorites, and the occasional jazz standard. Near the end of my first set, I pushed through the decades, landing in the early nineteen-seventies with John Lennon's *Imagine*.

Servers had stopped to admire the harp while I tuned my instrument. I was at best a novelty who was easy to ignore when their jobs kicked into high gear. But my foray into popular repertoire drew their attention to me like a siren's song. A marked difference between playing a single engagement like a wedding and performing on a steady (or potentially steady) gig was whether I focused on connecting solely with the guests or if I included the staff as part of my audience.

When I was on the Orpheus, I worked with the same crew members for weeks on end. Their demanding jobs kept them from socializing with the harpist most of the time. In lieu of conversation, I would treat them by playing their favorite tunes. While I played *Imagine* in the Vista, I read the name tags pinned to each server's navy button-down shirt, memorizing my new colleagues' names and faces when they again approached my harp. I hoped forging a bond with them through my selections could play a role in persuading Claude and Lily to hire me full-time. With each pop or rock song I played, my list of allies grew.

Across the room, an older gentleman pointed at me while he spoke to Helena. I changed my mind about what to play next. For him, I chose a song by the Gershwin brothers rather than the Gallagher brothers. Helena escorted her companion to my side. I faded out of the chorus of *Nice Work If You Can Get It* to shake the man's outstretched hand.

I sweated through the effort of retaining my smile rather than letting a wince twist my features in reaction to the pain caused by his bone-crushing grip. "Ellen is it? I'm Claude. Does this thing go any louder?"

Keep smiling, Ellen. "Would you like me to raise the volume on the amplifier?" I asked.

"I suppose that would help. We keep the piano in the center of the room at our other restaurant, but a similar set-up won't work here. The guests seated near the entrance probably can't hear you. If they don't know you're here, why are we paying a musician?" He swiveled his head toward the tables at the far side of the room.

Helena touched his shoulder, reengaging him in our conversation. "I've heard from guests throughout the room about how they've enjoyed the music. I'm sure raising the level on the amplifier will allow Ellen to reach everyone in the room." She returned my smile.

"Well, it's worth a try." Without a single nicety, he walked away. I raised a pair of crossed fingers at Helena. My eyes conveyed my concern.

"Leave him to me. I'll make sure he comes around. Sheldon was right: you are a fabulous musician! I've heard lots of great feedback from both guests and the staff. Let me know when you're ready to eat; I'll have a plate for you in the back."

A window-shaking bellow from the Orpheus' horn marked the end of my last set. Like the dockworkers untethering the ship from the pier, I prepared for my own departure. I hoped I'd be back again, but Claude's reaction had filled me with a sense of doom.

Helena adjusted my harp cover around the column of my harp as I slung the cover over the instrument. "Good news, though hardly unexpected. Claude has agreed you should play for us again. For the time being, can we book you for the next four Sundays?"

"Absolutely! I've loved playing here today. And everyone, well, almost everyone, is so nice."

"Claude and Lily are really lovely people to work for. Don't let his gruff nature put you off. He's often slow to commit to changes. I'm sure it will turn out just fine for you in the end. We'll see you again next week, in any event!"

"I FOUND THE **PERFECT** PLACE!" I pulled the phone away from my ear to lessen my exposure to Amber's eardrum shredding shriek.

Rubbing my ear to restore what was left of my hearing, I asked, "Could you repeat what you said, only say it a little louder? I'm not sure my neighbors could hear you."

"Ha, ha. No, seriously. I'm so stoked. When are you free to go see it?"

"We're talking about a wedding venue, right?" Amber had caught me in the middle of calculating the impact playing a steady gig at the Vista would have on my income. "Sorry, my head's not quite in the wedding planning zone at the moment. Where is this perfect place?"

"Princeton. Even though I have tons to accomplish before I leave next Sunday, I will drop everything to join you when you take a tour of it. When do you want to go?"

"I'll have to check Josh's schedule. And, oh, I suppose my mother's, too."

Amber's enthusiasm raised the decibel level of her voice again. "I can't wait to reconnect with Lorraine!"

I shook my fist at the phone. "She asked you to call her by her first name, too? I'll never adjust to my friends calling her anything except for Mrs. Blum. The sea air had quite the effect on my mother." One week aboard the Orpheus in February had brought about huge changes in my mother, changes I would never have imagined possible. I should have been happy for her when, for the first time since my father had his first stroke seven years ago, she relaxed. After a year and a half of mourning his death, she had begun to laugh easily and often. The problem was the transformation came on the heels of her having met a man aboard the ship. Although she hadn't mentioned what's-his-name — um, was it Don? Doug? Ah, yes. Douglas — since she had disembarked, she had retained some of her sunniness. I guessed I couldn't complain if, in the end, I had a happier mother who criticized me less frequently.

I said, "I'll check everyone's schedule for tomorrow. We're kind of running out of time. We have to find a venue before you leave."

"I'm not worried. I bet you'll love it. It ticks all of your boxes."

"What's the name of the joint? I wonder if I've played there before."

"You haven't. Friends of mine bought a nineteen-twenties-era Normandy manor home in Princeton. It needs a lot of TLC. They've already renovated the carriage house and are living in it while they tackle the main home. They were telling me this morning they have their doubts about whether they will have the funds to do all the renovations the home deserves. I had a brainstorm: they can renovate the downstairs first, rent it out for events, and use the rental income to finish the renovations upstairs. Sid and Maxwell loved the idea and promised me they'll have the first floor done in time for you to be their first client."

I cocked my head. "Your description of it reminds me of Oheka Castle. I'm intrigued. I'll let you know if we can go down to Princeton tomorrow."

Minerva, my minivan, rolled under the wrought iron arch rising above the gates at the foot of the driveway to the manor. Red gravel crunched beneath her tires along the winding drive. A huge stone mansion came into view. Its grandeur and its dilapidated state tugged my emotions between the poles of excited and wary. Even from a distance, I could conceive how perfect a site the manor would be for our wedding. But the chewed-up lawn and broken windows let me know it wasn't ready to host any event besides a demolition derby. I pulled the van into a spot next to my mother's white sedan parked in front of the carriage house.

Shielding her eyes from the sun, my mother jerked her head like a chicken, taking in the piles of gravel, metal scraps, and trash scattered about the unkempt lawn. Josh, Chloe, Gwen, Amber, and I gathered around her.

"It looked more promising from afar. I'm not sure we want to make plans to hold a wedding someplace where they're not ready for us."

"Don't you worry, Lor..." Amber caught my challenging glare out of the corner of her eye. "Mrs. Blum. Sid and Maxwell are experts. They renovated their three previous homes. Plus they did the work on each of their store locations. We're going to meet Sid in their apartment above the garage. You'll know what they are capable of after we see their renovations firsthand."

A man about my mom's age descended a flight of stairs at the far end of the carriage house. "It's Amber, in the flesh!"

In her air horn screech, Amber yelled, "Sid, baby!" She broke into a trot, her arms ready to scoop him into a big hug. We followed behind with tentative steps. "C'mon, guys. Let me introduce you!"

Sid began the tour of the property by comparing the exterior of the carriage house to the manor itself. "We've cleaned the stonework and pointing, making repairs where needed. We will need to repoint sections of the main house, but overall, the structure is in decent shape. Obviously, we'll replace windows and paint the trim to match the carriage house," he said, indicating the sage green paint on the window frames and doors next to him. "We'll also be replanting shrubbery out front and around the back patio in the next phase of renovations. Plus disposing all the scrap metal strewn about the lawn. Unless you prefer post-apocalyptic landscaping, in which case, I'd recommend you check that you are up to date on your tetanus shots before the big day." My mother shivered as if a zombie had tickled her spine.

The interior of their apartment wiped the cringe off her face. The pristine finish on the wood floors and a generic decorating style like every *after* shot on an HGTV show drew her attention away from the detritus and disrepair of the rest of the property.

Gwen, Chloe, Josh, and I stayed in the kitchen while my mother and Amber cooed their way through the tour. I said, "We're not holding our wedding in the carriage house. I've seen enough to know Amber's friends can be trusted to renovate the manor. I'm dying to know if the house has beautiful architectural details. Nothing here reminds me of a historic home."

Leaning against the marble island, Josh drew me toward him. "Hey, you should be glad your mom has started to recognize the potential of the property. She certainly was not impressed with the venue before the tour began." I snuggled against his chest, my head rising with each of his breaths.

Gwen peered through the windows facing the manor house. "I bet it's going to be amazing inside! It sure is from the outside." She was the eternal optimist.

The tour group returned to the kitchen. My mother squinted at me. "Oh, you weren't with us? They've done a beautiful job here. I was saying to Sid I might just have to have him come to Westfield to give me some ideas for updating my condo."

"We'll be tied up here for a few years, but if you're still looking to do some work down the road, it would be a real treat to help you, Lorraine. Now, let's go see about a wedding venue."

I spun around inside the foyer of the manor, keeping my eyes fixed on the discolored wood beams above me rather than on the muddy outlines left behind by work boots that had trampled across the flattened boxes protecting the slate floor. A wooden staircase to the left of the front door rose to a landing at eye level. I climbed the first six steps, stopping on the landing to gaze through the windows onto the front lawn. Josh followed me, his arm finding my waist. "I can just picture how beautiful you'll be coming down the stairs on our wedding day!" He pointed to the top of the staircase high above us.

"I guarantee if I descend the stairs in a long gown and high heels, it will be via a series of unintentional somersaults."

"Ellen, come quick! You have to check out the library!" Chloe called from the room on the opposite side of the foyer.

I grasped for the wooden finial atop the post at the bottom step. It wobbled free from its perch, and I slipped off the last step with the grace of someone returning home at the end of a long pub crawl. Regaining my balance, I examined the orb in my hand. "Um, should that have happened?"

"Be careful, Ellen. You know this home is in a state of disrepair." My mother took the finial from my hand, sticking it onto the post with a harrumph. It fell off, clattering against the slate floor.

"Oh, I should have warned you about the finial. It has a mind of its own. Are you OK?" Sid asked.

I nodded. "Yeah. Sorry about destroying the place. Are you having second thoughts about inviting us to rent your home?"

"Don't be silly. Let's join your friends in the library. We had the idea you could use both the library and the informal living room during the cocktail hour."

Chloe clutched my arm. "Look at the ceiling! I want this to be my practice room. How inspiring it would be!" The intricate maze of the dark wood coffered ceiling rendered me speechless. "Don't you love it?"

My head, bouncing in agreement, traced an arc between my shoulders. The room was windowless. One door led in from the foyer and another opened into a living room. The four walls each housed floor-to-ceiling bookcases. A hammer lay on the wooden shelf next to me. A dust rag draped over the edge of another. Neither of these simple tools alone could possibly be capable of conquering the work needed to restore the scuffed-up, dust-covered shelves to their former glory.

"It may be smaller than the library at Oheka, but it's grand in its own way," Amber said.

Sid ushered us into the next room. "This would be the main room for cocktails. The French doors lead out to a patio and the backyard. Did Amber say you were considering a date in June? If the weather permits, the party can flow outdoors if you'd like."

"Oh, I hadn't thought about an outdoor wedding! We could hold the ceremony outside. What do you think of that idea, Ellen?" My mother's eyes shone like she was the first ever to latch onto such a special idea.

Chloe knew my response before I had filled my lungs in preparation for a rant. Saving me from myself, she said, "You're right. Outdoor weddings promise to be lovely. Unfortunately, Mrs. Blum, they often are anything but. Between uncomfortable weather conditions, bugs, and the sound of airplanes flying overhead, I recommend staying indoors for the ceremony and venturing outside for photos or the cocktail hour."

My mother smiled at Chloe. "I'm so glad we have you to give us your practical advice, Chloe!"

I continued to bite my tongue, choosing to appreciate having avoided an argument with my mother rather than fighting with her for her having overlooked the wedding expertise I possessed.

The six of us followed Sid like a line of ants on a picnic-crashing expedition throughout the rest of the tour. A formal living room abutted the dining room. Sid envisioned removing the wall between them, enlarging the space he recommended we could use for both the ceremony and the dinner reception.

Throughout the tour, I alternated between determining the venue to be perfect and harboring significant doubts it could rise above its shabby state before our wedding. My mother fed my doubts. She pointed out each rotted floorboard and flaking bit of plaster, clucking her tongue with disapproval. Amber and Chloe tag-teamed her. She listened to each of their counterarguments. By the end of the tour, they had accomplished what I knew I couldn't have done on my own.

"Well, Ellen. Is this where you want to get married?" she asked.

Josh and I raised our eyebrows at each other. He took my hand. "I think it will be perfect. But my opinion doesn't matter."

I detangled my fingers from his. "Why would you say that? Please don't leave me to make every decision."

Josh took a step backward. "I'm not dumping the decision making on your shoulders. I said I love it, but I don't want to pressure you to agree simply because I want to get married here. We're planning our wedding together. I was wrong: my opinions are equal to yours unless me having an opinion will complicate things." He squeezed my arm, his brown eyes limpid with the concern he had hurt me.

I waited to speak, allowing the pacing of my breath to slow lest I hyperventilate. "I like it, in theory. Amber, you really understand what I'm looking for in a venue. But I'm concerned about the amount of work needed to restore it. Will it be ready in time? We'll also have extra planning to do: hiring a caterer, renting tables and chairs, things we wouldn't have to do were we to choose to marry in a hotel. Will it be hard to determine the sorts of flower arrangements and personal touches we'll need when we don't know what the finished space will look like?"

Amber clasped her hands. "I can already picture how I want to adorn each room. You know how I love to personalize each wedding. Hiring the caterers and furniture will work to your advantage. We'll be in control of both the budget and your tastes. And Sid and Maxwell will oversee the renovations like the experienced pros they are.

I promise it will be finished before your wedding." She wrapped her arm around Sid's shoulders.

"Is it settled, then?" My mother reached into her pocketbook for her checkbook.

"I'm sure any other place we visit will pale in comparison. I guess we've found our wedding venue." I agreed she should sign the contract with enough conviction for my mother to search for her pen. It wasn't my negative opinion about the venue — I really did love the idea of what it could become — fueling my lack of certainty. I brushed aside my increasingly familiar sense of anxiety.

"We're getting married!" Gwen grabbed my hands, spinning us around in an exuberant dance.

I let go of my darkening mood. "I hate to break it to you, Gwen, but I want to marry the studly man over there by myself."

AMBER FUSSED about having to ditch me six days later, despite my assurances I had everything under control. Her parting gift to me before joining up with the Orpheus was a red three-ring notebook. She had filled it with timelines, pages of vendor recommendations, blank planning sheets for each vendor, and the contact information for Tyler, a part-time employee at one of Sid and Maxwell's home decor stores. With it being her intention to steal him away from her friends and make him her assistant once she returned home to restart her wedding business, she trusted him to lend me a hand. Which I doubted I would need. I'd seen enough weddings up close to be able to make sense of each task outlined in the binder. Planning our wedding would amount to nothing more than a game of "fill in the blank." I giggled, imagining the Mad Libs version of a wedding worksheet. *When choosing a pickle, remember to ask to view the photographer's dingo first.*

Having paid the equivalent of my first child's college tuition into Chloe's jar in the days following my engagement, I had been pinching my pennies recently. My mother was still on a mental spending spree. She had continued to flood my voicemail with messages and my inbox with emails containing links for whatever wedding-related item had caught her eye on her most recent browsing episode. Considering how many of her emails arrived during office hours, I feared for her future at the law firm where she was the office manager.

My mail app dinged at me. The floral inspiration page I had been viewing had failed to inspire me, giving my mother's latest news the power to lure me away. Mom smiled at me from a photo. Her left hand on her hip, her right hand on the side of her head like a fifties pinup girl, she offered me a three hundred sixty-degree view of herself clad in a long, purple taffeta confection she modeled in front of a three-way mirror. The voluminous skirt collected in folds on the floor. Rhinestones bedazzled a belt buckle at her waist. A bolero jacket in a matching shade of Barney purple completed the ensemble.

"I took my hairdresser's advice. He swore I'd look ravishing in purple, and he was right if modesty allows me to say so," the message read. Her auburn bob did take on a pleasing glow above the fabric. It was hard to focus on something as small as her head, though, when confronted by the universe-swallowing blob of children's cough syrup-colored fabric dominating the picture. "I went ahead and purchased this gown. It makes me feel exactly like a mother of the bride. Don't you love it? Chloe and Gwen can wear dresses in a complementary shade of lavender. Your brother and Derrick could wear tuxedo shirts in the same color. How fun! Won't purple be the perfect color scheme for your wedding?"

I swallowed hard, pressing my fist against my lips in the event the retching sensation I struggled against in my mind became physical. The only thing worse than confronting the purple palette my mother forced upon me was envisioning Chloe's response to being told she would have to wear lavender. We had vowed long ago never to torture each other with hideous bridesmaids' dresses. Purple could be a friendship killer.

I knew I needed to tell my mother to return the dress. I suspected calling her would be the most effective way to inform her that under no circumstances would the color scheme for my wedding match a dress the color of a glass of grape soda. Dread weighted my body deeper into the couch. Maybe I should tell Chloe about my mother's plans. My mother thought Chloe walked on water. Hearing the news from her could soften the blow. I knocked on Chloe's bedroom door.

"I have a five-dollar bill itching to join its friends in the jar. Do you have a moment?"

"Yeah, I'm ready to take a break from practicing." She snatched the bill from my fingers, marching it toward the jar on the coffee table in the living room.

"I'm going to show you a disturbing image. I promise you it was not my idea, nor is it one I endorse." I winced, imagining Chloe's reaction.

"Your mother looks gorgeous! What a bold color choice for her. Is she going to wear the dress to a gala or something?"

"Or something. Read the message above it."

Chloe froze. Her eyes moved first, followed by her chin. Both pointed at me accusatorially. "No. Tell her *no*. If you make me wear any shade of purple, you lose a best woman."

"There's no way in hell I'm making you or anyone wear purple. How can I tell her she's not in charge of picking the colors? Since she has already bought the dress, she'll kill me if I ask her to return it!"

Chloe fished in the jar for my fiver. "It doesn't feel right taking money from you today. Maybe I should throw in money of my own to pay for your troubles."

"You can keep my contribution. Consider it to be a payment for breaking the news to her." I pressed my palms together in a fervent plea.

"But she's your mother. Don't try to manipulate me with your puppy dog eyes. All right. I surrender. Call her and blow tons of smoke up that big, purple skirt of hers. After you've inflated it with all your compliments, hand me the phone. I'll let her down gently."

After I cooed words of admiration regarding my mother's gown to her, Chloe worked toward the fatal blow with care, drowning my mother in a tidal wave of compliments. During the long stretches when my mother dominated the conversation, Chloe's facial expression was a model of patience. Only the hollowness behind her eyes gave away how little interest she had in the babble my mother was spewing at her. Little by little, Chloe injected the basis of her argument against the color scheme. Modern weddings don't require a matchy-matchy aesthetic, she explained. She had played at weddings where only the bride's and groom's mothers coordinated the dress color. Won't it be beautiful if we add tulips in the same shade of purple to the bouquets and centerpieces? I nodded my head in agreement, listening to a master at work.

My mother cut her off mid-sentence two or three times. With the subtlest hints of her patience fraying, Chloe countered each of my mother's parries. Her language remained diplomatic. It was a hard-fought battle, but when Chloe ended the conversation with an enthusiastic promise to include my mother on our shopping expedition for the wedding party outfits, I declared her to be the victor. And there was celebrating. And wine. Much wine.

A touch of nervousness accompanied me to the Vista sul Mare on the last Sunday in July. They hadn't given me any dates to play in August. Over the course of the previous four weeks, playing brunch at the restaurant had become increasingly easier. I focused less on auditioning for the gig than on having fun playing for the guests and interacting with the staff. The servers and I found ways to keep each other amused during the insanely busy times in order to relieve the building stress. I almost allowed myself to believe I had earned the position of steady harpist. Each week Helena reassured me she was happy, the guests were happy, and Claude and Lily must be pleased with the reports. I decided not to dwell on the fact that Claude had not made a second visit to the restaurant.

I approached today's gig with a workman-like attitude: do the job, do it well, and don't fret about the future. It might have been my intention to interact less with my coworkers, but they hadn't read the memo.

"Your meal, madam." Julio set a tray of dirty plates on the stand placed a few feet away from my harp.

"Yum! Looks delicious!" I pretended to grab for the top plate, empty save for a slimy trail of balsamic glaze.

"For you, always the best." He bent into a low bow. "Be sure to include my name in your review on Yelp."

With a grin, I played *Besame Mucho*, his favorite song.

On my last break of the day, I visited with Helena at the hostess stand. "Did you hear whether they want me back next week?"

"Yes, I did. Lily called a little while ago. She anticipates August will be a slower month in the restaurant. They can't justify bringing you in to play. She did ask for me to book you for the Sunday during Labor Day weekend. Are you free?" I confirmed the date was available.

I couldn't take the coming hiatus personally. Being invited to return, even if it wasn't for the following Sunday, kept my hopes of turning the job into a steady gig alive. I picked my favorite repertoire to play during the last hour, wanting to give the regular guests and staff reason to miss me.

Over the next month, I pushed concerns about my future at the Vista into an out-of-the-way corner of my brain. They itched for a chance to escape. The morning of my return, as I loaded my harp into my minivan, nerves corroded my gut. How could today's gig stress me out more than the first time I had played brunch at the restaurant?

I practiced all of my relaxation techniques on the drive to Weehawken. Deep breaths. Inspirational mantras. I even tried to embarrass the jitters out of me by drumming and singing along like the sixth member of Green Day on *American Idiot* while stopped at a traffic light. Mocking glances from other drivers only managed to give me another reason to be anxious. With one last pep talk to myself, I fused my sweat-dampened palms to the handle of my harp cart once I reached the restaurant. I relied on muscle memory to guide me along the circuitous path between the tables to my spot in front of the windows. Helena greeted me with a hug. "You've been missed, my dear. But now you're back, and we can't wait to listen to your wonderful music!"

"Was it super slow last month?" I calibrated my tone to reflect a lack of vested interest in whether the dip in reservations merited canning the harpist.

"Eh, we had a couple of slow days, but overall, it wasn't as slow as it had been last August. These things are unpredictable. But…" Her voice trailed off. With lips clenched and brow furrowed, her expression hinted she had a serious topic to discuss. I waited, gripped by tension "Oh, what was I saying? Never mind. In any event, we're fully booked today."

Too busy to offer me more than a welcoming hello, the staff prepared for the onslaught of guests. In previous weeks, I had hung out in the kitchen in the downtime between tuning my harp and the start of the gig. The bustling pace of servers entering and exiting the kitchen today kept me by my harp. Yet another flutter of butterfly wings tickled my stomach.

Like any performance for which I have prepared, my nerves melted with each note I plucked. I finished my first set feeling calm, but not secure. I ate my lunch alone in the back, plagued by guilty thoughts of being allowed to take a fifteen-minute break while everyone else darted about like hummingbirds at a freshly filled feeder. Four weeks away from people I had just begun to get to know had erased my sense of feeling like a part of the staff.

Later in the afternoon, the room finally grew quiet. Julio, setting a tray on the stand near me, offered to serve me a feast procured from a fresh array of dirty plates. With no tables to bus, he didn't depart after honoring me with his customary bow. "Was the violinist a friend of yours?" he asked.

I wrinkled my brow in confusion. "What violinist?"

"The one who played here last week."

My butterflies laced their tap shoes and began dancing their big number in my belly. Violinist? Was this the topic Helena meant to discuss with me earlier today? "I don't know a thing about a violinist. What happened?"

"Yeah, she was here instead of you last week. She walked around the room, playing at every table. She wasn't as good as you, though."

"Thanks, and thanks for telling me. I hadn't heard." Julio left me to digest his news. I needed to brush my concerns aside. If I had to compete with other musicians for the gig, I had to prove I was the better choice. I poured my heart into the last half hour of my last set, making the case for them to hire me.

I erased the shreds of insecurity from my voice when I asked Helena about the violinist at the end of the day. She wrung her hands before responding. "It was Lily's idea. The violinist is the daughter of a friend of hers. I couldn't prevent her from bringing her in. Tiffany doesn't compare to you. She is a rank amateur. I'm not opposed to helping a young musician gain experience, but she lacks more than experience. She wasn't an asset to the room. Her tone, her repertoire, even her demeanor fell below a professional level. I wish Lily had been here to listen to you today. Unfortunately, she has already offered Tiffany the remaining Sundays in September. I'm going to go to bat for you to return. I promise we'll be in touch soon with additional dates. You'll be back with us before you know it, I'm sure!"

FOR MANY YEARS, neither Chloe, Gwen, nor I had sustained a serious romantic relationship. I hadn't been looking for a boyfriend, Chloe preferred to avoid committing to a relationship, and Gwen was mum on the subject. I broke our singlehood streak first over a year and a half ago. While Chloe and I were aboard the Orpheus, Gwen got back together with her college boyfriend, Matt. We were big fans of his at Indiana University, but after he broke up with her, he was dead to us. Because Gwen had reveled in their reconciliation, Chloe and I had no choice but to forgive Matt for his earlier transgression.

Mindful of balancing my time between Josh and my besties, I'd remained faithful to our long-standing tradition of girls' night each Sunday at our apartment. It was no more appropriate to invite Josh to crash our intimate party than it would have been to invite Chloe or Gwen to hop into bed with Josh and me. And for the record, I wasn't down with the latter idea. We devoted quite a bit of time to discussing the male of the species over our dinners. A man in our midst would have spoiled such conversations. Boys might be a fascinating topic, but they inhabited only a fraction of our conversations. The gender makeup of our dinners wasn't the important detail; it was that the three of us had been a platonic thruple for eleven years, and we weren't ready to change the dynamic of our relationship.

On our first night back in Montclair in May, we sought to resume our routine. Since then, Gwen had ditched us to go to Matt's apartment in Manhattan more often than she had joined us for dinner. She lived in North Caldwell with her parents — who didn't quite support the rekindled relationship — and spending time with Matt presented a host of challenges for her. In order to lure her back to our table, we broke the rules. We invited boys to dinner Labor Day weekend.

I came home from brunch at the Vista in a foul mood. Matt and Gwen were cooking dinner in the kitchen, and Josh and Chloe were talking in the living room. I wasn't ready to be social. I still had a bit of solitary sulking I wanted to do.

Upon hearing the door open, Josh had sprung off his chair to help me bring the harp into the apartment. "Good gig?" Planting a kiss on my lips, he prevented me from answering right away.

"The gig was good; the news is bad. No more brunch gig. At least for now. The owner did a favor for some friend of hers, hiring her friend's apparently unskilled daughter to be a strolling violinist. I'm in a crappy mood."

If life were simple enough that a hug from someone who loves you could melt away a problem, I would lead a trouble-free existence. Josh wrapped me in his arms. Compassion flowed from him like a healing balm, but internally, I still seethed. Not wanting to squander such a precious resource, I wriggled free. With a kiss, I promised I'd be in a better mood once I had changed out of my gig clothes.

Chloe met me in the hallway between our bedrooms with a frozen margarita. "Josh told me the news. Suckage. Here. Drink this. There are chips and salsa waiting for you in the living room."

Adding the cool, slushy goodness of the drink to the lingering warmth from Josh's hug, I vowed to leave my mood behind with the balled up black dress I had shed in my room.

Our kitchen couldn't accommodate more than two chefs in it at a time without them running the risk of slicing and dicing bits of each other's clothing or sautéing an errant elbow. Chloe relocated the blender to the dining table to keep the five of us well hydrated while staying out of the way of our chefs. The savory scent of paella wafted into the living room.

Claiming the far end of the couch, I chose to keep my mouth occupied with chips and my frosty blender drink rather than to launch into a never-ending stream of whines about my bad day at work. Josh and Chloe managed to keep the conversation going strong despite my silence, landing on topics ranging from whether Edward Snowden was a hero or traitor to what Kim Kardashian and Kanye West should have named their daughter. Kar Wash emerged as the clear winner of the baby-naming debate.

With a flourish, Gwen set a bowl of paella on the table. "Dinner is served."

We shuffled around the table in a game of musical chairs. It hadn't crossed my mind earlier, but with two couples at our table, we had the potential to make Chloe feel like a fifth wheel. I couldn't decide which would make her more comfortable: sitting next to Josh or sitting at the head of the table between Gwen and me. She deducted the cause of my indecision. "I forgot to inform my date dinner was on the table." She excused herself to rescue Chester, cousin to the blow-up doll around whom we had intended to build our environmental protest aboard the Orpheus. In a voice loud enough for us to hear, she said, "You're not dressed yet? You've had oodles of time to put on a shirt, but instead, you lounged around naked on the bed. Really, Chester! Here. Put on this t-shirt." She carried the barely clad Chester under her arm to the table. "Sorry to keep you waiting." We've learned a slightly under-inflated Chester can bend at the top of his legs. A bungee cord attached to the back of a chair becomes a seatbelt, allowing him to sit upright like the civilized blow-up doll we're trying to mold him into.

"He needs a place setting." I rose to fetch a plate for our guest.

"He has been munching on pork rinds all afternoon. I doubt he has much of an appetite. Would you pass me the paella? Unlike him, I'm starving!" Chloe handed me the salad to clear a space for the paella. "Ooh, look at all the shrimp. You put in extra for me, didn't you, Gwen?"

Gwen smiled. "I know how you love your shrimp! Chester, that's not a dig at you, little man. Nor you, Ellen."

I scowled in mock indignation. "Ha. Just by stating your disclaimer proves you did mean to make a short joke."

"Ignore her. I wouldn't change a thing about you." Josh gave my cheek a quick peck.

I pushed him away. "Nice try. It's not like you've never made a short joke at my expense before."

Josh took the salad bowl I offered to him. "True. All right. We're not allowed to make fun of Ellen tonight. She had a rough day."

Gwen reached across the table to pat my hand. "I can't believe they replaced you with an incompetent strolling violinist. Do you want us to write a complaint about her online? We could have brunch at the Vista next week and make a fuss about how much we preferred the harp to a violin that sounds like cats fighting in a paper bag."

"If she is as bad as the staff made her out to be, maybe she won't last. I'm keeping my fingers crossed I'll be playing brunch again sooner rather than later."

Matt turned toward me. "Does this mean you need a gig for next Sunday? I have an idea: I'll be holding an open house on Sunday at a really swank co-op on the Upper East Side. Let me ask my client how they'd feel about hiring a harpist for the afternoon. Live music should make the unit even more enticing than the scent of an onion roasting in the oven."

"Matt, thanks for looking out for my friend, but what about your own girlfriend? Don't your listings come with grand pianos for me to play?" Gwen pretended to sulk.

"I haven't had any listings with a piano in the last couple of months, but you know you'll be my first call. Hey, I've found my side hustle: real estate musical impresario."

Josh said, "I could do with a side hustle. I had counted on returning to a steady schedule of subbing in the pits at *Jazz Hands* and *Waiting for Godot: The Musical*, but while I was on tour, they needed to hire new violinists to fill the spots on the sub lists I had vacated. Now they only call me when the subs above me on the list aren't available to play a show."

I rotated my wrists in an understated version of jazz hands, answering Josh's gesture. "What a shame. I would have thought the producers at *Jazz Hands* would have been able to guarantee you your spot since they're the ones who moved you from the Broadway production to the touring production."

"That's not how it works, unfortunately. I've been massaging my network, looking for other shows to sub on.

I'm hoping to pick up a bunch of dates when each of the concertmasters I sub for will be away on their vacations during the next couple of months."

"But you love it, right?" Chloe pointed her fork at Josh.

"I really do. Weddings are fun, of course. Especially when I play them with my favorite harpist." I gave him my *cute bunny* smile, scrunching up my lips, nose, and eyes. "I don't have a burning desire to take on high-pressure classical jobs. A concerto or solo recital once every year or two is OK, but I've been at my happiest in the pit. I like the style of the music. I never thought myself to be the day job kind of guy, but it turns out going to the same office and doing the same thing every day appeals to me. Who knew?"

"Just call him Dilbert. Hey, I was going to eat that!" I had to monitor my food and Josh's fork closely at each meal. Without fail, he regularly helped himself to the choicest morsels on my plate, like the well-browned hunk of sausage I had been saving for my last bite.

"And that's what makes it so delicious! Here, have my last mussel."

"A mussel for a sausage is hardly a fair trade, and you know it." I poked around in the serving bowl for a replacement sausage. Stabbing a chunk with my fork, I protected it with my right hand. Whether I needed it to be a protective wall or a slapping device, I was ready for Josh's next attempted incursion. Meat secured in my mouth, I rebuffed him with a defiant laugh.

Chloe pursed her lips. "Now you understand why I insisted Chester sit at the other end of the table. The man knows no boundaries at the dinner table." Chester beamed his vapid smile at her. I bet he had hatched a scheme to pilfer the leftovers once we've fallen asleep tonight. "Back to our discussion about work. I'm jealous of you, Josh.

You've found your groove. My groove has eluded me for some time. I've dabbled with the various means by which a musician can earn her living, and I'm not sure I have found my calling yet."

Gwen caught my eye. She must have heard the same subtext I had noticed. This was a side Chloe had hidden from us for who knows how long. "Is being a musician itself unfulfilling, or have the opportunities you've explored left you wanting?" Gwen asked.

"I'm not questioning being a musician. How can I put it? Each time I take my flute out of the case, I'm itching to play. When I practice, I don't have specific practice goals in mind. I mean, I'm practicing for the love of playing, but I miss practicing for a specific performance. The concerts I play haven't presented the challenges I crave. And although I love teaching, most of my students aren't headed for performance careers. I've gained immeasurable experience working with lower-level students, but I'd really love to develop my skills in teaching advanced students. Listen to me go on; I sound like an ingrate. How lucky are the four of us to be busy freelance musicians?" Chloe blotted her mouth with her napkin. "Who wants coffee?"

Chloe's allergy to dwelling on her problems publicly had flared up again. Before any of us had the chance to respond to her confession or even to offer sympathy, she ended the conversation and disappeared. Of the five of us remaining at the table, only Chester wore a smile.

THE TIME IT took to drive the seventy miles between my mother's condo in Westfield and my brother Nathan's house in Marlton with my mother riding shotgun should have been measured in dog years. Unfolding myself from my minivan in Nathan and Derrick's driveway, my head spun from the sheer quantity of words my mother had spewed on the drive south. Her conversation had ricocheted between wedding plans, her desire for Nathan and Derrick to live closer to her, and her panicked warnings for me to avoid the dangerous maneuvers of each driver within a fifteen-hundred-foot radius of my minivan. The slap of the screen door banging against its frame and the excited snuffles of Jax, their French bulldog, at my ankles revived me.

"How was the trip?" Derrick raced down the path to the driveway, leaving Nathan behind on the front porch.

My mother gave him a quick hug and kiss. "You would not believe the crazy drivers on the road today! They all have a death wish, I tell you!"

"I'm glad Ellen delivered you here in one piece, then. Let's move inside. I'm freezing out here without my shoes." A riot of purple, yellow, and blue stripes adorned his socks. I had a hard time conceiving how he, in his eagerness to greet us, could have forgotten to put on his shoes.

Nathan greeted us at the door. "Thanks for making the trip. I can't believe we lured you down here on a Sunday. No gigs today?" He hung my jacket in the front closet.

"I'm still in brunch limbo. I was at the Vista two weeks ago, and I'll be back next Sunday. I've been taking a bit of a financial hit this fall, holding dates for them, only to sit home on Sundays because they didn't hire me and I had turned down other gigs while I waited to hear from them. The thing is I'd hate to have to decline a date at the Vista because I had something else booked."

With his lips pursed, Derrick gave his head a little shake. "If the gig were a boyfriend, I'd tell you to ditch him. Thankfully, Josh isn't the type to jerk you around. Speaking of Josh, what's he doing today?"

"He's in an abusive relationship of his own with Broadway. *Jazz Hands*, having ignored him for the last three weeks, showed up with flowers, begging him to come back to play today's matinée. He couldn't say no."

Derrick said, "I hope your gigs learn to show each of you the love you deserve. But it's our gain to have you today. Speaking of which, let's head into the dining room."

Nathan and Derrick bought their house four years ago. The forty-five-year-old home was a generic structure in a generic subdivision of a generic suburb. With a little love and a lot of time pacing the aisles of their local home improvement store, they had brought style to a house whose appearance had faded with age. Derrick favored darker shades in his design. I had always marveled at how, despite the darkness of the slate gray walls of the dining room and the rich walnut finish on the kitchen cabinets, they achieved a warm and homey environment.

Jax circled three times and collapsed beside the black leather chair I had chosen. "Ellen, why are you sitting at the table? This isn't a restaurant. Come help your brother bring the food in."

Nathan said, "Mom, we have it under control. You can go join Ellen."

My mother craved being useful. She intercepted Derrick, taking a casserole dish from him when he emerged from the kitchen into dining room.

Nathan and Derrick brought in the remaining serving dishes. "Here's a Spanish omelet. We made the French toast in the slow cooker. Help yourselves to the roasted asparagus and bacon-studded monkey bread. Hope you're hungry!"

"You had me at bacon." I reached for the plate with the monkey bread Derrick offered me.

"You didn't have to go through the trouble of cooking for us. We would have been happy with bagels and cream cheese." The feast my mother had mounded onto her plate begged to differ.

"Nathan, do you want to tell them our good news?" Derrick's plate stood empty. He appeared unable to contain the excitement churning inside him.

Nathan pressed his lips together. Gathering our attention with his eyes, he began, "You know how they passed a marriage equality law in New Jersey last week?"

My heart raced. Derrick's happiness was contagious. "Are you saying what I think you're saying?"

My mother shushed me. "What do you mean? Ellen, let Nathan finish."

"We're engaged!" Nathan said calmly, a satisfied grin etched on his face.

"Oh, heavens me! Two weddings in the family! Come here! Let me hug the two of you!"

Nathan and Derrick hesitated. "We're not done with our news," Derrick said.

"Let me guess. Is it a shotgun wedding?" My lame joke amused me more than it should have. Nathan touched his nose. "Really? I was just kidding. Holy cow, you guys!" I leaped from my seat, uprooting poor Jax in the process.

With me hanging from his neck like Flavor Flav's clock necklace, Nathan said, "In case you missed it, Mom, we're expecting."

"Expecting? What? I'm going to be a grandmother!" My mother rose from her chair with such force, the seat fell over backward.

I wiped away a tear and swallowed the lump stuck in my throat. "Congratulations, you guys! I want to know everything!" I punched Nathan in the arm. "How come you've never said anything? I didn't know you were planning to start a family."

Derrick had joined the blubbering mass of Blums for a group hug. "These things take time. And without guarantees, we didn't want to take you along on our conception rollercoaster ride. We're four weeks in. The due date is July second." I did the math in my head, and I didn't like the numbers. My face telegraphed my concerns. He patted me on my arm. "We have a window of nearly two weeks between your wedding and the baby's birthday. We won't miss it. And I promise neither our nuptials nor the baby will overshadow your wedding day."

I banished my worries. "Are you kidding? I'll gladly share the spotlight with you and the baby. Who's incubating the little critter?"

"Now really, Ellen! That's no way to talk about my precious grandbaby. But I am curious how surrogacy works."

Derrick explained, "Our dear friend Laurel loves being pregnant. I know, we all think she's weird. But she and her husband don't want to have a third kid. At a party a couple of years ago, we joked about her carrying a child for us. The four of us discussed it again when we were sober, and it still sounded like a good idea. We went the in vitro route. Nathan is the biological papa, and an anonymous woman is the egg donor. It took two tries, but this time it looks like it stuck. It's a tad early in the game to know for sure. We were nervous about telling anyone, but you're not anyone, of course."

"Have you done the legal paperwork? I'd hate for you to wind up in some awful custody situation."

Derrick patted my mother's shoulder. "We've dotted the Ts and crossed our eyes. Laurel won't be walking away with our baby. Well, she will, in a sense. Early next year, they're moving to Chicago. We're going to miss doting over her baby bump at every possible moment, but at least she'll be here for our wedding. Oh, I nearly forgot. Mark your calendars: we're getting hitched on December twenty-seventh."

My mother was a whir of wedding and baby talk on our drive home. By focusing her attention entirely on Nathan and Derrick, my mom made the hour-and-a-quarter-long trip the sweetest I had ever spent with her in a car. Not once did she say, "Purple." While my brother's well-developed plans for a small gathering at a local restaurant left no room for my mother to add her magic touch, she could churn out ideas within the shelter of my minivan without anyone opposing her. In a remarkable show of maturity, I never once interrupted her to speak on behalf of Nathan and Derrick.

I dropped my mother at her condo in Westfield, taking a moment to listen to a voicemail before driving home. "Ellen, this is Sheldon Strauss, the pianist from the Orpheus." He opened each phone conversation with the same introduction. It probably had never occurred to him he was the only Sheldon I knew, that his voice was unmistakable, and oh, yeah, there was this little thing called caller ID. "I thought I'd surprise you by dining at the Vista sul Mare today. I received quite a shock when I learned you were not playing. Let me tell you, I gave Lily an earful after she told me she was responsible for hiring the woman who plays the violin so horribly in place of you. I'm not having it. Helena tells me you will play again next week. If Lily doesn't offer you a full-time position, I will continue to intervene on your behalf. No need to return my call." Ah, Sheldon! I could always trust you to speak the truth bluntly. I drew my fists together under my chin, contemplating the situation. I hoped Lily would follow his advice.

"Mom, step away from the purple." True to our word, when Chloe, Gwen, Sheila, and I went shopping for their dresses, we let my mother tag along with us. While my three friends discussed their preferred dress styles with each other, my mother descended on the rack of lavender and eggplant-colored dresses like a homing pigeon returning to its roost after a cross-country flight.

"Come here, Ellen. I've brought a swatch of fabric from my gown with me. Don't these colors look lovely next to each other?"

I knew bringing my mother to pick the dresses would turn the day into a "take a deep breath and count to five" sort of event. I feared I'd hyperventilate if these moments squished together in quick succession. "Purple and lavender is a pleasing combination, Mom. I won't deny you that. Sheila says her coloring is all wrong for this shade, though. Besides, if the women are in lavender, then the men will have to wear lavender ties and pocket squares. Before you know it, we'd have to go with purple linens and flowers and food to make the colors all match. The reception room will look like a giant glass of grape juice. There has to be another color besides lavender that will compliment your dress." It was clear the arguments against purple Chloe had presented to my mother three months ago hadn't made a lasting impact.

My mother held her hands together. "Promise me they'll at least try on a lavender dress? It shouldn't be much of a bother for them now, should it?"

"You're right, mom." I knew she wouldn't win the Battle of the Color Palette in the end. You could lead Chloe to a purple dress, but you couldn't make her wear it. Anticipating the outcome, I had no reason to argue with my mother.

Standing in the middle of the store was like being stranded inside a rainbow. With every shade represented by a dozen different dress styles hanging on the racks, I could no longer identify individual colors or value them. Amber loved red, Chloe suggested black, Sheila preferred yellow, and Gwen would never venture into such a controversial topic. My friend Amy couldn't attend the wedding (and therefore wouldn't be in the wedding party) due to a schedule conflict. At least we wouldn't have to factor in her tastes, which, back in third grade, centered on bubblegum-pink. I wanted the color of Nathan and Derrick's ties to match the bridal babes' dresses. Derrick had his heart set on royal blue, in case I needed to add another opinion to the mix.

"Mom, let me see your swatch." I wiggled my fingers at her.

Her face lit up. "Aren't you glad I thought to bring it? Should we show Chloe how beautiful it is next to the dresses I selected?"

"Hold your horses. Here's my plan. I'm going to use the fabric like a divining rod, taking it on a spin around the store. Any color that doesn't clash with yours is fair game. It will be easier to choose between a curated collection of colors. I'm finding it overwhelming to look at fifty shades of gray and pink and green and—"

"Gray!" Chloe grabbed the swatch from my hand, running off to the least colorful section of the store. She tugged the skirt of a silvery-gray satin dress in front of her. "This color reads a little like lavender. They're a similar intensity."

I took a long glance at the fabric. "It could be really elegant. Gwen and Sheila, would you wear gray dresses?"

With her arm around my waist, Gwen said, "Honey, it's your wedding. Don't worry about my opinion."

"How does it look on me? Does it make me look washed out?" Sheila unhooked a hanger from the rack to hold a dress in front of her. Her thin, light blond hair livened up against the gray, turning a shade of platinum. Her pale blue eyes sparkled.

"You look like a movie star! Ta-da! We've picked the color. Now we have to pick a style." By we, I tacitly meant Chloe. She was on a quest to find dresses they could wear again. We knew what she didn't want in a dress: ankle-length, lace, a sweetheart neckline, rhinestones, and about ten other details I had already forgotten. I opted for the protection of a cream-colored velvet love seat in the demilitarized zone of the store, far from Chloe's fashion battleground.

She swept dress after dress to the left, filling the store with the squeak and scrape of hangers rubbing against the metal racks. Sheila and Gwen hovered behind her. My mother sat with me, fingering the fabric swatch. If you asked me, I'd say that visions of lavender still danced in her head, but she kept her opinions to herself.

"I've found the perfect dress!" Our saleswoman walked over to examine Chloe's selection, a tea length sleeveless dress with a boat neck, fitted bodice, and a full skirt.

I jumped off the love seat. "Ooh! So pretty! Try it on!"

The saleswoman took their sizes, returning with three dresses of the same style, each in a different color. "I don't have Silver Mist in stock in any of your sizes, but we will be able to order the dresses for you." She handed Gwen a dress in hot pink. Sheila gave me a hopeful glance. I smiled, shaking my head at the dress in her favorite shade of buttercup yellow that she held. The salesperson handed Chloe her dress, and my mother bellowed a triumphant laugh. Chloe's eyes seared a hole in my forehead. With a lavender dress dangling unloved from the hanger hooked on her finger, she skulked into a fitting room.

CLAUDE STOOD with his palm pressed against the hostess stand at the Vista, surveying his realm. Helena rushed across the room to greet him. Four months had passed since I had first met the owner. While Sheldon might have put the hurt on Lily last week, I had come in here today believing my future remained tenuous. I wanted to make the most of my chance to play for Claude a second time. Even more, I hoped I would finally meet his wife Lily. I couldn't imagine I would have the power to secure the gig without her listening to me.

Helena led Claude, another gentleman, and two women to a table not far from the harp. My heart pumped blood like it was restocking shelves during a going-out-of-business sale. I rubbed my inner arms against my sides to blot my pits. Claude held a chair for one of the women. A cap of steel gray curls framed her kind face. She met my eye-bulging stare with a smile. I coaxed my lips into a nervous grin.

Intensifying my focus, I dug deep into my bag of tricks to make my sure my music appealed to our VIPs. Ignoring the rumbling of my belly, I played through my first break. Claude and one of his companions regarded me at random intervals, but I couldn't judge whether their reaction to me was in response to my music or to me giving them the creeps by constantly ogling their table.

With the restaurant's owner in the house, the other staff members were on their best behavior. Julio abandoned his usual routine of presenting his dirty dishes to me, adopting an efficient manner of dropping off a tray before rushing to fill the next. We had exchanged fewer than ten words before he came to ask me to play *Happy Birthday* while a server brandished a birthday candle-bedecked dessert to a guest. In a whisper, Julio said, "Would you believe Tiffany doesn't even know how to play *Happy Birthday*? We have to sing it whenever she's here instead of you. I'm not sure which rendition of it would sound worse: ours or hers."

It didn't make sense to me. Every other detail at the Vista was flawless. How could they choose an unqualified musician over me? Did Tiffany's mother know where Lily had buried a body? Maybe Tiffany was playing for free. Claude had rendered me powerless. I couldn't imagine how to improve my performance, and I was loath to lower my price below market value.

A palpable sense of self-doubt crept across my chest, pushing me away from trying to win over Claude. As I had done a couple of years ago when I believed Josh's ex had shoved me aside in the race for his attention, I succumbed to defeat. Without control over the outcome, why bother to fight for it? I couldn't let these people rule my life. Heck, I shouldn't even let them keep me from eating. At 2:00, I gave myself a much-deserved lunch break.

A full belly took the edge off my morose thoughts. I ignored Claude and his guests, performing instead for the other guests, the staff, and myself. I loved playing the harp.

While working aboard the Orpheus, I discovered I didn't need a concert stage to find my happy place. Plucking out easily digestible tunes to the accompaniment of the clinking of glassware and the clattering of forks against plates fulfilled me more than I had ever thought possible.

Their dessert plates cleared, the foursome rose from their chairs. Helena must have possessed a sixth sense. She appeared by Claude's side before he had taken a step away from the table. The two of them and the woman with the halo of gray curls skirted between tables on a path toward my harp.

I swiveled to the right side of my bench to greet Helena and the woman. "Ellen, may I introduce you to Lily? Lily, this is Ellen, about whom we all have been raving since we first heard her play."

Lily took my hand between hers. "Sheldon has never let us down. Now I know why he and Helena have been singing your praises." I bowed my head, biting back an emerging grin. "Would you be available to come play for us each week through the end of the year? We'll hold it to these next few weeks. I don't want to get ahead of ourselves, but I know with the holidays coming, harp will be an ideal complement to our Sunday brunch." Helena smiled a knowing smile at me.

"I am available, and I'd love to continue playing brunch here. Thank you." I wanted to break into a jig, but I had another hour left to play, and the guests were likely to prefer my music over my dancing. I knew the job still hadn't become permanent. A steady gig would be at its most valuable to me in January and February, but I was glad to have my Sundays booked for the next few weeks. I had to believe playing here several weeks in a row would convince Lily and Claude they couldn't imagine the restaurant operating without me.

"Your news deserves better than pizza and beer at my apartment, but this is the best I could do on short notice." Josh pried the cap off a bottle of beer, tipping its contents into my pint glass.

"Pizza and beer sound perfect." I really meant it. From the moment Lily hired me to play until I finished the gig, I couldn't wait to tell Josh the news. Gwen was in the City with Matt, and Chloe had a gig, freeing me from attending our regular girls' night. Josh and I spent most nights together. Because I didn't want to impose on Chloe by having him stay in our apartment every night, I spent a couple of nights each week at his home.

His place was less comfortable than ours. And he didn't have Chloe to keep it from attracting the attention of the health department. New parents bragged when their little rug rats developed a sense of object permanence. The furniture in Josh's apartment might never reach this developmental stage. The chairs, tables, and bed couldn't rediscover takeout containers or piles of music following a prolonged period away from them because the objects were permanently in residence on top of them. Before I met Josh, I believed my housekeeping habits (or lack thereof) were legendary. Josh made me look like a neatnik.

"Sorry I have little to offer you beyond my paltry feast. And me, of course!"

My elbow accidentally swiped a violin etude book off the table, and I bent to retrieve it. "What's going on with your feet? Even in the bad lighting under the table, I can tell the difference between a blue sock and a brown one."

"You're acting like you've never noticed my relaxed approach to sock selection." Josh crossed his ankles in an attempt to hide the evidence.

"Some say relaxed, others say too lazy to fold laundry."

"I call it efficient. Think of the time I save by leaving the clothes unfolded in the basket. When I need socks, I pick two from the top," he said with a shrug.

"Can I make a request for you to buy a pair of black socks to put aside for our wedding day?"

"Why spend money on socks when I have such a beautiful collection? Now quit picking on me. Enjoy the penalty-free environment in which we can talk about our wedding. Chloe's not here to extract your life savings from you each time you utter the word *wedding*."

I folded my pizza slice, priming it for my first bite. "Would you believe me if I told you I haven't had to pay a dollar into the jar all week?"

He cupped his chin in his palm. "Hmm."

"What do you mean by *hmm*?" I dropped my slice on my plate without having taken a bite.

"Does this mean Chloe has gone soft on you, or have you taken the week off from planning?"

"Not you too! Even with the distraction of Nathan and Derrick's wedding and baby news, my mom can still find the energy to drill me daily on our wedding. She can't believe I'm not eating and breathing wedding plans twenty-four/seven. Everything's fine with our wedding! We have a venue, the women in the wedding party have ordered their dresses — and have done so two months ahead of schedule, according to the timeline Amber gave me. Our photographer is on hold. A couple of days after Amber comes home next month, she and I have meetings with a florist and the party rental store. Wedding planning is a piece of cake!"

"Speaking of cakes, is sampling wedding cakes on our to-do list?" Josh, sensing the growing tsunami within me, deflected potential waves of anger by introducing a favorite topic of mine: dessert. It worked.

"You know the cake tasting is my favorite thing on the to-do list! Amber says we don't need to take care of the cake until early to mid-March, though. Oh, well."

"Maybe we'll start earlier. I imagine we'll want to visit dozens of bakeries. Cake tasting is serious work. I'd hate for us to make a decision without having ample information to aid us."

"Mmm. Cake. Oh, no! Cake tastings and dress fittings will be at cross-purposes. I've decided I'm not going to diet my way into the smallest sized dress possible, but I can't eat cake with abandon, either."

"Have you found a dress? You don't have to tell me anything about it. I think your plan to keep it a surprise is a perfect one."

So much for averting the storm. Panic surged in my chest. "My mom is going nuts over me not having tried on a single dress. I don't know. I'm just not in the mood to think about dresses, or even the wedding, right now."

"I didn't mean to bring on any more pressure. I appreciate everything you are doing for our wedding. You know I'm not one of those grooms-to-be who leaves all the work to the womenfolk. I don't play that game. I'm evolved."

I let the waves recede. Josh was the one person who hadn't been kick-starting my angst by complaining about my sluggish pace of making wedding plans. "And how! We'll take care of the fun stuff — like buying rings and choosing our invitations — together. But not until February. In March you'll need to select what you and the groom dudes are wearing. Everything is on schedule." I hoped we had reached the end of the discussion.

"How about the music? Or the celebrant?" His tone lacked the intensity and judgment underpinning my mother's questions about our wedding plans.

Although I would have preferred to move on to another topic, it was only fair to let Josh continue to talk about the wedding plans. And since he wasn't in a tizzy about it, it gave me the chance to manage my defensiveness. "My mom wanted us to hire the rabbi who performed my father's funeral. I'll admit he gives good funeral, but his weddings are more like cabaret acts at which he's the star. Besides, neither of us is Jewish. I swear, after all this time, my mother still gets confused about life events that involve religion. I had to remind her how having a Jewish father doesn't make me Jewish. We'll sort out the celebrant issue some other time. Music should be easy though, right?"

"And fun. But we should do it sooner rather than later before everyone we know picks up another gig on our wedding date if that's not too stressful for you."

"How about F-bomb?" I covered my mouth, lest the crust of pizza I had been nibbling on become a projectile. In the early, flirty days after we had first met each other, Josh and I had invented a band, F-bomb, who never played gigs. They spent so much time in a basement talking about buying musical equipment, they never got around to rehearsing.

"Your mom did complain about how loud wedding bands can be. Here's one band I guarantee won't drown out the conversation."

"But man, if they had only bought that amp, the one they saw on Craig's List. Then they'd be the loudest band in Princeton."

Josh nodded his headed, feigning regret over a missed purchase. "Our first dance might be a tad conceptual, what with the band not actually playing anything."

"Hey, if F-bomb's not available, how about we give the guests their own personal music devices and earphones?

The room would remain quiet for the guests who complain about how loud wedding bands can be. Anyone who wanted to dance could groove to their own beat."

Josh grew serious. "There's another item to add to our list: we have to pick a first dance."

"Ugh. We were having wedding planning fun for a moment. We don't have a song. How can we pick a first dance?"

Reading the folds between my eyebrows, he said, "*Creep*?" He played me perfectly, choosing to make a joke.

I relaxed. "Could work. How about *Gold Digger* by Kanye West?"

"Yeah. I'm digging it. Get it?"

"Cute. *Baby Got Back*?"

"Well, that would just be me getting my brag on 'bout my sexy new wife. But seriously, I have an idea for a band. How about the bar band I used to play with? You heard them once, at Amber's last wedding. They come super cheap."

"Yeah, they were really good! And there you go. We've checked another item off our list. See how easy planning a wedding is?" Josh regarded me askance. Of course I had confused him, swinging from the panic of buying my dress to the swagger behind my last question. I hadn't come clean to him about my weird episodes. I still believed planning a wedding was easy. It wasn't the effort of planning our wedding driving me bonkers; it was some unidentified entity attached to the planning process making me deranged. I wasn't ready to try to explain to him something I didn't yet understand. "Ooh. Speaking of weddings we've played together. Didn't we play a bunch of opera arias at the F-bomb gig? We may not have a song, but I fell deeply, madly, passionately in love with you while we played the Intermezzo from *Cavalleria Rusticana* together."

"Yes! I'm already choked up conjuring an image of you walking down the aisle to that piece. Would it be weird to have a violin/harp duo play our ceremony?"

"I'm pretty sure if we had a harp, I'd swat the harpist aside and take over the gig. Would you be OK with a string quartet instead?"

"Sure! I promise I won't yank a violin from another musician's hand. Let me call a friend of mine. See, I'm useful!"

"Why don't you prove how useful you are? I'm out of beer." He took my glass from me after planting a kiss on my parched lips.

"Didn't we play *Nessun Dorma* for the recessional of the same wedding? It might not be original to copy our former client, but we don't need points for originality."

"I'm down with a little Puccini. What should the wedding party process to?"

"*Baby Got Back*?"

AMBER REGALED ME with four months' worth of gossip from the Orpheus during our drive to Flemington to pick out rental furniture and flowers for my wedding. Her best friend, Nessa, had received a promotion, becoming an activities director aboard a different ship based in the Mediterranean. Amber speculated about whether Mary, Nessa's replacement on the Orpheus, had been having affairs with various passengers. Romantic liaisons with passengers carry the same consequences as gluing place settings to the deck. Unlike Chloe and me, Mary never got caught.

Part of me missed the cruising experience. With the weather growing colder in New Jersey, I grew wistful for the tropical climate in the Bahamas. Living and working with the same crew members for months on end reminded me of being in college. I enjoyed having easy access to food, drink, entertainment, and a social life. On the other hand, once Chloe moved into my cabin, alone time became a precious commodity. Between reveling in having temporarily secured the brunch gig, learning repertoire for upcoming concerts, spending time with Josh, and planning our wedding, I knew I had no interest in leaving my life behind for a second dose of life at sea.

Amber said, "I told you a new harpist signed on a week ago? She's right out of school, from North Carolina. Now that they've finally fixed the sound insulation problem above the show lounge, the harpist no longer enjoys the cush digs you occupied on the ship. She has a solo cabin below deck. Am I making you regret that you blew your chance at another contract aboard the Orpheus?"

"I'm good, thanks. I have plenty to anchor me to New Jersey. Like planning a wedding. Are we going to swing by Sid and Maxwell's today, or are we only visiting the florist and the rental place?"

"Sid says the manor is a mess right now. They're making great progress, though. We'll check in on the updates one of these days. You have no need to stress over the renovations. Once we've selected the tables, chairs, linens, and the other rental goods, I thought we'd stop for lunch at a great bistro I know of in Princeton before our appointment with the florist."

We pulled into a parking spot in front of the rental warehouse in an industrial complex. The curb appeal did not scream wedding. The responsibility of hawking goods for events fell on the interior, a riot of every item one could conceivably desire for a party. Tall tables, square tables, round tables, each set with different place settings in front of unique styles of chairs. Napkins in so many different hues, a rainbow would be jealous, fanned out from within a trio of wine glasses displayed on a small table. Matching shades of tablecloths hung from hangers on the wall behind the table. Shelves on another wall groaned under the weight of cake holders and chafing dishes. I had expected to pick out our furniture and tableware from a catalog. How could I focus on a single element when every item in the store vied for my attention all at once?

Amber ran through the door to accept a hearty handshake from the man standing behind a counter. "Harry! It's been forever! How've you been?"

"You get prettier and prettier. Must be the sea air! So, you're back in the wedding business?"

"Almost. I want you to meet my first new client, Ellen. She's a fabulous harpist. Your paths have probably crossed on the wedding circuit."

"Nice to meet you. Amber tells me you're looking for quite a number of items for your wedding. Now, where is that piece of paper? Oh, yes, I've left the list over on that table, the one with the white tablecloth and the towering candelabra."

We followed Harry to a table in the center of the warehouse. Each place setting included more cutlery than I used in a week. The crystal glasses glittered in the light thrown off by a chandelier hung from an overhead pipe. Swirls of ivy spilled out of silver urns filled with white roses. I searched for Mr. Carson, expecting Downton Abbey's butler to be standing guard over the perfectly laid table. Choosing place settings might be a difficult task, but at least I knew what I didn't like. This was way too fancy for my tastes.

Amber made the first choices: two service bars and a dozen seventy-two-inch round tables. I preferred the Chiavari chairs with their elegant frames to the simple wooden folding chairs Amber suggested. A difference of three dollars per chair convinced me she was right.

"I'm guessing your mother was unhappy when I didn't invite her to join us today. I knew she'd have a lot to say, but I wanted to be able to hear your opinions. I see three shades of purple linens. She probably would have fixated on those had she been here. With her in purple and the bridesmaids in gray, I suggest avoiding tablecloths in any shade except for white. Do you like this table setting?"

"The white is fine, but I don't want our tables to be so formal."

Amber left the table. Fingering the napkins on display near the register, she plucked a dark gray napkin from a glass. "We could have a white cloth draped over a gray underskirt. The white will make selecting your flowers much easier, but we can tone down the formality of the tablescape with the gray."

The sense of overwhelm I experienced upon first walking in the door subsided. Amber had a subtle way of asking me for my opinions after she had made a decision. With her amazing sense of style and concern for my budget, she guaranteed agreeing with her would not lead to later regrets. If the rest of our wedding planning could go this smoothly, I doubted I'd have another panic attack.

"OK, Harry. We'll go with a dozen each of the ninety-inch tablecloths in charcoal and in white. I'd suggest white for the napkins, too. We'll hold off on the place settings for now. Once we have selected the menu, the caterer will give us the specifics for which plates and silverware we need. Since Sid and Maxwell plan to furnish the living room, we'll order only a few extra tables and chairs for the cocktail hour. We'll also have their outdoor furniture to use if the weather permits us to venture out onto the patio. Looks like we're done here. Anything you want to suggest or change?"

"Nope." I tucked the paperwork Harry handed me into my wedding binder. Admiring its growing thickness and the fraying edges of papers sticking out between the dividers, I enjoyed the evidence of our wedding plans being well underway.

"Oh, no. Don't look now. OK. Look up, but slowly. On the far end of the bar, you see the guy eating a burger by himself? I'm pretty sure he's an ex-boyfriend of mine from college," I said to Amber.

She craned her neck. "Where? Oh, I see him now. He's kind of cute. How can you not be sure if he's your ex?"

"I mean, I'm pretty sure it's him. I haven't seen him in about ten years. He was from outside of Philly. Princeton's close enough to Philly for it to make sense for him to be here."

"Was he a music major?"

"No. He was a Poli Sci major. We met in a cafeteria. He was the guy who dipped our student ID cards into the card reader. I made a habit of eating lunch at his cafeteria every day because he was really funny. He turned out to be a crappy boyfriend, though. We dated for only a few months my freshman year. I haven't thought about him in years." I neglected to tell Amber the story I had once told Josh, the one where he wanted me to try on his mother's sexy underwear. My spine quivered like a gelatin mold at the memory of the episode.

Amber smiled at me. "Well, there's no better time to run into an ex than when you have someone else's ring on your finger, or so they say." Reflexively, I spun my engagement ring. "I think he has spotted you. Uh, oh. You have a little ketchup on your face." I dabbed at the corner of my mouth. "Other side. Almost. A little higher. Yup, you're good."

I dropped my napkin into my lap. A glance to my right brought my eyes within intimate contact of a man's groin. My eyes darted back to the safe terrain of my lap. "I thought that was you, Ellen! What brings you to Princeton?"

69

I stood to prevent another crotch-related greeting. "Hey, Sam. This is my friend, Amber. She's my wedding planner. I'm engaged, and I'm getting married at a home in Princeton next June. I mean, it's a really big, historic manor, and they're renovating it in order for it to become a wedding venue. Josh and I — Josh is my fiancé — are the first people to book a wedding at the site. Amber and I are in the area doing all sorts of wedding-related stuff like picking out tables and chairs and linens and—"

"It's nice to meet you, Sam." Amber cut me off from continuing to spew a stream of word vomit. I had no reason to be nervous, but then again, I never needed a good reason to work myself into a lather.

"You're engaged, huh? I guess that means you would turn me down if I asked you to go out sometime." Cockiness oozed from him. As I stared at him, my own pose deflated. By not fawning over him in return, I poked a hole in his confidence, too. "Er, so, uh, you still playing that harp of yours?"

"Yup. I've been lucky to be able to make a career out of it. And you? Still, um, poli sciencing?"

"Nah. It was just a degree. I worked for my father — he's a contractor — right out of school. I preferred filling out the work permits to the other tasks he had me perform. So I switched sides. Now I'm a building inspector for the Borough of Princeton." I fiddled with my ring, not interested enough in him to respond.

Amber saved the conversation from sliding into an abyss. "If you're a building inspector, perhaps you're familiar with my friends Sid Johnson and Maxwell Balter? They've purchased the old Harrington Estate on Elm Ridge."

"What a great property! I handled the permitting for the work they did to the carriage house. I haven't been involved since. Hmm. Interesting they're considering using it as a commercial space."

Amber elaborated on the plans for the property. I struggled to draw a deep breath. What did he mean it was interesting? Were Sid and Maxwell's plans kosher? Amber shouldn't be revealing potentially damaging information to a building inspector.

"They've filled out the permits, right? They have let the town know their intentions?" I twisted my napkin between my hands, eyeing Amber nervously.

Sam gave me a knowing wink. "Of course they would have. Their contractor is one of the best around. I've never known him to skirt the law. I'd be happy to check on the site if you wanted. Better we catch a problem earlier rather than later. I'd take care of anything for you, for old time's sake."

Amber said, "I'm sure everything is in order. But it is reassuring to know we have a friend in the Building Department, just in case. Can I have your card?" Amber put the card Sam offered her into her purse. He handed another one to me. The glossy card refused to release itself from my sweaty fingers when I slipped into my pocket.

When I didn't offer him my card in return, he asked, "How come your fiancé isn't helping you today?"

"Oh, I didn't want to torture him with a full day of shopping."

"I love to shop. It wouldn't be fair to make the hypothetical woman I may marry do all of the planning." Glancing sideways at me, he raised his brow in an unsettling gesture.

"I'm not here without him because he doesn't like to shop or refuses to help me. I just didn't ask him to come." My words came out clipped.

"Hmm." Sam had a way of appearing to take notes on everything I said to add to a mental notebook.

I knew anything I said would fling me deeper into the defensive spiral already spinning within me. I petitioned Amber with a look of desperation. She nodded. "Well, we have to keep moving. It was nice meeting you, Sam."

"Likewise. I'd love to continue our conversation another day." He helped himself to a hug before I was ready. His cologne lingered after we parted, clinging to every bit of me that had come into contact with him.

His scent dogged me for the rest of the afternoon. I thought I had escaped it while we were in the florist shop. The subtle sweetness of the roses and the spiciness of mums in the tiny shop erased the musk left behind by my ex. Once we returned to my minivan, even with a nosegay of flowers tucked into the water bottle in the divider next to me, I again sensed Sam's presence. I was glad I had a few hours before Josh came to my apartment. A hug from an ex-boyfriend was hardly an act of infidelity, but bringing home evidence of another man having touched me, even platonically, sent a shiver down my spine.

THE MUTED STRAINS of flute music met me in the hallway outside our apartment. I accented the last note of Chloe's final phrase with the thud of the closing door. She swabbed out her flute, returning it to its case. "Did you and Amber accomplish everything on your list?" she asked.

I offered her the small bouquet of flowers the florist had given me. "Nice." She took a sniff before handing them back to me.

"My mom will be thrilled. Look how purple they are!" It shocked me that I had gravitated toward the mix of orchids, tulips, and delphiniums ranging in shades from lavender to eggplant the florist had put together for me on Amber's suggestion. A spray of acid green button mums cut the cloying purpleness. "The centerpieces will be in low glass rectangular vases. He'll line each vase with long leaves. We'll have a couple of smaller square vases for the tables in the cocktail room. He might throw bits of white hydrangeas into those to tie in with my bouquet, too." I paused, eyeing the jar on the coffee table. Chloe hadn't interrupted me yet to remind me to pay my fee. Maybe it was because I hadn't said the word *wedding*.

"So, our wedding flowers are done." Crickets. "So are the furniture rentals. Ooh, we're going to have a white tablecloth on top of a charcoal gray one. The napkins and plates will be white."

"Sounds nice." Chloe sat at the dining table, rifling through the mail. "You mentioned you designed your bouquet? I'm not sure you should have chosen the flowers before you bought your dress. You'll want to make sure they work together perfectly." I had been baiting Chloe with my free-range wedding talk, yet she managed to incite a reaction from me instead. I opened my right fist, letting the stems of flowers spill onto the table. The giddiness from having knocked off two big items on my list today evaporated.

"Amber says it shouldn't matter since I know I'm going to go with a true white."

"Are you sure? Just say the word, and I'll take you dress shopping. I can't wait to help you to select the perfect dress." She didn't look up from her magazine.

"I'm not ready to shop for a wedding dress." I sounded like a petulant child. I had nothing against going shopping for my dress, but whenever Chloe or my mother mentioned it, I'd grow defensive. It wasn't like they were telling me to do something I had no intention of doing. Weird. I shrugged off my odd behavior, shifting my focus to Chloe's. "How come you haven't made me cough up a dollar for droning on about the wedding, anyway?"

"I'm slipping, I guess. My mind is elsewhere. Thanks for reminding me. Go on, pay your fee."

I extracted a bill from my wallet to feed to the jar. "What were you practicing?"

"Oh, nothing, really. Just going through my orchestra audition repertoire for the fun of it. I thought it would be a smart idea to get the pieces back into my fingers. You never know when you'll have the chance to perform a big work or teach it to a student. I have a lot of work to do on them, though. Everything I played today sucked."

"I'm confused. Didn't you just say you were practicing them for fun? And the little I heard sounded amazing! You were playing *The Afternoon of a Faun*, right?"

"Thanks, but I disagree." Chloe has always been hard on herself, but saying she sucks when she wasn't even working toward a specific goal was harsh, even for her. "So, how's Amber?"

I recognized she had employed her usual conversation evasion tactic, but remembering I had additional news to share, I let it slide. "You'll never guess who we ran into at lunch: Sam!"

"Like, *Sam* Sam?" She closed her magazine, swiveling to the side of her chair. "That must have been a nasty shock."

"I know, right? He's a building inspector in Princeton. He's familiar with Sid and Maxwell's house, or at least the renovations they did on their apartment."

"I can't remember. Did Sam cheat on you?"

"Not that I knew of." Marcus, the guy I dated right before Josh, was the only boyfriend who had cheated on me. I thought — or hoped — it was only the one time. I'd forgiven Amber, but I'd never forgive him for kissing her while I took a potty break during a date with him. Since I hadn't suspected him of cheating on me, at least I didn't have to live through the suspicions and lies. "I know I'm safe with Josh on the fidelity front, in any event."

"That you are. Did you ever cheat on anyone?"

"No way! I don't have the stomach for infidelity. How about you?"

"I never did, either. Perhaps a few of the doucheburgers in my past had a little something going on the side while we were together. One guy I dated had a wife. No shower could help me to remove the dirty feeling I had of having hurt his wife despite not having known she existed. Why are we talking about cheating exes again? Oh, right. Sam. He wasn't my favorite of your exes."

"Mine neither. I think he was testing me today on how serious I was about being engaged. He made a joke about me turning him down for a date without having asked me out. And he had this lecherous glint in his eye. Maybe I'm mistaken. He wants to catch up, whatever that means. I don't see the point. Here. Would you smell my shoulder? He left his cologne stank all over me. Should I change shirts before Josh gets here?"

"It's not slaughter, it's laughter. Sadly ever after. Murder most fun!" Josh entered our apartment like a cabaret star taking the stage, breaking into song between fragments of conversation.

"What the hell are you singing?"

"The contractor for *Jazz Hands* came by during intermission today to give me a copy of the book and cast recording of another show he wants me to learn. It's called *Murder Most Fun*, and it sounds like a ridiculously silly romp of a murder mystery. I listened to the first act on the way home. Now the title song is stuck in my head. Since I was in the market for a new earworm, I shouldn't complain. I'll be glad to have another show to sub on, now that *Waiting for Godot: The Musical* has closed."

"Is it possible to do a stabby version of jazz hands?" I gripped an imaginary knife in my right hand and Bob Fosse'd the heck out of my left. My right hand couldn't help but quiver unless I slowed the rotation of my left hand. "I'm thinking nope."

"I'll be auditing the show next week. I doubt I'll see the action on the stage from the pit, though. I'll be sure to get a pointer or two on how to dance one's way through a fun murder from the dancers after the show."

"It's important you do. If they add you to the sub list, we'll need to learn the appropriate gestures in order to distinguish which show you're playing." Doing jazz hands every time Josh spoke about the Broadway musical, *Jazz Hands*, was a long-running joke of ours. When I visited him in Dayton last spring with the hope of spurring a reconciliation between us, I began my pitch with our joke. Note to self: work jazz hands into my vows. I giggled to myself, picturing petals flying from my bouquet mid-shake.

"What's so funny?" Josh laughed with me without knowing the joke. I gave him a quick kiss. I loved how humor was our relationship's default setting.

"Nothing. Just picturing campy ways to stage a murder. Oh, speaking of starvation, Chloe will be home soon. She suggested we order Chinese for dinner. Gwen's not joining us; she's in the City with Matt again."

Josh knit his brows in confusion. "Were we speaking of starvation?" My stomach growled on cue. I pointed to my midsection with both hands, my face emphasizing the fact that my belly will not stand being ignored. "Oh, I see. You're the murder victim in this scene. Let me order you a mess of mu shu pork before they haul me to the local precinct house for foul play."

While Josh studied the Chinese restaurant menu, I stole another glance at an email I had received this afternoon. Sam had found my address even though I hadn't given him my card. It was clear I hadn't been imagining him leering at me.

Dear Ellen,
I'm so glad we ran into each other on
Thursday. You look really, really good! I
haven't been able to stop thinking about
you. You and I should get together the next
time you're down in Princeton. I'd love to
give you a personal tour of some of my
favorite buildings.
xo
Sam

I had told him I was engaged, yet his email implied he thought he stood a chance with me. What should I do? I couldn't tell Josh another man might be propositioning me. But not telling him that I had run into an ex would be deceitful. I didn't want to risk pissing off Sam by ignoring him altogether. Amber mentioned how useful it could be to have an ally in the event Sid and Maxwell ran into any permitting problems.

My fingertips danced a nervous tango on my thigh. "Hey, Sweetie? Did I tell you Amber and I ran into an ex-boyfriend of mine from college the other day?"

"Sounds fun. Or not?"

"Whatever. I hadn't thought about him in, like, forever. We dated freshman year. He decidedly was not a keeper."

"Must have been a good ego trip to show him what he missed out on." If Josh only knew!

I flipped my phone up with a swish, letting it click against the coffee table when I lowered it. Swish, click, swish, click. "One thing, though. He's a building inspector. In Princeton. He knows about our wedding venue. Amber suggests we stay on his good side, using his influence in case we need it during the renovation process."

"Yeah, sounds like a good idea."

"In his email today, he said the next time we're in Princeton, we should let him know. Maybe we'll all have lunch together." I touched my nose, hoping the story of Pinocchio was not true.

"Meeting your ex, huh? We've managed to avoid introducing each other to our ghosts. Well, with the exception of Monica."

"I would say I spent enough time dealing with her to be exempt from meeting any of your other former girlfriends." Monica and Josh came into my life on the same day. While they had broken up prior to the concert we played together, watching Josh flirt with me set her on a course of winning him back. Her plan worked, albeit only in the short term. It wasn't enough for her to interfere with my love life; she also made me miserable with her constant harangues on every gig we played together afterward. Even with Josh's ring on my finger, I remained wary about running into Monica on a concert.

"If she hadn't hired you to play on that concert, we wouldn't have met. I give her the teensiest bit of credit for making me the happiest man alive. But about your ex: next time we head to Princeton to see how the construction is going, I'd love to have lunch with him. Let's focus on tonight's dinner. I'm going to order mu shu pork, Happy Family, broccoli in garlic sauce, and steamed dumplings. Will that be enough food, or should I order soup?"

"I'd love some hot and sour soup. And now we're set for lunch tomorrow. Nothing's better than finding a stack of leftover containers waiting for you in the fridge when you're hungry for your next meal."

WHAT A WASTE of a good panic attack. I had stressed over what my mother's reaction to the request for me to play at the Vista on Thanksgiving would be. I was accustomed to her annual burst of anger for me having gigs every Christmas Eve and Day, but I had never worked on Thanksgiving before. With the threat of having to compete not only with my work schedule but also with visits to Harrisburg in the future to spend holidays with the Yates, my soon-to-be in-laws, her guilt trips concerning holidays had increased as my relationship with Josh matured.

Thanksgiving had been sacred turf. Before my father suffered his first stroke, we would fly to Florida to spend the long weekend with his family. After he fell ill, we relocated our feast to my parent's condo in Westfield. Chloe often came along as my date. Following my father's death, Nathan and Derrick inherited the hosting duties.

Nothing I had imagined could have prepared me for our conversation. She didn't sound like she minded me missing the family meal. In fact, she brushed it off, musing over the possibility she, too, would decline the invitation. I was sure she had deployed a new weapon on me. I waited for her to declare, "Well, if you don't go, I won't go. And then what kind of Thanksgiving will it be for the boys?" A second shoe never dropped, unless you count her not weaponizing her decision to skip the meal as the second shoe. She tasked me with telling Nathan and Derrick we would both miss the feast. I couldn't decipher the message behind her decision. Maybe it wasn't just a second shoe but an entire rack of jackboots descending on my head.

Derrick answered Nathan's cell phone when I called him. "Hey, kiddo! Your brother forgot to take his phone with him to the grocery store. You're stuck with me."

"Maybe it's for the better. I have news to break to you guys: Mom and I both won't be able to make it to Thanksgiving."

"Say it ain't so! We'll miss you guys. Are the three of you going to spend Thanksgiving with the Yates?"

"No. I'm playing at the Vista."

"Please let Josh know the invitation to celebrate with us is still good. Unlike his fiancée, we're not going to ditch the poor guy because we found something better to do."

I held the phone in front of me, wishing Derrick could see my scowl. "Way to make me feel heartless. Depending on his gig schedule the days before and after Thanksgiving, he may head to Pennsylvania to see his parents."

"So, what's your mother up to?"

"I have no idea. She was being all cagey. Her missing the party had started out as a hypothetical situation. By the end of our conversation, she had come to the decision to go ahead with her secret Thanksgiving plans."

"Now I'm intrigued. Where could she be going?"

"You've got me. I was sure it was a ploy to make me feel guilty for my gig. The shock of her not eviscerating me had blinded me to her actual motive. I never asked. If she were debating whether to accept an invitation from a friend of hers we know, she would have mentioned who invited her. She's keeping a secret from us! You're good at this sort of thing. Can you call her to suss it out?"

"I'll wait for Nathan to weigh in. I don't see how we'll survive the intrigue. I'll miss having you guys for Thanksgiving, for sure, but Nathan's more likely to have a bit of a sulk over losing bodies from his table. He's outdone himself with the menu planning. We might have to extend invitations to additional friends to have them help us conquer the mountain of food he plans to prepare. Laurel and her husband are joining us. We can't count on her to eat for two this early in the pregnancy. At least she's eating, though. She hasn't been felled by a wicked case of morning sickness."

"I'm bummed I'll miss meeting the baby bump."

"The kid's the size of a kidney bean right now. You wouldn't even suspect Laurel to be pregnant. We've scheduled the first sonogram for December twenty-third. We should have pictures of our little heir or heiress to share at the wedding."

"I can't wait to see the pictures! Speaking of weddings, how's yours coming together?"

"Easy as can be. There's practically nothing to it."

I grunted. "That's what I keep saying, but no one believes me."

"I believe you. But your wedding sounds a lot more involved than ours."

I rolled my eyes. "See what I mean?"

"Sorry. I promise I won't bug you about it again. Between you and me, I wanted a big blowout. Drag queens on a float, me descending from aerial silks, the whole shebang. Nathan would prefer to have our ceremony at town hall with only the requisite witnesses in attendance. Our compromise is to invite a small group of people to join us at our favorite restaurant. A quick exchange of vows followed by lots of good food and wine."

"It will be awesome, even without the RuPaul of it all. I'll wear false eyelashes, a headpiece, and lots of sequins if you'd like."

"Oh no, you won't. It's bad taste for the guests to dress like the groom. I won't permit anyone to be prettier than me. Speaking of beauties, have you found your dress?"

I huffed. "Didn't you just promise me you wouldn't bug me about wedding stuff? Despite what my mom and Chloe say, I've decided to not think it about the dress until the beginning of the year. I watched a couple of episodes from that wedding dress show. The whole spectacle of it — bringing your wedding party with you, the tears, the fights. No thanks. I don't know how I'm going to avoid including my mother in the hunt, but I know my sanity depends on me searching for a dress without her."

"Based on your conversation with her about Thanksgiving, maybe she might surprise you. In the event she's heartbroken, I'll gladly schedule a mother/son-in-law day with her. She and I can try on wedding dresses to our hearts' content!"

I yelled to Chloe as she headed for the door, "Bring home some stuffing for me!" Chloe had made plans to spend Thanksgiving with Gwen's parents in North Caldwell. Gwen needed an ally because Matt was joining them for the holiday. Her parents knew him from college, of course, but after he had broken their daughter's heart, they were reluctant to welcome him into their home for the first time following the reconciliation. "And wish Gwen luck!"

The roads leading toward Weehawken were blissfully clear on Thanksgiving morning. I wished I could spend the day with Derrick and Nathan, but I wouldn't miss the bumper-to-bumper traffic we normally encountered in the early afternoon trip to Marlton. I especially hated having to spend the day without Josh. He had driven to Harrisburg yesterday and wouldn't be back until Saturday morning.

Working on a holiday had a way of detaching a person from reality. I'd sit alone behind my harp on such gigs, observing happy families enjoying the holiday together. We existed in two separate worlds. While I stared longingly into their realm, they didn't even acknowledge me, let alone imagine swapping lives. I'd adjusted somewhat to the experience of working on Christmas, but driving to my gig today differed from heading to work on Sundays or Christmas. I was weightless. Not in the sense of being free from burdens. More like floating in outer space because I had forgotten to tether myself to the spacecraft.

The quiet of the waterfront and the parking lot at the Vista fed the lingering sensation of unease. I unloaded my gear from my van, purposely making noise to drown out the silence around me. A seagull abandoned its nearby perch, scared away by the clatter of my bench falling to the pavement. Across the river, Pier 88 was empty. I had never been to the Vista when the Orpheus wasn't in New York. I wondered how the crew would be celebrating the holiday. Probably monitoring endless games of bingo and parading large trays bearing turkeys down the aisles in the dining rooms.

Helena's warm hug and the bustle of the restaurant gave me a sense of security. I had found a home at the Vista in the weeks since I had become the regular musician. The staff became a second family. Everyone working today had to spend time away from their families, but at least we could commiserate with each other.

"Claude and Lily will be here today." Helena continued to insert today's menu into the black leather menu holders.

I leaned over her shoulder to read what the chef had prepared for today's feast. The Vista specialized in seafood with a Mediterranean bent. I'd become addicted to their seafood lasagna, but my taste buds knew today was Thanksgiving. They wanted turkey with all the fixings. The chef had counted on his guests making similar demands. His description on the menu of Italian sausage stuffing with roasted chestnuts convinced me I wouldn't miss out entirely on my Thanksgiving celebration.

Closing the last menu with a *thwump*, she said, "Oh, and they're bringing a special guest."

"Sheldon?" I asked. She nodded. "You've made my day!" I'd barely seen him since I disembarked last spring. We met for lunch once over the summer, but I hadn't been to visit him since. I couldn't wait to show him what I'd done with the wisdom he had imparted.

When he arrived, Sheldon embraced Helena, kissing each of her cheeks. Butterflies fluttered mercilessly in my gut. He crossed the room to examine the angle of my harp and the music on my tablet. "You have the job under control, my dear Ellen. Don't let me disturb you."

I launched into a peppy rendition of *Love is Here to Stay*, shocked he had no critiques to lob at me. Knowing he approved of how I handled the job did nothing to calm my nerves. My head bobbed up from my music to check in on his table every couple of minutes while I played. I didn't mean to seek his approval, but with each smile or nod he returned to me, I relaxed.

Claude and Lily entertained another couple at their table with Sheldon. One of their guests regarded me with an expression on her face I would have expected from her had I farted in her box at the opera. More than once, Lily interrupted her mid-glare, grasping her arm to bring her attention back to their table.

The comforting scent of Thanksgiving foods wafting into my corner distracted me from my detractor. I asked Julio to put in an order for me to eat during my first break. Because my break was only fifteen minutes long, I made like a turkey, quickly gobbling my meal. I savored my first bite of the stuffing, but the clock wouldn't allow me to linger over additional mouthfuls. I hoped the chef didn't catch sight of me wolfing down the rest of my food like a barnyard animal.

Sheldon came to visit me after I returned from my lunch break. He rested his hand on my left shoulder. "You've made me very proud, Ellen. My, how you have grown musically! This job is just the beginning of your career."

"I owe it all to you. I didn't know how much I had to learn until we met. You've been so generous to me!" I wrapped my arm around his waist.

"Pshaw! You needed my help, so I helped you."

I angled my head toward Lily, Claude, and their guests. "It seems one person at your table doesn't appreciate my harp playing."

"Oh, Mrs. Trydel? I wouldn't lose sleep over her. She's an investor in the restaurant. She's probably miffed because you're playing instead of her daughter. I told you about the violinist I heard committing unconscionable acts to her instrument at brunch last month? The daughter and the violinist are one and the same. Claude and Lily understand why they can't hire an inferior musician despite their dependence on her parents' money. Like I said, no needs to pay any attention to Mrs. Trydel. Now, don't let me keep you from your job. Play some show tunes for me. Maybe a medley from *The Fantasticks*."

"ONE WEEK into the Christmas season, and I'm already sick of Christmas music." Chloe changed the station on Minerva's radio in time to escape listening to the next piece they announced, John Rutter's _Shepherd's Pipe Carol_.

I hovered my finger over the station preset button. "I like that piece. I hate to break it to you, but tonight's bride requested we play a few Christmas carols during the prelude and cocktail hour." Pressing the button to return us to the classical station, I let loose an evil laugh. Chloe's shoulders drooped in disappointment.

Chloe had called shotgun when we loaded the van, relegating Josh to the seat behind her. He chimed in, "I'm in the mood to play holiday music. I had been dying to be busier subbing at _Jazz Hands_ and _Murder Most Fun_, but now they're about the only gigs I've been playing. Careful of what you wish for, I guess. Don't get me wrong. I still love playing Broadway shows. But a change of pace will be nice. Especially since I get to play with the two of you."

"Whatever." Chloe pulled her phone out of her gig bag.

Ignoring her rudeness, Josh said, "I hear you're heading to San Francisco to spend Christmas with your mom. When do you leave?"

Chloe closed her message app. "December twenty-third. I can't wait to ditch New Jersey."

"What's wrong with New Jersey?" I'm always quick to defend my home state.

"Winter in New Jersey is blah. Blah weather, blah gigs."

"But the state comes with kickass friends."

"True. I miss my mom, though. And the view of the Pacific from her house. I just have to survive two more weeks of gigs, and then I'll be on vacation."

"Exciting stuff awaits your return. My birthday, for instance," I reminded her.

"I promise I'll be back in time to help you celebrate. Big year for all of us, turning thirty."

From the backseat, Josh said, "Speak for yourself. I have an extra year to enjoy being twenty-something."

"I like 'em young!" I reached my arm behind me, giving Josh a condescending pat on his knee. He tugged my hand to his lips to plant a kiss on my fingertips.

I owned this awesome pair of shoes in kindergarten, pink jellies with a blue flower on the toe. Having bought them after school on a Friday, I spent the weekend wearing them around the house, bursting with the excitement of wearing them to school on Monday. I hoped my classmates would notice them. It wasn't that I wanted to brag about my new shoes. Because they were so special to me, I needed everyone to know I was wearing them. I took unnatural strides to put the shoes on display. At story time, I plopped myself down in the middle of the reading carpet circle and stuck my feet out to form a V with my legs.

Instead of complimenting me on my cool new shoes, my classmates were mad at me for hogging the carpet.

When the ring on my left hand was brand new, I wanted brides at the weddings I played to catch a glimpse of the stones sparkling on my finger. I had joined their little club and took pride in displaying my membership ID. None of them ever noticed, or if they did, the connection between us wasn't special to them.

The impulse to show off my engaged status had faded. Deep into my own wedding planning, I'd spent free moments at each recent wedding I played to study the proceedings. I would have welcomed any bit of inspiration I could pilfer for our wedding, but mostly I wanted to confirm I was doing it right. I prepared to panic at each gig, expecting to find proof I was failing in my efforts, but I had yet to discover any items or rituals not itemized on my own checklist. With the exception of the notorious wedding at the Central Park Boathouse two years ago, I had never played at a wedding where something had gone horribly wrong like the bride forgetting to buy her dress. Leave it to me to be the first to have to throw on a random dress from her closet because she neglected to go dress shopping. Ugh. I was going to have to face it soon. Just not in the thick of my busy holiday gig schedule.

Chloe, her New Jersey Christmas Blahs aside, regarded the line of women at the altar swaddled in emerald-green taffeta with glee. Poofy sleeves jutted out from their shoulders. A bow the size of Texas sat as coyly as a bow the size of Texas could above each woman's derriere. Their bouquets of red, green, and white flowers befitting a herd of elves heralded the early arrival of Christmas in West Orange. "Even lavender dresses would be better than these," she whispered to me once we had finished playing the processional. "Don't get any ideas, though. I still would never agree to wear lavender. We picked the perfect dresses, thank goodness."

Josh leaned over to join our scrum. "I don't have to wear one of those vest thingies with my tux, do I? Especially not if it's green."

Rolling my head backward and sighing dramatically, I feigned disappointment. "You've ruined the surprise! I've ordered you an entire suit, vest included, in bright green."

"That changes everything. The green vest looks silly with the black and white, but if everything's green, well, I'll be the most gorgeous groom ever. Can I wear a green hat?"

"You'd be naked without one. I ordered you a walking stick, too."

"Good. I will cane anyone who dares to laugh at my attire."

"They'd be laughing with pure delight, my love."

"Son of a b..." A sound like a gunshot drowned out the beginning of my exclamation. A mouthful of nylon muffled its end. I brought my hands to my face, dabbing my nose to search for blood. There were red splotches on the back of my right hand, but they weren't blood. Each angry spot marked a place where my skin burned. I sneezed, only to exacerbate the bruising sensation spreading across my face.

"How could you possibly get into an accident turning into our parking lot?" Chloe coughed as she spoke. She batted away the deflated airbag from her lap.

"I think someone clipped the rear of the van. I had the vaguest sensation of being bumped from behind, but everything happened in a split second." In another moment of imperceivable brevity, my brain spewed data at me. Best Friend. Fiancé. Harp. Minerva. My hands. The two people I love more than life could be hurt. The two objects of the greatest value to me could both be irreparably damaged. I wiggled my fingers and wrists. No pain. My elbows and shoulders moved according to their blueprints. I could still play the harp, provided I still had a harp to play.

"Are either of you hurt?" Josh unbuckled his seatbelt and leaned forward.

"I might look like I took a sucker punch to the face tomorrow, and my right hand is burning, but everything else checks out," I said.

"You probably got sprayed with the explosive that inflates the airbag. Thank goodness you're not hurt too badly. And you, Chloe?"

"It hit me on my chest. I'm having trouble taking a breath. Otherwise, I'm fine."

"Me, too," Josh said.

Time regained its normal pace, but the adrenaline coursing through me sped me up. I needed to know what had happened, how much damage there was to my car, whether my harp had been impacted by the crash, and I needed the full report immediately. If I had been hit from behind, why did the airbags go off? A streetlamp loomed far closer to my windshield than it had any right to. The twisted blue metal of Minerva's hood rose from her chassis with a sneer.

Josh left the van without warning. I opened my door, taking tentative steps away from the vehicle to follow him. He walked north on Fullerton, his phone raised in front of him. Beyond him, a man examined the front of his car. I approached Josh. He was repeating, "Exegesis 64, Exegesis 64," to himself.

"What are you saying?"

Josh shushed me.

In a whisper, I asked, "Is he the guy who hit me? Should we go talk to him?"

"Stay here. I don't trust him." He continued to film the scene. The driver of the other car got into his vehicle and drove off.

"He's getting away! We have to stop him. He caused the accident!" I watched in horror as he sped out of view.

"I suspected he'd pull a runner. I have his license plate — that's what I was muttering to myself. I turned it into a mnemonic device. I have video footage of him bending over the front of his car to examine the point of impact. The police will find him. Let's see how bad a hit poor Minerva took."

Chloe was examining the crumpled front of my van. "She may be a goner, Ellen."

"No! Not Minerva! Maybe the damage to the rear is minor." I passed behind the van. The driver had hit her right flank. The side panel and the taillight were both damaged. She had a flat tire, but the rear gate hadn't been hit. I opened the hatch. My harp, packed with pillows between the passenger seats, had shifted only slightly. I hopped into the van to unzip the cover. With a swoosh of my fingers against her strings, I played a glissando, listening to the pitches of the notes. The C-flat major scale I played was in tune, a good sign she hadn't suffered structural damage. I wouldn't know for certain until I had her upstairs in my apartment, though. Four out of five of us walking away from an accident was reason enough to be grateful. Releasing a deep breath, I expelled some of the tension from my constricted chest.

"Ellen, I'm so sorry I blamed you before. The accident totally wasn't your fault." Chloe rested her head on my shoulder, her arm wrapped around my back.

"I didn't even notice you saying anything. This totally sucks! How am I going to get to work tomorrow? I can't imagine a worse month to have an accident. I have no extra time to deal with insurance adjusters and body shops this month."

"Here's a little perspective. You can use my SUV tomorrow. I can carpool with another musician to my concert. Be thankful none of us was injured. And finally, if you're going to have an accident, where better to have one than at home? No tow trucks needed. We can push your car into a parking spot."

"You're right. But still, it sucks. Oh, look. The cops are here. How did they know?" It hadn't yet occurred to me to call them.

"I made the call when you and Josh were checking out the other car."

"You're too good to me. I love you, you know." She shivered within my embrace. "Where's your jacket?"

"In the car."

"Well, go put it on, young lady. We can't have you survive a car crash only to freeze to death."

If Josh and Chloe hadn't been with me, I probably would have exploded like the propellant in my airbags. Being the only driver present, I had to make the case for not having caused the accident. The surge of righteous indignation coursing through me would have hampered my ability to explain my version of the events in a calm, objective manner. Chloe had helped me to lower my blood pressure before I had to give a statement. Josh's easy nature had him joking with the officers. His video would be strong evidence for the hit-and-run crime.

Enlisting the help of a man walking by, the four of us pushed Minerva into the closest parking space once the police had finished taking our statements. I hated to leave the crumpled, forlorn car behind. I wanted to let her know I hadn't meant to hurt her, that I would do everything I could to get her back on the road.

On Friday, I met my insurance adjuster at the shop where I had sent Minerva to recuperate from her trauma. "Your car is totaled," he said without warning. He fiddled with the papers attached to his clipboard.

My hand reached for Minerva, covering her metaphoric ears to spare her from hearing the awful news. "Totaled? Are you sure they can't fix her?"

"Any car can be repaired. From our point of view, we have to consider the cost of the repairs against the car's pre-crash value. For a vehicle worth, at best, three thousand dollars—"

"Only three thousand despite the thousands of dollars I poured into the car payments? She's in great shape, except for the recent damage. I've had her oil changed regularly. I just fit her with a set of new brakes over the summer. This was my first accident."

"Cars depreciate. We're talking about a ten-year-old minivan with over one hundred twenty-thousand miles on it. Your car has had a good run. If you had gone to a dealer the day before the accident to trade it in, you'd be lucky if they offered you two thousand for it. I'll take into account how well you maintained your vehicle in my report. But whatever number I come up with will be far less than the cost of getting the vehicle up and running. Accidents happen. My job is to make sure you can return to normal as soon as possible. If the police can complete their report in a timely fashion, we should be able to send you your check soon, maybe even before the New Year."

thirteen
long live minerva

I HAVE TO BUY a new car? On top of planning a wedding? Because, really, I needed one more thing to stress over. I knew Minerva was an old lady, but she took care of me. Yes, she was unhappy at speeds above seventy miles an hour. And she did have a weird rattling sound my mechanic never could identify. I had finished paying off her loan two and a half years ago. She didn't owe me anything. None of these realizations made saying goodbye to the only car I had ever owned any easier.

I drove Chloe's SUV to a few gigs after the accident. Like an unfaithful lover, I admired features in her car I didn't have in mine. Its four-wheel drive scoffed at snow that would have made Minerva skittish. Backing up was a breeze with the rearview camera. I made good use of the USB port in the dash. Burdened by guilt, I tempered my lust, troubled to care for a car other than Minerva.

Chloe could lend me her car because she wasn't using it. The blow from the passenger airbag bruised her chest, making breathing uncomfortable. With breathing being a key component to playing the flute, she had to send a sub to her rehearsals on Wednesday and Thursday. She found a way to practice each day without having to blow air across the mouthpiece. The clatter of flute keys replaced her flute's sweet tone in our apartment. Her increased drive to practice remained a mystery to me.

I came home from the auto body shop to find her fingers flying on the keys. She turned the flute upright between her hands upon noticing the dejected slump of my shoulders. "The news isn't good?"

"Minerva is dead. Long live Minerva."

Chloe laid her flute across the blue velvet interior of her opened flute case. "It doesn't surprise me, but still. She was a good girl. We had a lot of great conversations in her. Wow, we've come to the end of an era."

"It's like the band is breaking up. Minerva's gone, Gwen and I have both fallen in love. But the three of us still have each other. Matt and Josh know they'll sometimes have to play second fiddle to our relationship."

Chloe's brow crumpled in confusion. "How'd you segue to this topic? You really must be taking Minerva's demise hard. We'll find you a new car to love."

"I don't know what's going on with me. I have to snap out this mood. Speaking of cars, here are your keys. Since I left my harp at the church last night, and I won't be bringing it home until tomorrow, I don't need a harp-sized car today. Josh will chauffeur me to my rehearsal tonight, and I'll rent a car tomorrow. It's time for me to move forward, I guess."

"You know I'm here to help any way I can. Oh, hey, Josh! I didn't hear you come in."

"Hey yourself!" Thrusting a bouquet of gerbera daisies into my hands, he asked, "Do you remember when Donald gave Minerva a flower? Wasn't it this kind?" Donald was Josh's previous car. A few hours before we had our first date, Josh had tucked a flower under Minerva windshield wiper with a note from Donald.

"Ah, Donald! Is he still pining for her from the grave? Maybe they've reunited. At least one of the accident victims might have found her happy ending."

"You'll find yours soon enough. I'd like to imagine our two former vehicles frolicking together in the car afterlife. Where do cars go when they die? To a version of the Autobahn without any other cars, perhaps?"

"Sounds like my version of heaven. You guys, would it be weird for me to put a few of the flowers at the base of the lamppost, you know, like a memorial to Minerva?"

"Not weird at all. C'mon. Let's head to the parking lot to say a few words in tribute to the old gal." Chloe led us to the scene of the crime.

In an odd mix of self-consciousness, despondency, and humor, I poured out my gratitude and sense of loss. Chloe and Josh each added a few words. To passersby, we might have appeared to be mourning the loss of a human, not a car. Or perhaps they thought we were lamppost fetishists.

The mourning party shuffled back into our apartment. "You know, the worst thing about today was how little value the adjuster attached to her. He said she was worth less than three thousand dollars," I said.

"You don't have to accept their first quote, you know. Here, let's get a couple of estimates online." Josh typed away on my laptop. "There. I've submitted Minerva's deets to two different sites. While we wait for the quotes, let's check out the prices of used minivans for sale. The more you know, the better your negotiating position will be."

The insurance adjuster's offer was close to the prices we found online. The highest price we found for one of Minerva's siblings was only thirty-five hundred dollars, and it had features my car lacked. In my search for comparable vehicles, I considered the affordability factor of buying a used car. The high mileage on the vans scared me. The best way to ensure I would avoid having to cope with car problems in the next few years would be to buy a new car. Regardless of how much the insurance check will be for, I resigned myself to having to cough up a bit of cash from my savings for the down payment on a car. "Should I buy another minivan or an SUV like yours, Chloe?"

"Do you like mine? I've enjoyed driving it. Since your parents picked out Minerva, here's your chance to find your dream car."

"Minivans are ideal harp cars, especially for harpists with kids. I've had fun driving your car, Chloe, but what happens when Josh and I have a kid? I'd spend half my time converting it from a harp mobile, complete with a mattress in the back, into a kiddy mobile."

Josh recoiled with a start, a wild expression carved into his face. "I know we've talked about having kids one day, but you can't talk about the *what-ifs* of parenthood today. That's a long way off, right?"

"I'm planning on the new car lasting another ten years. What if we have kids before then?" I gasped for air. First weddings, then a car, and now kids were setting me off? I shouldn't be looking for a new car. Print me up a boarding pass 'cause I was ready to ride the crazy train.

Sensing my tension rising, Josh held his anxiety in check. "I'll tell you what: I'll be in the market for another car in a couple of years, tops. I'm man enough to drive a minivan. If you don't buy one, I will. We'll transport our future kids in a minivan whether it's yours or mine."

"You'd buy a minivan? Thank you!" I exhaled with a *whoosh*, letting my shoulders fall away from my ears. "I really like Chloe's SUV. To be honest, I snuck a peek at what they cost. I could swing a base model if I dipped into my wedding savings to bolster the down payment. It shouldn't be a problem. We don't have to buy the fanciest invitations. I can eliminate a few of the extra things we don't really need for the wedding. I don't have to hire someone to do my hair and makeup, for instance. I'll cut my dress budget in half."

"I wouldn't advise it. Your dress budget was already too low. I still stand by my belief you won't find the perfect dress for less than two thousand dollars."

Josh gasped. "Two thousand for a dress you're going to wear only once? Sheesh! What do you get for that price? Free internet service? A lifetime supply of socks?"

Chloe kept shaking her head. "You're going to end up with awful fabric and cheesy details. I don't know, Ellen."

My chest constricted yet again. "I'm not talking about buying a dress today. Or even a car. I have to prepare for my rehearsal. I'll deal with everything else later."

I had forgotten I had mentioned to Sam I would be playing a Christmas concert not far from Princeton. He startled me, coming up beside me while I was tuning before the performance. "This brings me back! I remember having to carry this thing up a flight of stairs for you once or twice."

I remembered too late about the perils of hugging him. The toxic, inescapable cloud of his cologne clung to me with fervent desperation. "Thanks for coming tonight. Are you here alone?" I held out hope I had misinterpreted his first email where I thought he had been coming on to me. Maybe he had a girlfriend.

"Uh-huh. None of my friends are interested in classical music. I'm not, either, but how could I pass up the opportunity to see my favorite harpist? Does your boyfriend come to hear you play?" He scanned the audience, perhaps expecting to recognize a man he had never met.

"Fiancé. And no. Unless we're on a gig together. He's playing a Broadway show tonight."

With his hand on my harp's neck, he said, "I wouldn't let you out of my sight if you were my fiancée."

I had forgotten how possessive he could be. Needling me about my plans every time we parted whilewe were dating plus his obsession with seeing me in his mother's underwear? I really had dodged a bullet by dumping him. "We have careers. We lead our own lives."

"So, if I asked you to join me for a drink tonight after the show, would he get mad?"

I crossed my arms. "I don't have to ask his permission to do anything."

"In that case, would you like to grab a beer later?" He shot me an eager grin.

While I would rather invite my mother to come on my honeymoon than spend an evening with him, I agreed to have drinks with him if only to prove to him I can act independently without it hurting my relationship with Josh.

Sam could not compete with Benjamin Britten for my attention during the performance of *A Ceremony of Carols*. I remembered his existence only when he returned to my side at the end of the concert. Sharply rebuffing his know-it-all suggestions on a better way to move my harp, I relegated him to the role of harp bench carrier. I also declined his offer to ride with him, preferring to have the option of leaving the bar on my own if he became intolerable. *The reason I agreed to have a drink with him was to nurture him as an ally of the renovation*, I reminded myself when I considered reneging on the invitation.

Thankfully, the beer softened his aggressiveness, reminding me of his better qualities. Although he was nowhere near as funny as Josh, Sam did have a decent sense of humor. It was fun to laugh with him over highlights of our lives from the last ten or so years and recollect the friends we had in common from IU.

While he nursed a second beer, I sipped a cup of coffee. "We had some good times together, didn't we?" Setting my cup on the bar table, my hair fell across my face. I tucked it behind my ear.

"We did. And we're still having fun together."

I appreciated the detour from my crazy life Sam offered me tonight. I was happy to linger a while longer with him, to talk about my life with someone who wasn't a part of it. "… and now, every time I say the word *wedding*, I have to put a dollar into the jar. Yet Chloe's the one who is all gung-ho about getting me into a wedding dress. I'm not ready to tackle the whole rigmarole of trying on dresses in front of my friends and my mother."

"Do you think the dress, or your lack of enthusiasm for buying one, symbolizes your reluctance to get married?" WTF? Narrowing my eyes to question and condemn Sam's line of analysis, I scared a nervous laugh out of him. "Man, I don't know why I said that."

I couldn't help but wonder if he hoped to coax me into admitting I had my doubts about marrying Josh. The last thing I wanted to do was to trip over myself denying any such problem existed. Of course I wanted to marry Josh! Being the queen of awkward defensiveness, I had to find the escape hatch that would allow me to dismiss with grace the emotional mayhem he concocted. "See? Weddings are like catnip. No one — not even you, a disinterested outsider — can resist stepping in and turning them into a big drama."

"I wouldn't call myself disinterested. I'm happy to be a part of your life again. Oh, speaking of your wedding, how are things going with your venue?"

"We haven't been back since the beginning of July. I hear they're ahead of schedule. We'll see the progress soon enough."

"Doesn't it make you nervous not to know for sure? They could be lying to you, telling you everything's fine when in fact it's not."

Great. I had succeeded in putting any doubts about the venue being ready for us in the back of my mind. Sam had a knack for dredging up all of my phobias. "We just have to trust them, I suppose."

"So long as you're not worried. I'd hate for something to go wrong with your wedding. Look. I did it again. I promise I'll stop talking about your wedding. I can't help it, though. Since we're back in each other's lives, I care about what happens to you." He reached for my hand, a nauseating grin stretched across his face. With a shudder, I retracted my hand.

Sam the creepster had returned. I was sure I had done nothing to encourage his behavior. He had already unsettled me with his off-base psychoanalysis and hints about reasons why I should freak out over the renovations. This assumption of rekindled familiarity was too much. I removed my jacket from the back of my stool. "I'm going to hit the road. Thanks for coming to my concert. It was fun seeing you again."

"It's almost like it was meant to be."

His fingertips on my arm burned my skin like they had been dipped in acid. I took a step away from him. "Um, yeah. I'll be in touch when Josh and I revisit our site."

"I'd like to meet him. And anything I can do to help, I'm your guy."

THE SILVER PICTURE FRAME I pulled from the box of decorations weighed less than I had expected. Before adding it to the collection of pictures I was arranging, I took a peek at it. I recognized the photo. I had taken it of Nathan and Derrick posing in front of the Orpheus in February when they and my mother had vacationed aboard the ship. They had tasked me today with arranging framed photographs on the mantle in the private dining room of the restaurant where they were hosting their wedding.

I reached into the box, pulling out a painted wooden frame. Cartoon images of a lion, an elephant, and a giraffe marched below a dark photo of faint swirls and shapes outlined in white. "Derrick, is this the kid?" I held the frame aloft. Derrick left his mother and mine to continue filling vases with mottled blue and green hydrangeas, thistle, and eucalyptus leaves.

He took the frame from me, his thumb caressing its edge. "In all the wedding excitement, I forgot to show you the sonogram. Look — our little nugget has figured how to suck its thumb! We have a genius in the making!" He set the photo in the center of the mantle.

"So precious! With those Blum genes, brilliance does come with the territory. As does a little moodiness, in case you hadn't noticed." I added a photo of Nathan holding Jax, their French bulldog, to the growing tableau of frames. "I'm surprised Jax isn't here."

"You want to talk moody? The one guest Nathan insisted we invite to our wedding isn't allowed to attend because of the health code."

"So, um, inviting his dog but not his sister or mother was his original plan? I'm offended. I'm taking myself home." I snagged the photo of Jax and Nathan from the mantle. "And his little dog, too!"

"I refused to say my vows without the two of you in attendance. And Josh." He turned away from me. "Yikes. Your mom has the proportion of thistle and eucalyptus all wrong. Gotta go prevent a floral disaster."

With an appreciative squeeze of his arm, I returned to decorating the mantle. I placed three votive candles between the groups of frames scattered across the beam. I held a fourth candle, unsure where it belonged. The small room offered few surfaces where Nathan and Derrick could infuse it with their personalities. Two hefty tables of dark wood stood end-to-end against the far wall. Combined, they would seat thirteen guests once moved into the center of the room after the ceremony. A cove in the opposite wall beckoned. The empty ledge at the bottom was an inch wider than the base of the candleholder. I regarded the candle in its new home. He was lonely. I pilfered a stem of thistle and another of the eucalyptus, weaving them behind the votive. "Here you go, little buddy." I surveyed my handiwork. Perfect.

My stomach did a backflip. Nathan and Derrick's wedding was a gateway drug, a wedding foreshadowing my own. Their small event made ours look like a three-ring circus. Were Josh and I thinking too big?

Servers passed flutes of Champagne and trays of hors d'oeuvres. I nibbled a slice of pumpernickel bread topped with smoked salmon and crème fraîche. Josh draped his arm around my shoulders. "Excited?"

"I am. I've always known they were going to grow old together — don't tell Derrick I alluded to the fact he will, in fact, age. But for them to have the right to make their bond legal, it means the world to me!"

"This will be us in six months." A contented smile spread across his face.

I licked a smear of crème fraîche from the back of my pointer finger. "I'm a fan of the simplicity of their wedding. To celebrate with only a few people is so intimate. I'm not complaining about getting our buzz on before the ceremony, either. Do you wish we were planning ours on a smaller scale?"

"Honestly, no. I think ours is going to be perfect!"

I clenched. This was ridiculous. I had no reason to panic about our wedding today. Even having taken the month off from planning due to my overstuffed gig schedule and car troubles, we were in great shape with our wedding plans. I beckoned the server holding the tray of salmon, happy to placate my nervous belly with delicious food. With my mouth obstructed by a hunk of fish, I said, "If our caterer will serve these puppies, everything will be perfect." Josh planted a kiss on my lips before I had a chance to swallow.

While my mother fussed over Laurel, tea cozy to her future grandchild, Nathan hailed me to the back corner. Their friend Dave was presiding over the signing of the marriage certificate. He had become ordained online in order to perform the ceremony. Dave's partner Pedro and I bore witness to the marriage, adding our signatures and addresses below Dave's. Nathan and Derrick stood behind us, their hands entwined. "Are we ready?" Nathan asked.

Dave stood in front of the far wall. The guests congregated in small clusters facing him. Still holding hands, my brother and Derrick walked between us, their faces radiating joy. Less than twenty minutes later, Dave pronounced them married. I fumbled in my pocketbook for a tissue. Josh turned toward me, sniffing loudly. For a moment, I believed we were the couple whose job it was to end the ceremony with a kiss. I wanted the overwhelming sense of love and commitment to be ours. I couldn't wait for our wedding day.

Food, wine, and conversation flowed. Throughout the meal, guests randomly clinked their glasses, demanding attention for yet another toast. Josh and I eagerly joined the chorus of well-wishers and speechmakers.

My mother could barely contain her happiness when she stood to deliver hers. "I was done making babies by the time Ellen arrived. Two children were plenty. The first time Nathan brought Derrick home, back when they were students at the University of Pennsylvania, I recognized how much room I had in my heart for more children. I knew I had gained a son the day I met Derrick. I promise it wasn't only because you did the dishes after dinner. And did them the right way." With a proud snicker, Nathan kissed Derrick's hand.

"A mother wants nothing more than for her children to be happy. Derrick, you make Nathan so very happy. You are both such wonderful gifts to me. If the child you are expecting brings you even a smidgen of the love and happiness the two of you have brought each other and me, you will be blessed with a most wonderful life." She pushed her chair out of her way, running around to the other side of the table to kiss the grooms.

On the morning of New Year's Eve, Josh drove me to a car dealership in Edison. Everyone had spun the news of my accident into a win for me, how I would be able to negotiate a great price on a new car at the very end of the year. I had never bought a car before since my parents had picked out Minerva for me at a used car dealership, her down payment serving as my college graduation present. I wasn't sure either Josh or I had the negotiating skills to pull off a good deal.

My mom had given me the business card of a man we had met on the Orpheus last February. I remembered Douglas to be an affable guy. He accompanied my mother on shore excursions and invited her to dine with him and his two daughters, freeing me from having to entertain her non-stop during the week. Him owning a car dealership where I could buy an SUV like Chloe's should be convenient. At least I didn't have to choose a dealership. But I would be on his turf today. I hoped he didn't bamboozle me. I had crunched the numbers every way possible. I had a monthly payment in mind, and nothing except for a low price on a base model would help me to stick to my budget, even with money pilfered from my wedding savings applied to the down payment.

Douglas strode across the showroom toward the welcome desk where we had checked in. Even without a Hawaiian shirt, he projected a good-natured and relaxed vibe. His curly brown and gray hair was longer than it had been last February. His coffee-colored skin lacked the kiss of sun and sea from last winter, but his grin remained unchanged. He greeted me at the reception desk with a bear hug. "Well, here we are on solid ground! And you must be Josh. I've heard a lot about you. Ellen talked about you nonstop on the ship." Josh extended his hand, but Douglas scooped him in for a hug. Josh and I eyed each other suspiciously. Were we being lulled into a trap by his friendliness?

"I've reminded your…, er, I mean, when we were on the ship, I told your mother to come see me the next time she needed a new car. I'm sorry to hear the circumstances of why you need to buy a car today. But at least you weren't hurt, which is a blessing. And did she say they caught the man who hit you? He'll face some stiff penalties, for sure. Well, let's not reflect on the past. We're going to get you into a new car today. Am I correct in understanding you like our smallest SUV?"

The three of us walked through the crowd of frenzied last-chance car buyers at the dealership. I peered into each car we passed, a nervous excitement rising within me. I tapped a balloon tied to a sign. The side with *Year End Sale* rotated away from me, showing me the side with the manufacturer's logo. Here I was, doing the very adult thing of buying a car, and I wondered if they would give me a souvenir balloon with my purchase.

Douglas led us to an office in the back. Lacking the comfortable leather furniture and family photos of my father's welcoming office at his law firm, this room served only to isolate the owner from the rest of the staff and to offer the minimum of desk space and chairs needed to close a deal. Filing cabinets lined the wall behind Douglas. Josh and I sat opposite him in dingy gray chairs. Douglas and I occasionally met each other in the middle of his desk, leaning over each document he offered that required my signature. My legs bounced along with the tinny strains of holiday music coming through the sound system.

"Now that I've amassed a collection of autographs from the famous harpist, Ellen Blum, let's go take a test drive." Josh and I followed him toward the front door. Armed with a purpose, I walked a straighter, more focused line past the showroom vehicles.

A white cousin to Chloe's car waited in the no-parking zone by the front doors. Even under an overcast sky, the vehicle gleamed. Douglas opened the driver's door for me. "Have a seat." Josh rounded the car to hop in the passenger side.

I slid my right hand back and forth against the cold curve of the steering wheel. The gas pedal was a mile away. I spotted two buttons with seat icons below the sound system controls. "Are these the seat adjusters?" I would love to have power seats, but I knew even these simple options were out of my budget.

"Those are for the heated seats. The seat controls are to the left of the seat cushion." While I fiddled with the seat adjustments, Douglas reached across my face to push a button on the ceiling. A sunroof opened. Josh whistled, his head thrown back in amazement. I shook my head. I knew this would happen. Douglas wasn't really our friend. He had purposely picked the most tricked-out model he had in stock, confident I would be unhappy with a car sporting manually adjustable seats and no sunroof once I compared it to this beaut.

I shifted my legs out of the car, planted my feet on the ground, and squared my shoulders. "I wish I could afford features like these, but they're not in my budget."

He grinned. "Would you believe me if I told you they are?" My blank stare answered his question. "I had someone come in yesterday. She bought this vehicle from us a year ago. Ten thousand miles later, she decided she wanted the next larger size. I can sell it to you for eight hundred dollars less than the best offer I could make on the base model of a new car. The vehicle is not in perfect condition, though. You'll find a dimple about the size of my fist on the rear bumper."

"Not perfect sounds just my speed. Affordable works, too." My anxieties floated away like a bunch of *Year End Sale* balloons on the lam.

"Would you like to take it out for a spin?" Josh leaped out of his seat, offering shotgun to Douglas.

Three and a half weeks of driving both Chloe's car and a rental had helped wean me from Minerva. What I loved about my minivan was that she took me from point A to point B without insisting I reward her for her service with frequent trips to the local car repair shop. I had enjoyed not making car payments each month. But she was tired. This vehicle made not a sound when the engine was running. With the slightest tap on the accelerator, it veered forward. The lightest pressure on the brakes stopped it immediately. Its cup holders didn't hold crumbs, grit-covered paperclips, and coins. I was sure I had never viewed the road through such a crystal-clear windshield.

During the test drive, Douglas continued to point out features to me. Navigation system, satellite radio, heated mirrors. I hadn't imagined having such luxurious features. Slowly, I adjusted to the notion of owning a fully loaded car. I poked at her buttons while stopped at red lights, memorizing their functions and placements. All she lacked was a name. Maybe Luisa, the name of the heroine from the musical, *The Fantasticks*. Nah. In my head, I heard the scene where Matt calls out for her at the beginning of the song, *Metaphor*. Describing Luisa as too vibrant for a name, he tries a few others on for size. She answers to all. Would my car? Juliet? It sounded too prissy. Helena? Well, that would be awkward when I told my friends at the Vista about my new car. Guinevere? The car purred, enjoying the extra shot of gas I fed her. Guinevere!

CHLOE CHALLANGED ME to make a New Year's resolution our freshman year at IU. I generally gravitated toward the beige and light brown food groups served in the cafeteria. French toast in the morning, breaded and fried chicken patties on a roll for lunch, and potatoes in any preparation to accompany the least mushy entrée on the steam table for dinner. Beige is not the most flattering color on me, especially when worn in the form of an extra ten-pound blanket of fat on my hips and thighs.

My resolution was to explore other colors of the food rainbow, especially the dark greens my roommate extolled like a clone of her mother, a famous nutritionist. Between her overeager guidance and my stubborn streak, by the middle of January, I once again painted the surface my tray beige, often accenting it with shades of chocolate brown. I resolved never to make New Year's resolutions again. Here was a resolution I had no problem keeping.

This new year felt shinier and newer than some. Guinevere shimmered in the parking lot of my apartment complex. Because Claude and Lily had decided to make me a permanent fixture at Sunday brunch following a successful holiday season, I no longer had to compete with Tiffany, the violin strangler, for the gig. Best of all, Josh and I would become husband and wife in less than six months. I made a resolution not so much to change my life, but rather to keep the shiny and new feeling going for as long as possible. The first blemish in my perfect new year appeared on day two.

Chloe had spent the holidays with her mother in San Francisco and was due home on the third. She had left me a message while I was playing brunch today to say she had changed her return ticket to the ninth. Without explaining herself, she simply stated she wasn't ready to come home. I couldn't help but hear an insult buried within her words like she wasn't ready to see me. Her delayed return meant she would have to miss my birthday on the seventh.

Gwen swooped in to nurse my wounds. She and Matt arrived at my apartment with a bag of groceries. Josh and I had become one with the couch, recovering from our gigs. "Ah, shoot! I forgot the potatoes!" Gwen poked her head out of the kitchen. "Ellen, could you run out to buy a pound of fingerlings or another small type of potato? And wine. Or do you have a couple of bottles of red?"

"We're fully stocked in the wine department. We have rice. Would that work?" I had no intention of peeling myself off the couch.

"I'm craving roasted potatoes. Please?"

I sighed. "OK. Josh, wanna come with?"

He shook his head. "I love you, but I can't move. The commute out of the City did me in. Hurry so you can resume lounging with me."

At least there was an upside to running the errand. I could spend a little QT with Guinevere. The closest store was too close. My heated seats wouldn't have the chance to reach peak butt-comfort level. Since I had to go out, it wouldn't be so bad to head to the store at the far end of the next town over. Guinevere and I zipped along the tree-lined street meandering through Brookdale Park. We passed a few people braving the cold. Dogs sniffed at the bases of trees stretching their skeletal gray arms into the twilit sky. With my tush enveloped by warmth, the stillness beyond my windows lost its bleak, wintry edge.

Potatoes procured, I made the trip from my car to the apartment quickly in order to retain the warmth in my core. Gwen, Matt, and Josh stood near the dining table, arranged in a scattershot pattern. They had risen in haste upon hearing my key click in the door. Expressions of guilt inhabited each face. "What's going on?"

Gwen snatched a piece of paper from the table. "Um, er, nothing."

"Yeah, right. I'll pretend I didn't see anything." I grinned to myself. I bet they were planning a surprise party for my birthday. How was I going to be able to contain the anticipation without spoiling the surprise for myself?

Gwen tried to distract me from whatever it was they were hiding. She put me to work preparing the potatoes while she babbled on and on about nothing important. With one final stir of the pot on the stove, she lowered the heat under the beef stew. "The food requires a little alone time. Let's open a bottle of wine and join the guys."

The rich, meaty scent of the stew wafted into the living room. My stomach gurgled in response. The bell on the kitchen timer saved me. Gwen set the stew on a trivet on the dining table. "Come and get it!"

"Isn't Chester going to join us?" Josh looked around the room for our third roommate.

"He decided to ring in the New Year with a cleanse. He prefers to sulk in Chloe's room while we eat."

"It's just not a party without the two of them, is it? Should we video chat with Chloe during dinner?" Gwen rose from her chair, ready to grab her phone.

I said, "We'll call her later. It will be easier. Speaking of Chloe, is it just me, or do you suspect something's been off with her over the last several months?"

Gwen reached for the salad bowl I passed to her. "What do you mean?"

"I don't know exactly. Throughout the fall, she practiced as if an evil spirit possessed her. Nothing she accomplished pleased her, though. I think she has lost her confidence. And she has been more secretive than usual." I broke the end off of my roll, debating whether to add butter to it. In a show of self-control, I withstood the desire to slather it in rich, buttery goodness.

"I have wondered once or twice whether she is taking a mental inventory of her life. She has five months before she hits the big three-O, but she could have gotten a head start in preparing for the milestone."

"Maybe. I've decided I'm not going to get my undies in a twist about turning thirty in a few days. I like what I have going on in my life. Age is just a number, right?" And a roll without butter is just a roll. I cut a sliver off the cube of butter Josh had placed next to me. "Matt, you're thirty already. Is it different than being in your twenties?"

"Nah. Growing up is good. If I hadn't done a bit of it, I might not have gotten back together with the love of my life." I swear I saw bluebirds arrange garlands of flowers around the two of them while they kissed.

"Aw! You two are super cute!"

Gwen leaned over to whisper in Matt's ear. Her eyebrows arched, her expression cajoled him into agreeing with her. He nodded. "So, we were talking over the weekend and came to a decision. I'm going to move in with Matt!"

"You're moving to the City? Wow! How are your parents taking the news?"

"I wouldn't know. I haven't mustered the courage to break it to them. I mean, they surprised me on Thanksgiving, what with how well they treated him when they reconnected with him. But I'm still nervous about how they'll react to us taking this next step in our relationship. I'd better tell them before the next semester starts at Montclair State University, while they're both still in vacation mode."

"Moving in together, huh? You're one step ahead of us." Josh put his fork, Brussels sprout still attached, on his plate. "Were we supposed to have had this conversation?" he asked me.

"Yes. Yes, I believe we were supposed to have chosen where we'd live once we got hitched. How the hell did we forget?" I gasped for air, triggering a coughing attack.

Josh patted my thigh. "Have some water. Catch your breath. It's really not a big deal."

My teeth clamped the rim of my glass, and my eyes bugged out. "How can it not be a big deal? Besides the fact that we've failed to communicate on a vital topic, Chloe and I had to sign our lease six months ago, right before you proposed, two months before the lease expired. It ends July thirty-first. Chloe would kill me if I moved out on her a month early! Even if I don't move out until a month after the wedding, she'd probably want to leave at the end of the lease. There's no way she would welcome a new roommate into her life."

"Mine's up on July thirty-first, too. We can keep doing what we're doing, alternating nights at each other's apartment. We'll figure out where we'll live before our leases expire. Who said couples have to live together? Woody Allen and Mia Farrow never did."

"Yeah. And look how that turned out." I chugged the remains of my wine, glaring at him over the rim.

"Bad example. We don't have to solve the issue of where we're going to live at the moment. Promise me you won't let it stress you out?" Josh brought my hand to his lips, his limpid brown eyes pleading with me. I couldn't remain upset when he puppy-dog-eyed me.

"OK. Since landlords ask for two months' notice, I can put off talking to Chloe until late April. Done. Speaking of things stressing me out, my ex Sam keeps emailing me to remind me he's available to smooth over any problems with the reno. I don't want to pay attention to the renovation details on a day-to-day basis. It's not our problem. Amber was keeping tabs on it for us, but she joined up with the Orpheus today. She promised me yesterday everything is still on schedule. Is it foolish of me not to be following the renovation more closely?"

"No. Don't let Sam's offer influence your mindset. I believe Amber. The manor will be ready for prime time well before June twenty-second without your intervention. We'll check out the work they've done firsthand in a month or two. You need to take worrying about the renovation off your plate." To illustrate his point, he pilfered my last roasted potato.

"I see what you did there. I'll get my just desserts. Ooh. Dessert! Your last bite of brownie sundae is mine!"

"We'll have to wrestle for it."

"Matt, that may be our cue to hit the road. Speaking of the road, how's your new car?" Gwen cleared the plates from the table.

"I love it. I can't believe the good deal I got on her. How could a year-old car with all the bells and whistles be cheaper than a new car? If I didn't know any better, I would say Douglas gave me a family discount. But why would he do me a favor? He's just a guy we met almost a year ago on the fourth day of a weeklong cruise. I'm not complaining about him being nice to me, mind you."

"I guess it makes sense, seeing how much your van had depreciated. They say a car loses its value the moment you drive it off the lot. I wouldn't worry about the dealership losing money. They probably made a killing by selling the same car twice."

Matt returned to the table with our brownie sundaes. "Gwen was planning to stick a candle in yours, but I didn't want the ice cream to melt."

"Does this mean the two of you won't be hanging out with me on my birthday?" I couldn't help myself from digging for information about any possible surprise parties.

Matt shook his head. "I'm showing clients two apartments Tuesday evening. Count me out."

"I can't make it, either. I have a rehearsal." Gwen pulled her lower lip over the upper in an exaggerated pout.

"Ellen, don't kill me, but I just picked up a gig to sub on a show on Tuesday night. I promise to make it up to you later in the week. You can pick the restaurant." Josh raised his brow, hopeful I would let him off the hook for missing my birthday.

I didn't believe them. Their alternate plans on my birthday had to be a ruse to keep me from suspecting anything about the party they were planning. I was happy to play along. I bet Chloe plans to come home earlier than she told me. They had better be lying to me. I'd kill them if I had to spend my birthday alone.

MAGS, MY FRIEND AND NEIGHBOR, invited me to her apartment for a birthday lunch. I was glad to escape my empty apartment to take a break from wondering what festivities Josh and my friends had planned for this evening. Mags lived on a lower floor in my apartment building. We met each other a couple of years ago in the locker room of my local Y. Although she was over forty years older than me, she epitomized strength and vitality. If I grew up to be half as wise as Mags, I would consider my time on this planet to be worthwhile.

"Here's the woman of the hour! What an honor you chose to have lunch with me on such an auspicious occasion. You do like broccoli quiche, I hope?" She released me from her arms, closing the door behind me.

"Mmm! I do! Your hair looks great. Did you just get it cut?" Mags kept her grayish-white curls in a short hairstyle. The first time I saw her, the cap of curls around her face reminded me of Dame Judi Dench. She patted her hair, a pinkish glow forming in the center of her barely lined mahogany cheeks.

"The stuff keeps growing, so I keep having to have it hacked off. But thank you for noticing."

We sat across from each other at her table. The pie server clanged against a plate when Mags lowered a slice of quiche onto it. "This will be mine. The first slice of a pie is always the ugliest."

"If you go and call something pie, you know my mouth couldn't care less about how it looks. Heck, I salivate at the mention of pie charts."

"Here's a perfect slice for the birthday queen. How do you feel? Is thirty any different from twenty-nine?"

The air I inhaled refused to travel deeper into my lungs. A hot flash prickled my neck. I swore I wasn't going to let turning thirty mess with me. I believed my own hype: age was just a number. Even if I regarded my thirtieth birthday to be a chance to measure my life thus far, I had to give myself props for hitting key milestones. I was alive (that had to count for a lot, right?), and I was doing well in my career. My fingers clasped the ring on my left hand to give it a quick twirl. I had never challenged myself to be married by the time I turned thirty. Josh was my bonus achievement. The moment of calm I achieved upon reflecting on how much I loved him vanished under another cloud of panic.

Mags leaned forward, her eyes wide with concern. "What's the matter, dear? Your leg is bouncing a mile a minute. You're a bundle of nerves!"

"I'm having a panic attack. I had my first one back in June while my friend Amber and I discussed picking a wedding venue. I've had a couple of mini meltdowns since. For the life of me, I don't understand why wedding plans make me go apoplectic. But we weren't even talking about weddings. You just made a little comment about me turning thirty. Maybe I've been losing my cool because everything reminds me I have to be an adult."

"While marriage certainly is an endeavor requiring maturity, it alone doesn't define what it is to be mature."

"True, but I think our wedding is the trigger for my anxiety. I used to obsess about growing up because I wanted to be an adult. I thought after I had graduated from college, when I had moved out on my own, my mother would let me live my life uninterrupted. I craved an end to the days of being treated like a baby. I bet she will go to her grave with one last critique to hurl at me still on her lips." How did I get onto the topic of my mother? First I overreacted to a comment about my age. Then I lost it at the mention of the word *wedding*. Now I was in a lather because of my mother? Forget shopping for a wedding dress. I was ready for a straitjacket.

"So your mother triggered your panic attack? She's an important person in your world, but remember: you are in control of your own life." Mags reached across the table to massage the back of my hand. It calmed me to focus on the slow circles she made with her fingers.

I took a moment to consider my mother's recent behavior. I had expected her to make planning our wedding difficult, but truthfully, she hadn't. While I had complained a lot about how often she checked in with me about the details, nothing she had done had derailed my plans. She came close with the purple dress, but even the situation with the color scheme was salvageable. In fact, if I were truly honest, I would say she was having fun with the planning process. Whether we implemented her ideas or went another direction, she was giddy with excitement either way. Come to think of it, she had been far less critical in general. No, I couldn't blame my mother for my rash of panic attacks. "I've always chafed at her telling me what to do and then criticizing me because I did it wrong, but she hasn't been on my case recently. I used to wish she'd just do everything for me so I could avoid her judgment. Hmm. Maybe I don't want to be responsible all of the time. But being responsible is what it means to be an adult, right?"

I could tell Mags didn't agree with me. She tipped her head to the left, a squint burying her eyes under her brows. I waited for a response, but none was forthcoming. My head buzzed with thoughts I hadn't yet explored. I couldn't let the lull in our conversation force me to listen to the drone in my head. "I love my career and watching it develop. My relationship with Josh is the best thing to come into my life. I'm cool with the trappings of adulthood provided they don't present complications. Planning a wedding is a metaphor for what I imagine life should be for someone who is over thirty. It is a nonstop stream of things I have to care about and take responsibility for, whether or not I want to.

"I'm not ready for a life filled with responsibilities. For instance, taxes are kind of a pain now, but when we're married, Josh and I will have to file joint returns. Whose accountant should we use? Will we have to merge our bank accounts? Only two days ago, we realized we hadn't talked about where we would live once we're married. We're both stuck in leases until the end of July." I clutched my thighs, gasping for breath.

"Breathe, Ellen. There you go. Let's tackle one thing at a time. It is true the older we are, the more responsibilities we have to assume. If a pipe bursts in your home, you have to call the plumber. When you develop a toothache, you can't expect someone else to make the dentist appointment for you. Just remember: you will have Josh by your side each time you have to face an unpleasant situation. And you have a wonderful network of friends and family who support you, too. But there's more to life than bad days. Who says you have to grow up, anyhow? I've refused to do it. The best way to make life worth living is to have fun living it. Does any of this help?"

"You've offered me great advice, Mags. But I'm not sure it delves into the heart of the matter, though." I planted my elbow on the table, resting my chin on my fist. "I'm pretty sure a combination of wedding nonsense and my fears about adulting are fueling my freakouts. Planning a wedding really isn't that difficult. If everyone would leave me alone, stop telling me what I'm supposed to do, I wouldn't mind making the plans. Weddings, at their most basic level, are about filling in the blanks. But everyone wants to turn it into some kind of race. *You have to do this NOW! What? You haven't planted the seeds to grow the wheat the baker needs to make your cake yet? You can kiss having a wedding cake goodbye, young lady!* I don't see what the big rush is. It's not like aliens will vaporize every wedding dress on the planet five months before my wedding if I haven't selected mine yet. Even when everything is going according to plan, I'm under so much pressure. Amber goes on and on about how perfect our venue is. Chloe has promised to help me find the perfect dress. I think everyone expects me to plan the perfect wedding. It's overwhelming!"

"Oh, I'm sorry, dear. I think I'm partly to blame for your little episode today. Didn't I offer you a perfect slice of quiche? I believe we have identified the source of your panic attacks. You've been hearing the word *perfect* tossed around carelessly for months. Your anxieties stem not so much from how to manage your responsibilities as from your concerns about what people will think about how you handled them. Nothing is perfect. I assure you no one expects you to be perfect. Let go of expectations. This is a major lesson, my dear. Don't expect an outcome to exceed your input. Never expect other people to do what you've imagined they should do. And free yourself from living up to the expectations you perceive others have for you."

The buzzing in my head stopped. My legs no longer pumped up and down like a quarter-fed bed in a cheap motel. I let out a deep breath. "You're brilliant, Mags! My panic attacks were about the notion of perfection. I kept imagining that because I had been to a gazillion weddings, I had to prove I'd been paying attention, that I knew exactly how to make my wedding perfect. Not perfect for Josh and me, but perfect for the record books. I have a Greek Chorus living in my head. It dictates a litany of expectations to me. I need to find a way to stop listening to it."

"Get a pair of earmuffs?" Mags burst into a fit of giggles. I'd never been able to resist her melodious laugh.

When I stopped laughing, I noticed the uneaten quiche sitting in front of me, beckoning me to take a bite. I lingered over the first silky morsel I put in my mouth.

"I'm afraid we've let our meal get cold. Would you like me to reheat it?" Mags asked.

"No. The quiche is delicious as it is. Your food always is. But I swear I don't expect you to prepare yummy, perfect food for me." I let my eyebrows dance to let her know I was teasing her.

"You're learning. Let's keep searching for ways to manage your expectations about your wedding. Your brother married recently and did so on short notice if I'm not mistaken. Tell me about their wedding."

"It was joyful and intimate. During the ceremony itself, it was clear how special the day was, how seriously Nathan and Derrick took their vows to each other. Even still, the friend of theirs who officiated kept the mood light and personal. Nathan and Derrick's love for each other permeated the service." The clatter of my fork dropping on my plate startled Mags. "I just had an idea for the perfect…" I stopped myself. "Scratch that. I don't mean perfect. I know who would best be able to convey both who Josh and I are and who we are to each other in our ceremony."

Mags set her fork on her plate with more care than I had mustered. "Don't keep me in suspense."

"You."

"Me? Heavens! What makes you believe I could perform a wedding ceremony?"

"You know me so well. You have a gift for understanding the complexities of love and being human. I don't know anyone better qualified to solemnize our vows than you. Would you do it, Mags? Would you consider being our celebrant?"

"My, what a thing you have asked of me! Of course, I'd love to. I won't agree to officiate until you and Josh have mulled it over together. I won't be hurt if you decide to go another direction."

"I know I won't change my mind." I cocked my head, a slight smile creeping across my lips. "Where do you put all the weight I leave behind each time I talk to you?"

With her brow lowered, she jutted out her chin. "I don't know what you mean."

"Like, do you sweep rocks onto a growing pile in the closet after I leave? I swear, every time I visit you, I leave behind so many worries and concerns, surely there must be some physical evidence of me having unburdened myself."

"Well, if we don't keep eating, you'll leave me with more leftovers than I had bargained for. Another slice of imperfect quiche, dear?"

I PUNCHED the *Year End Sale* balloon floating in my living room. It sunk to about a foot above the floor before rising to eye level. Like me, it was a deflated soul. By seven-thirty in the evening on my birthday, I had to admit the truth: Josh really was in the City playing a performance of *Jazz Hands*. Chloe hadn't returned home ahead of her revised schedule. I had to celebrate my thirtieth birthday alone with only a frozen dinner, a bowl of ice cream, and a free balloon from a car dealership for company. No surprise party. No presents. No cake. I hoped Josh knew the furies would descend upon him later tonight.

A little past eleven, he let himself into my apartment. Holding his violin case in his right hand and a gift bag in the left, he said, "Let's get this party started!"

"You're too late. I'm ready for bed." I had changed into my pajamas once batting around a tired old balloon had lost its thrill. I kept my feet, cozy in their fluffy slipper socks, on the coffee table, forcing Josh to come to me.

"How was your birthday?" He looked so hopeful, so eager to be a part of the festive mood he mistakenly had expected to find.

"Isn't it every person's dream to spend her thirtieth birthday alone, abandoned by her fiancé and friends?"

"You know I hated to abandon you on your birthday. If they had called me months ago to play tonight, I would have turned it down. But on such short notice, and with every other sub unavailable, I had to come through for them. We'll celebrate later in the week, I promise!"

"When? I'm teaching tomorrow evening, you're playing a show Thursday, we're having dinner with my mom on Friday — you're not going to ditch me on Friday, right? — and I have gigs on Saturday and Sunday."

"I'm good for Friday night at your mom's. I wouldn't dare let down both of you on the same night. No one could survive upsetting the two of you simultaneously." His feeble excuse of a laugh petered out under my withering glare. "We'll find a free night soon. Think of it as a way we can extend your birthday celebration. And speaking of celebrating, are you ready for your gift?" He held the pink and green bag out to me.

Snatching the bag from his hand, I jettisoned the green tissue paper from the bag onto the coffee table in my search for pay dirt. Peering inside, I spotted a box from the same jeweler where Josh had bought my engagement ring. This could work. But I maintained my poker face. I wasn't ready to let him know he may have found a way to make up for having left me alone tonight.

Lifting the lid, I gasped. "I love them!" I held my left hand next to the earrings in the box, comparing the stones. "They're the same!"

"Yup. Peridot with diamonds." The grin on his face expressed the confidence he had in making me forget his earlier sin. I could barely pucker my lips to kiss him, so wide was my own smile. "Let me see them on you."

I ran to the bathroom. Turning my head to view each lobe in the mirror, I studied the earrings. Teardrop-shaped peridots the size of the tip of my pinky bordered by tiny diamonds dangled from the diamond-encrusted loops winding through my earlobes. "They're super fancy!"

"Are they too fancy?"

"Not at all. They'll be perfect for gigs."

"Maybe a wedding, too?"

"Of course! I'll have to consider wearing my hair up. They'd look great with a dress where my shoulders are bare. I love them!"

"Maybe you can give me a preview of what they look like above bare shoulders?" He tugged me by the elastic of my pajama bottoms, steering us toward my bedroom.

I guided Guinevere into a spot near the entrance to my mom's condo in Westfield on Friday. At least *she* had thought to schedule time to celebrate my birthday. Chloe had flown in late last night only to disappear this morning for a full day of teaching before she headed to a gig.

"Is it silly to wear my new earrings?" We sat in my SUV for a minute while Josh finished sending a text. "I could put them in my purse and go without."

"No, keep them in. Your mom will want to see them."

"OK. You ready?"

"Yup. Let's do this!" Josh had developed a habit similar to mine of exhibiting forced enthusiasm whenever our plans involved my mother. He probably did it for my amusement. Like anyone who wasn't one of her offspring, he didn't share my negative opinions of her.

Standing on the slate pavers in front of my mother's front door, I rang the bell. Josh held his hand against the small of my back. It took my mother forever to answer the door. She stepped outside, the screen door closing behind her. The dishtowel in her hand served to remind me I had taken her away from another task. I had a key to the condo, but whenever I'd let myself in, I'd felt my invasion was equally inconvenient for her.

"Well, here's the birthday girl. Show me your earrings." She bent over to poke at the left stone. "Josh, you have exquisite taste in jewelry. Jewelry buying skills are an important quality for a husband to possess, I've always said. Now, why are we standing here in the cold? Come on in." She held the door for me. I hesitated. Josh gave me a little push before taking the door from my mother to allow her to follow me into the condo ahead of him.

"Surprise!!!" I planted my feet in front of the coat closet, too startled by the greeting to move. Chloe sprang into my path, planting a huge kiss on my cheek. "I didn't have any students or gigs today. I've been here all day, helping your mother. I'm sorry I made you cranky by abandoning you earlier today. Will you forgive me?"

I had forgotten how to speak. Guttural sounds accompanied the chicken-like pecking motions I made while I took inventory of the guests.

"Come on in! Look, Josh's parents and brothers are here, too!" Chloe guided me by my arm after Josh took my jacket from me. I plodded around the room in a daze, giving hugs to his family, my brother and Derrick, Gwen, Matt, and Sheila, my best friend from high school.

"Did you suspect anything?" Gwen's eyes sparkled.

"I knew the three of you were up to something last Sunday at dinner, but when nothing happened on my actual birthday, I forgot about it. I'm totally surprised!"

"It was Josh's idea. We just helped him pull it off. I'm amazed you didn't figure it out!"

"To think I was going to interview for a new set of friends because all of you forced me to spend my birthday alone! I don't deserve friends like you."

Pink, green, and lavender balloons still high on their helium buzz danced above the curling ribbon that tied each of them to pieces of furniture throughout the room. Paper plates in the same color palette with *Happy Birthday* emblazoned on them held half-eaten noshes. With a quickly chugged glass of Champagne working its magic on me, I flitted from friend to relative in a happy haze of love.

"Hey, have you seen my mom?" Josh asked. I shook my head. "You know, my dad has disappeared, too."

"They'll turn up sooner or later." I helped myself to a hunk of Brie. Reaching for another pig-in-blanket, I noticed my mother setting holders for chafing dishes on the dining room table. With willpower I didn't recognize, I withdrew my hand from the tray.

From the hallway by the bedrooms, a female voice announced, "Presenting: Mr. Misterioso!" The room grew silent. Josh and I met each other's eyes with a perplexed stare. Josh's father walked into the living room wearing a black satin cape lined in red over a tuxedo. A top hat threatened to jump ship from atop his head.

He whipped out his right hand from under his cape, revealing a white-tipped black wand. "And my lovely assistant, Zelda." Mrs. Yates pranced into the room. The top hat perched on her glossy black hair was a third of the size of his. As was her costume. Three black bows climbed the front of a white corset. Flounces of black tulle formed a skirt far shorter than one I would have been comfortable wearing. Black pumps, black fishnet stockings and a pair of long black gloves completed her ensemble.

"Mom!" Josh's younger brother Brian's horrified tone matched his expression. She ignored him, the smile plastered on her face refusing to budge. She extended her left arm above her and gestured with her right hand in a balletic gesture toward her husband. Josh collapsed on a chair, pulling me onto his lap.

"Ladies and gentlemen, prepare yourselves to enter a world of wonder and amazement." Mr. Yates pulled three silver rings out of his cape, brandishing them in front of us. One ring dropped, rolling under the couch where Nathan, Derrick, and Chloe sat.

Derrick began to bend forward. "Can I retrieve the ring for you, or will it break the magic spell?"

"You can't have too many assistants, I suppose."

"Honey, maybe start with some close-up magic." "Zelda" Yates offered to take the ring from Derrick.

"Right." Mr. Yates turned his back to us, working the pockets inside his cape like a magic trick of its own. "Brian, could you place the snack table near you in front of the birthday girl? Thanks, son. Take the plate and napkin away, too if you don't mind." He stepped behind the small table, twisting away from me. "Hmm. Technical difficulties. My flash paper won't light."

"You're not supposed to give away your secrets, dear."

"Right. Ignore what I just said, folks." The scrape of a lighter flint sounded in the background, replaced by a faint crackling sound. I caught a glimpse of the smallest spark of fire jumping away from the deck of cards he brought to the table with a flourish.

"Honey, your cape!" Mr. Yates looked over his shoulder at the smoldering hem of his cape. Josh booted me off his lap. Grabbing his glass of Champagne, he dunked the cape into it. My mother wrung her hands.

"We're good. No need to call the fire department. But Dad, what the heck is going on here?" Josh helped his father to remove his cape.

"Your mother gave me the hat, cape, and a book of tricks for Christmas as a gag gift. We've been having so much fun with it, we decided to buy her a costume and work out a little bit of an act. We had hoped tonight's show would entice you to hire us for a bigger gig. Like your wedding?"

Josh held his fist to his mouth. His parents were the normal ones. His mom hadn't bought a dress in a hideous color before I had picked my color scheme. His dad didn't call us ten times a day with suggestions about the food we should serve. Beyond offering to host a rehearsal dinner, they had stayed out of our way throughout the planning process. Who knew they had saved their credit just to blow it on selling us a form of entertainment one typically doesn't associate with weddings?

"Don't call us; we'll call you." Josh erupted into a fit of laughter. One by one, we fell victim to the contagion of his braying. His father, his mother, even my mother, once the threat of fire had dissipated, guffawed at the magic act that wasn't.

Once Mr. Yates had introduced the topic of our wedding, it was impossible to avoid talking about it throughout the rest of the evening. Without having had my breakthrough with Mags on Tuesday, I would have considered the party ruined. Instead, my defensiveness and my urge to resist accepting everyone's assistance had evaporated. How could I have failed to appreciate the warmth and support of my family and friends? I finally understood: Josh and I would have our whole lives to love each other, but the wedding itself was for everyone who loved us. If they wanted the perfect party, damned if I wasn't going to give it to them.

I REREAD Sam's latest email for the umpteenth time. I hadn't missed anything or imagined what I thought I had read. He truly believed Josh and I were going to break up and that he had a shot at winning me back.

> Dear Ellen,
> It sounds like you and Josh may be discovering you're not meant to commit your lives to each other. I'm not wishing for your engagement to come to an end. I just want you to know I'm here for you if you need me.
>
> We had a good thing going back in college. As we are both older and wiser, I think we'd be right for each other now. If things don't work out for you and Josh, I'll be ready to help you through your breakup.
>
> Love,
> Sam

How could he have gotten the idea Josh and I were on the skids? I scrolled through my *sent* folder. Oh. I had emailed him in the bleak, post-dinner hours on my birthday. Mm-hmm. Yeah, I did come across as a woman scorned in the email. But, still. It was a bit of a stretch for him to interpret me being mad at Josh for leaving me alone on my birthday as a harbinger of our relationship's imminent demise.

With shaking hands, I began to type a reply. A few words into each attempt at a new sentence, I pounded the delete key, erasing yet another version of the phrase, "Back the f*#& off." The guilt for having inspired him to write his message intensified my discomfort. How unfair I had been to Josh to complain to an ex about him! I had to make this problem go away.

I could commit only so much abuse to my delete key before it seemed prudent to slam the laptop shut and leave the unfinished draft to linger until I gained clarity. Time for a practice break.

Puccini did the trick. I'd be playing the arias from the end of Act I of *La Bohème* on a Sunday afternoon concert in a couple of weeks. Last year, before Claude and Lily had promised me steady work at the Vista this year, I finally made the decision to take guaranteed gigs rather than to hold dates for a permanent job that had yet to materialize. Tiffany would be able to play to her heart's content on the days I need a sub.

While I blissfully worked through the arpeggios in *O, suave fanciulla*, Chloe cursed her way through every fast passage from the top ten list of flute audition repertoire in her bedroom. Josh's trio of knocks on the door brought our practice sessions to a halt.

"Listening from the hallway, the muffled sound of multiple musicians practicing reminded me of the music building in college. You guys were going at it pretty hard."

Josh distributed hugs to each of us, embellishing mine with a passionate kiss. "Were you playing *Peter and the Wolf*, Chloe?"

"Yeah."

"Do you have a performance of it coming up? I've never had the chance to play the piece. I'd love to perform it."

"Nah. Just working on some orchestra excerpts on my own." She rifled through the stack of mail on the table without looking at him.

"Are you preparing for an audition?"

"No!" The ferocity of her answer pushed Josh and me back in our chairs. "Sorry. I'm a bit keyed up from practicing. I chose to run through the Prokofiev because winter is always a great time to get some solid work in."

Remembering she had been practicing the same repertoire at the same frenzied pace throughout the fall, I opened my mouth to correct her. She averted her eyes. Her complexion lacked its usual glow. I swallowed my words, ready to change the topic. "Hey, I need your help. For the life of me, I can't figure out why, but Sam is coming on really strong."

"In what way?" Josh asked.

"I have a weird feeling he wants to get back together with me."

Josh furrowed his brow. "But he knows you're engaged. Why does he have the impression you'd be available?"

"Perhaps it's just wishful thinking on his part." I didn't want to tell Josh I had shared personal information with Sam. I had to make my explanation credible, stick close to the truth, though. "Since I ran into him on a day I was doing wedding stuff, and because he has a connection to our venue, he has insinuated himself into my life, I guess. I might have said something to him once about trying to strike a balance between each of our ideas for the wedding like we did regarding the size of the wedding party. Depending on my mood, it could have come out sounding like we were having a fight." My cheeks grew warm. I shrugged my way out of my sweater.

"Surely he knows from experience you're not the sort who would dump a guy — or cheat on him — if a better opportunity came up." Josh reached for my hand, confident he knew the answer.

"I certainly never cheated on him, and I didn't leave him for another guy. I've been faithful to every man I've dated." I stroked Josh's hand, drawing a contented smile from his mouth. "Compared to you, he doesn't even rate. Even if I were the cheating sort — and the thought makes me nauseous! — no way would I trade you for him! Not a chance. I have to find a way to make sure he understands he cannot prevent me from marrying you."

"Speaking of our wedding, when are we meeting with the caterer? Please say tonight, because I'm starving."

"Next week, my love."

Chloe, her left hand on her hip, pointed to the half-filled jar on the coffee table with a giggle. "My arrangement might be with Ellen, but 'rules is rules.' You talk about the wedding in our apartment, you pay. Josh, go toss a dollar in the jar, would you?"

The wind kicked up small ruffles on the Hudson River. I tightened my grip on my harp on my way from my car to the Vista. The giant mitten-shape of a harp in its cover turned it into a sail on windy days like today. Catching sight of the bright blue of my harp cover, Helena held the door for me. She rubbed her hands against her upper arms. "It's a nippy one today!"

"At least it's warm in here. I love how different the river looks, depending on the weather. The view is always changing."

Helena followed me to my corner on the far side of the room. The pace of the staff readying the restaurant was slower than it had been during the busy holiday season. "Claude and Lily couldn't have been luckier to find this space. A location with a million-dollar view doesn't come on the market very often. Even in the dead of winter, the view is still a draw. The food and service deserve some of the credit, of course."

"And the harp music!" I couldn't help but sing my praises. I loved playing here every week. Having a steady gig was everything I had hoped it would be. Working with the nicest staff in New Jersey made it even better.

"How could I forget your wonderful music? Well, I'll leave you to finish setting up. We have four early reservations today."

Despite the lack of traffic on the roads on Sunday mornings and the familiar routine of the gig, I still left home early enough to ensure I would arrive an hour before the gig began. Bandleaders I'd worked with had taught me how important it was to be early, especially for musicians with a lot of equipment to load in. Besides, I'd rather avoid the stress of arriving at a gig at the last minute.

Once my harp was in place and I had stored my cover, cart, and jacket in the coat check, I wandered into the kitchen to help myself to a cup of coffee. I made my rounds, chatting with chefs, dishwashers, servers, and other staff members who had become my friends. Fifteen minutes before the first reservation would arrive, I returned to my harp to tune it.

Across the room, a woman holding a violin case leaned forward in a hostile pose. Neither Helena nor the hostess was at the front desk. The violinist strode through the room with purpose, like she had been here before. Was this the infamous Tiffany? And why was she here today?

She wasted no time asking me the same question. "What are you doing here? They told me you needed a sub today." A pair of legs clad in basic black slacks stuck out below her oversized green parka. Its hood, ringed by matted fake fur, hid her face. "You!" She set her violin case on a chair and pushed her hood from her head. "You're the skank who dissed my playing last summer!"

I stared into her charcoal-rimmed eyes, searching my memory. The subway violinist! Amber and I had run into her in a subway station after our first wedding consultation. I hadn't dissed her. I had reflexively covered my ears to protect them from the caterwauling strains of music reverberating against the subway tiles. "I didn't say a word to you that day in the subway station. And why are you here today? I don't need a sub until next week."

"You didn't have to say anything. I could tell by the way you looked at me you would have said something mean if you had the balls to say it." This was the woman I had been competing against for the gig? Not only was she a terrible musician, but between her attire, her deportment, and her lack of respect for the job, having breezed in for a gig fifteen minutes before downbeat, nothing about her made the case she was a professional.

"Let's find Helena. She'll sort it out."

"There's nothing to sort out. Doncha get it? You stole my gig. I bet you badmouthed me to Helena, and that's why they picked you. Wait till my mother hears. You'll be out on your sorry ass!"

Helena walked from the kitchen to the hostess stand. Tiffany's last word echoed in the quiet room, drawing Helena's attention.

"Oh, dear. We seem to have a little mix-up. Tiffany, we have you down for next Sunday. Am I correct, Ellen?" I nodded. "I hate to send you back out in the cold, but we don't need both of you, and it is Ellen's job, after all."

For a second time, Tiffany said, "Wait till my mother hears." She stabbed at the screen on her phone. "Mom! I'm at the restaurant. It's my turn to play, but that harpist is here, and she won't go home. She's a bully!" Helena gave me a quizzical look. I denied Tiff's accusation with an emphatic gesture. "Here. My mother wants to talk to you." She handed her phone to Helena, giving me the stink eye while we tried to interpret the unheard side of the conversation.

Helena returned Tiffany's phone to her. "It looks like we're going to have to send you home, Ellen."

"Why me? I'm the regular musician for brunch. I'm positive I let you know I need a sub next week, not today. And I've never spoken to Tiffany before today let alone bullied her."

"While that may be the case, the Trydel's are important investors. We have to be respectful of their wishes." Tiffany — no, make that *the Tiff* — wore a look of triumph on her face like a child who had made a boom-boom in the potty for her first time.

I trudged toward the coat closet to retrieve my gear. Helena walked with me. "I apologize for the mishap, Ellen. You can see for yourself she is not well-suited to play here. I blame myself in the event I asked her to come in on the wrong date. We'll smooth it out in your absence.

Everything will be normal again for your return in two weeks."

The restaurant phone rang. I went to retrieve my harp from enemy territory while Helena took the call. With my bench thrown over my harp and my gig bag and amplifier in its bag hanging from my shoulder, I prepared to exit the restaurant. Helena rushed to hold the door. "I just heard from Lily. Mrs. Trydel had called her, spinning some tale or another about her poor, maligned daughter. I'm sorry to have to tell you, but Lily has asked me to let you go."

"Let me go, like fire me?" I brought my hand to my mouth. "But I've done nothing wrong!" I fought the tears welling up in my eyes.

"The situation is grossly unfair, I know. Please don't take this personally. You're a gifted musician and a delight to work with. Opportunities will come pouring in, of this I am certain. With Sheldon on your side, everything will turn out just fine for you."

I shimmied my bags off my shoulder to give her a hug. "I sure hope so. I wish I could point out to Lily that she hasn't heard an accurate version of the story."

"I will do everything I possibly can to make your case, I promise."

"Thanks. I'm going to miss working here. Please tell everyone I said goodbye," I sniffled.

"You will be missed. Good luck with your wedding! And if I have a say in the matter, you'll be back with us soon!"

nineteen
shades of gray

I SHOULD BE an old pro at losing gigs by now. Josh's ex, Monica, fired me after she and Josh broke up a second time. The logic behind the Monica incident was even more twisted than the Tiffany situation. I thought I had blown it with another bandleader by forgetting to show up for a gig a couple of years ago. Thankfully, he forgave me. And then, of course, there was the whole unfortunate incident on the Orpheus.

My dismissal from the Vista stung the most of all the firings. I wanted this gig more than any of the others. And I was blameless in its demise. Sheldon had blown a gasket when he heard the story, but like Helena, he had been unable to sway Lily and Claude into rehiring me. Now they're stuck with the Tiff terrorizing their guests with her musical abuses. Served them right.

While my Sundays remained empty, my wedding binder expanded with each contract and purchase order I added to it. Josh and I had picked out our menu, rings, and invitations. We had reserved a block of rooms at the hotel in Princeton where his parents were hosting our rehearsal dinner. They had even hired a party bus to take guests from the hotel to the wedding. I couldn't wait to show Amber how much progress I had made in her absence.

I hoisted my bag higher onto my shoulder, heading from Port Authority to a café near the waterfront in Chelsea where I would be meeting Amber while the Orpheus was in port for the day. A host of memories flooded my mind. On another cold, gray day almost a year ago, I had walked along the Hudson River a few days after Josh and I had put our relationship into stasis. Even with the strap of my bag digging into my shoulder, I was weightless compared to last year's version of myself.

I'd tried to reconcile how a little gray always manages to throw a shadow on the brightness in my life. Happiness might not always be fleeting, but it definitely didn't exist in a vacuum. Multiple emotions could play out simultaneously. Life tempered happiness. Even when I was counting my blessings, a few cursed events would always lurk in the background, ready for a starring role. Like how I used to have a steady brunch gig until an evil, immature violinist robbed me of it.

Chloe had remained enshrouded by gray. She took me by surprise a week ago, announcing she was flying back to California for a few days. She returned on Friday, her mood quieter than it had been before she left. It could be the jet lag. Yesterday was the first day in ages she didn't practice. She appeared fragile, anxious. Her attention laid elsewhere, pinned to a focal point invisible to me.

Amber could only spare enough time for a cup of coffee while she reviewed the progress Josh and I had made on our wedding plans. I envied her tan and the ship-mellowed ease she had about her. "Four more months, baby! Can you believe it?" She squeezed me in a tight hug.

"I go from kind of normal, like planning a wedding is just this thing I'm doing to super-psyched when I focus on why we're making these plans. And then to full-on anxious when I remember the leap of faith we're taking with our venue. It would calm my nerves to see it again. Would that be possible?"

She clapped her hands three times. "That's what I've been dying to tell you. Tyler is helping Sid and Maxwell throw a party at the home next month. They want to show off the progress they've made to their friends."

"Ooh! Are we invited to the party?"

"Sorry, no. Since they're renting tables the same size as yours, Tyler thought you and Josh could tour the space before the event to see how it looks in party mode. Sound good?"

"Totally! If that doesn't make it feel real to me, then nothing will!"

"Show me what's left to do."

Amber and I pored through the binder, double-checking my progress against her timeline and checklists. Besides my dress — and I swore I was going to make plans to go dress shopping with Chloe and my mother any day now — we only needed to schedule a cake tasting and a suit fitting for Josh and the men in the wedding party. Both could wait until March.

"You're killing it with the plans, Ellen! My contract ends just in time for me to handle the last-minute details. In the meantime, since you're free on Sundays now, promise me you'll come into the City just to say *hi* every once in a while?"

"I promise! Now go welcome the next boatload of pax aboard the ship. And enjoy a drink in the crew bar for me, will you?"

"You got it!"

I took a different route back to Port Authority, enjoying the quiet along the blocks of brownstones. A poodle sniffed at a square of dirt cordoned off by a tiny fence at the base of a tree. I turned up 8th Avenue. The noise level increased as the brownstones yielded to buildings with commercial space at ground level. I stopped in front of a white plastic A-frame sign on the sidewalk. Positioned to the side of a glass door behind which stood a staircase, it read, "Bridal Event Today, 2nd floor."

The lack of specificity fed my curiosity. I didn't need to be anywhere. What did I have to lose? I opened the door. Scuff marks on the off-white steps blurred during my ascent. My fingertips grazed the surface of the banister made from an industrial pipe. Reaching a landing, I made the one hundred eighty-degree turn to mount the second flight of stairs. Masking tape held a sign to a massive, gray door held open by a wooden wedge. A red arrow pointed me inside to the bridal event.

On each wall, dresses entombed in clear plastic garment bags gasped for air on racks. The din of women's voices and hangers scraping against metal rods greeted me.

"Hello! Are you here for a dress?" A woman my progress into the small warehouse.

"Um, I saw the sign. I hadn't planned to go dress shopping today, but, yeah, I might as well see what you have since I'm here."

"Great! I'm Emily. Did you bring anyone?" She led me to a pair of chairs off to the side.

"Nope."

"We don't allow any photographs. If you need a second opinion on a dress, you can ask me or someone else in the shop. Can I tell you a little bit about our event?" I nodded. "We're selling high-end, previously worn bridal dresses. Normally, we're an appointment-based shop, but for today's sale, walk-ins are welcome." The words "high-end" raised a prickle on my skin. With a portion of the money I had saved for the wedding siphoned from my account into Guinevere's down payment, I had nowhere near a high-end budget. She continued. "Every dress in the shop is nine hundred fifty dollars or less today, many of them under five hundred dollars."

Dresses for less than a thousand dollars? I wanted to hug her.

Emily led me to the rear of the warehouse. Three dressing rooms with curtains for doors stood on each side. A window on the back wall overlooked the traffic on 8th Avenue. Two women in fluffy, white gowns admired their reflections in a pair of three-way mirrors. A best friend and a mother cooed their support.

Armed with my measurements and details about my wedding, Emily went to select gowns for me to try on. She returned with a single dress, still in its bag, draped over her arm. "Let's get you started with this dress. We have plenty of other options if this isn't the one."

She unzipped the bag, transferring the gown on its hanger to a hook in a dressing room. I examined the dress from outside the fitting room, gathering the blue and white polka-dotted fabric of the fitting room curtain in my sweaty fingers. The dress screamed *matronly* at me. If I dyed it purple, my mother would swoon over it. Two small sleeves, protruding from its sides like the pencil holder I attach to my music stand, aligned with the straight edge at the top of the bodice. Swirls of gathered fabric encasing the bodice added both heft and texture. A simple satin skirt fell below a straight waistband.

Emily beckoned me into the fitting room. "Some dresses need to be worn to come to life. There's no harm in trying it on, is there?"

I had yet to have tried on even a single wedding dress. I supposed I had to start somewhere. One of the brides-to-be admired her gown in the communal area. Tall and lithe like Chloe, she wore a long-sleeved, off-white lace dress. A deep scoop in the back melded sexy with elegant. I cursed the family genes that had rendered me short and a tad pudgy with most of the weight carried on my hips and thighs. I knew I would look awful in a dress like hers.

The dressing room had no mirror in it. I disrobed and stepped into the dress. The sleeves ringed my biceps, leaving my shoulders bare. I twisted and reached, unable to bring the zipper to the top of the dress. I pushed the curtain aside and presented my back to Emily. As she tugged the zipper closed, the dress compressed my torso but not so tightly as to encumber my breathing. It bound me in a secure embrace. Emily guided me to a mirror, taking a spot behind me and clasping her hands together over her mouth. I had no words.

"Well?" Emily tugged on the skirt, draping it over the side of the box on which I stood in front of the mirror.

While the dress appeared matronly on the hanger, it transformed into an unexpected vision of *va va vavoom*! But in a totally modest, sophisticated way. My curves worked in my favor. I wasn't particularly well-endowed in the breast department. The swirls of fabric on the bodice filled me in where I needed filling in. The waistband made the most of the slight narrowing of my waist, and the satin skirt clung for just a moment to my hips before falling away. The roundness of my shoulders played against the straight edge at the top of the bodice skirting the bottom of my collarbone. And the sleevelets masked the jiggly bits of my arms, working some sleight of hand to make my arms appear long and lean.

I pivoted on the box, examining myself from different angles. "How did you know?"

"You like it?"

"I LOVE it! Is it possible to buy a dress having tried on only one?"

"You're welcome to keep searching if you'd like."

"I'd only be wasting your time and mine."

"Then let's ring you up."

I wouldn't recommend walking for blocks with a wedding gown in your arms. I had never considered the weight of one of these things. But the lightness in my heart buoyed me even when my arms ached from carrying it. I squished through the aisle on my bus, glad the passenger load was light enough to allow me a full row to myself. The two blocks between the bus stop and my apartment in Montclair stretched endlessly. I arrived home out of breath but eager to show Chloe my purchase.

"I can't believe you bought a dress! I might never forgive you for doing it without me. I've decided your penalty is to pay ten dollars into the wedding jar." Chloe was quick to free the dress from the bag. She examined the label and the price tag. "You're a friggin' shopping genius! Your dress probably retailed for four times what you paid for it. Put it on. I want to see you in it."

I had worried the thrill I experienced admiring it in the showroom would not have followed me home, that I wouldn't love it outside of the store. Chloe stood behind me while I peacocked in front of the mirror hanging on the back of her door. "Stunning! I never in a million years would have picked this for you had I seen it on the rack. But they designed it for you. I can't believe how well it fits. All you'll need to have done is to get it hemmed."

I squealed with excitement. "I'm getting married!"

"ARE YOU SURE you don't want to go to Princeton with us tomorrow?" I asked Chloe. I was beside myself with excitement to witness how eight months of renovations had transformed the manor. I would have loved to light a similar spark in her.

"Nah. I'm not in the mood to make the drive." She hadn't been in the mood for much the last couple of weeks beyond scanning her phone at more frequent intervals than usual, only to put it down in a huff afterward.

"Are you expecting a text? Ooh! You met a guy!"

"I did not meet a guy. And since when do you think I'd be the sort to wait around for a text from a man? I thought you knew me better than that."

"We could video chat with you while we're touring the joint." Josh steered the conversation away from a potentially dangerous detour.

"No need. Just take a few pictures." A phone chirped. Chloe pounced on hers, but it was Josh's making the sound.

"Hey, what's up?" Josh, with his phone against his ear, wandered into the hallway leading to our bedrooms and the bathroom.

I drowned out his muffled voice with the clatter of the silverware I set on our table. Even after I had signed for our food delivery a few minutes later, he still hadn't joined us. Chloe and I helped ourselves to salad and pasta.

Josh finally sat down at the table after we had opted to start eating without him. "So sorry I had to ditch you. Wow. I have some news: the concertmaster on the *Jazz Hands* tour broke his arm skiing today. The tour's in Denver for another week. That's neither here nor there. The thing is, they don't have anyone available to replace him until the end of the month. The money is really good on tour. We could use it, you know."

I recoiled as if I had been smacked in the face by a skunk. We had gone through a series of problems during his tour last year. And the benefits they promised him of how going on tour would improve his Broadway career had been slow to materialize. Could I — and his career — survive another absence? "Did you take it? I mean, we have a busy month of wedding tasks planned. We're visiting the venue tomorrow, you're going for a suit fitting on Saturday, and we're scheduled for a cake tasting next week. And what about the gigs you have booked?"

"The timing's not great, I know. I'm not going to have to give up a lot of work, at least. While we were talking, the contractor researched flights to Denver tomorrow. The only flight he could book me on isn't until the evening. We can still head to Princeton. Just drop me off at the airport on the way home. The guys can keep the appointment at the tux shop. Derrick was going to be the style maven, anyway. All they need from me are my measurements and my credit card. Plus I trust you to make an impeccable cake selection without me." His eyes pleaded with me to accept his news.

"Is the contractor waiting for you to call him back?"

"Um, I already told him I'd do it." His thumb caressed the back of my hand.

"I guess you're going, then. Is Peyton still on tour?" The androgynously named woman who played the keyboards on the tour last winter had provided the spark that torched my limited ability to cope with missing Josh. I'd have to go on tour with him if she were still playing the show to make sure she kept her hands off of Josh.

"Last I heard, she was in Boston. The tour will be over so fast, you won't even miss me. One week in Denver, two in Albuquerque, and I'll be home on the thirty-first."

"I miss you already!"

My left hand cramped on the steering wheel, burdened with the task of steering the car by itself. My right hand clung to Josh's. Every few miles, I'd turn toward him, reassuring myself he was still by my side. Without ample notice about his departure, I had to squeeze every drop of togetherness into our last hours together.

"You think the party bus will clear the gate?" Josh rolled down his window to examine the wrought iron gate spanning the entrance to the estate.

"We'll make it fit. Grease 'er up, give her a swift push in her behind. She'll slide right through."

"On second thought, if the truck parked by the carriage house could fit through, our bus will, too."

"We'll be sure to ask about the kind of grease they coated it in."

"Silly!" Josh planted a kiss on my waiting lips.

We parked next to the truck marked with the logo of the place where we were renting our tables and other sundries. Puddles in the red gravel were the only reminders of this morning's rainstorm. Plywood sheets stretched between the driveway and the back patio. Hands entwined, Josh and I tiptoed across them. A man stood in the open doorway leading into the great room.

"Hi, I'm Tyler. You must be Ellen and Josh! So nice to meet you in person! Come on in."

I scanned the room. "Not much has changed in the last eight months." A pinkish-brown water stain on the wall above the French doors had a crack running through it. Curls of plaster peeling away from the walls speckled the room. I clutched Josh's hand tighter in mine.

"You'll be having cocktails in here, right? It might not look like much yet, but this room is next on the to-do list along with the downstairs bathrooms." Tyler led us into the library. "They just finished the woodwork in here and on the staircase last week. How fabulous is it?" Tyler stroked the burnished wood of an empty shelf. With a fresh application of stain and multiple coats of varnish, the golden-brown wood came to life. I wished Chloe were here. The library had been her favorite room.

"Come see the staircase." We followed Tyler into the foyer. The glaze on the deep mahogany treads and banister captured droplets of light sparkling from the chandelier in the center of the ceiling above us. I reached for the finial on the post at ground level. It rattled in my hand. I withdrew my hand, remembering my first visit to the site. "Don't mind the finial. Sid thought it would be fun to retain one imperfection during the renovation."

In the photos Amber had emailed us early in the demo phase, the combined living and dining rooms had appeared dark and raw. Being in the open space today caused my heart to pirouette. Light flowed through windows on three of the walls. The new beams in the former living room matched those on the ceiling in the dining room. The massive fireplace, lovingly restored, swelled with pride.

I gazed at Josh, imagining us walking into our wedding reception for the first time as husband and wife. The equivalent of the spinning pizza of death on a computer screen appeared before me, bring the joyful scene to a halt. Tall tables with tiny tops dotted the floor. "They're not doing a sit-down dinner tonight?"

"That's right. Just passed hors-d'oeuvres."

"But I thought you said they had ordered the same sized tables as ours."

Tyler flipped open our purchase order. "They did. We have you down for a dozen 27-inch tables."

"But we're having a sit-down reception for over one hundred twenty guests. We ordered 72-inch tables."

Josh mumbled something about the Druids to himself.

"What are you saying?" I dropped his hand with a huff.

"It's the intro to the song, *Stonehenge*, by Spinal Tap."

"How can Spinal Tap help us?" We had a potential wedding disaster on our hands, and he all he could do to help was to quote silly song lyrics?

"You know the part in the movie when they had a bit of a scale issue with the set?" He bent over in laughter, his cackles bouncing off the windows behind us.

Between the stress of confronting a snafu and my anger at Josh for ignoring the problem, I meant to scowl my way into a solution and an apology. An image from the movie of the crew lowering a tiny Stonehenge monument onto the stage while the band performed the song materialized in my mind. My scowl melted, and my own set of burbles, chirps, and snorts joined Josh's, echoing back to us from the farthest reaches of the large room.

Tyler shared a polite, somewhat confused laugh with us. "We can change the order, no problem." Josh danced an awkward jig around the too-small tables, purposefully backing into them a couple of times.

I gasped for breath and wiped away the tears from the corners of my eyes. "Yeah." Snicker. "We'll be wanting the full-sized versions for our reception."

I dug into my juicy cheeseburger, happy to return to Amber's favorite bistro in Princeton. Rivulets of grease dripped into the webbing between my fingers, tickling my skin. I dabbed at the backs of my hands with my napkin. I waited for Josh to raise his burger to his mouth. The moment his teeth sank into the bun, I said, "Stonehenge."

It was too late for him to save himself. He dropped his burger onto his plate, covering his mouth until it was safe to speak. "Not fair!"

Taking my next bite, I dared him with a flicker of my eyebrows to do the same to me.

"Fancy running into you here!" Not the phrase I had expected to hear. With a mouth full of burger, I glanced upward to see who had spoken to me. It was Sam.

I fought to clear my mouth to speak, my chin diving toward my chest with each awkward swallow. "Hey, how's it going? Oh, you haven't met Josh, have you?" It hadn't occurred before to me to notice the physical similarities between the two men. Both were tall with dark, curly hair and glasses. Sam's face had none of the depth or spark of life of Josh's, however.

"Nice to meet you. Are you checking in on the progress at the Harrington estate? I bet the property is starting to shape up real nice."

"We visited it this morning. The space looks amazing. We can't wait for June!" I reached across the table for Josh's hand, love in our eyes.

"Glad to hear! I don't want to be a third wheel. Let me leave you lovebirds alone to enjoy your meal!"

Josh rotated his head over his shoulder, measuring Sam's departure. "Seems like he got your hint all is well between us." He glanced at his watch. "Not to rush you, but I'm going to ask for the check. We still have fifteen minutes or so before we need to leave."

"Two more bites, and then I'll hit the head."

When I returned from the bathroom, I said to Josh, "I wrote an epic song about the tiny wastebasket in the bathroom. You want to hear it?"

He dismissed my offer, seemingly immune to Stone-henge jokes. His eyes didn't meet mine. "You ready?"

"Yeah. You OK?" I reached for his hand, coming up empty. He walked away from me without answering me.

Since Josh wasn't responding to my questions, and with the Stonehenge jokes having lost their magic touch, I filled the constricting silence on the ride to the airport with mindless prattle about how we would set up the dining room for the ceremony. "So, they'll have the tables fully set but pushed off to the sides. We could use screens to hide them. What do you think?" I couldn't decipher the meaning of his grunt. "We'll use the centerpieces to line the aisle. I've ordered two bigger arrangements to mark the altar. I definitely don't want an aisle runner. The thing is— Hey, are you even listening to me?" I snapped my head to the right.

"I have a lot on my mind. Maybe we don't talk for a bit?" Josh closed his eyes.

The silence between us grew prickly. Was he mad at me? Maybe he had a case of jitters. I desperately wanted to ask him if seeing the venue today elicited any wedding anxiety for him. I wouldn't want him to spiral out of control like I had.

Of course! It wouldn't be the wedding weighing on his mind. It had to be jumping back into the tour on such short notice. The first time he joined the tour, he had two days to acclimate himself to the experience before he played his first show. He'd arrive at his hotel late tonight and have to play a matinée tomorrow afternoon. I'd be a bundle of nerves, too. I squeezed his hand to reassure him I understood what was bothering him. Neither his hand nor his face responded to my gesture.

Josh hadn't even asked me if it was OK for him to accept the gig. By the time he told me about it last night, it was a done deal. Neither of us should make important decisions — decisions that will impact both of us — independently. Hadn't he considered how hard him going away will be for me? Shouldn't we be soaking up every last bit of being together before the drought of loneliness creeps in? I hardened myself against his rejection.

Curbside at Newark Airport, his hug wasn't tight enough; his kiss never materialized. "Call me once you've checked into the hotel?" I asked.

"It will be late. I might not have the chance."

"Sometime tomorrow, then?"

"I'll be in rehearsal in the morning. Maybe between shows tomorrow. You know, with the time difference, I won't return to the hotel each night until at least midnight your time. I'll text you when I have a moment."

Rather than being his fiancée, I could have been a random friend whom he had suckered into giving him a ride. Without a backward glance, he wheeled his carryon into the terminal. The automatic glass doors opened to swallow him into the milling crowd and out of view.

"HOLD YOUR HORSES! I'm having a moment here!" I screamed at the driver whose horn blared a warning for me to surrender my curbside spot at the airport terminal. A rush of anger animated my numb body. I wished my left indicator had a sarcastic setting, one that's blinking pattern might translate as, "What a novel idea you've suggested! Why, yes. I do believe I would like to spend my day elsewhere. Sitting in front of an airport, abandoned by my fiancé, is less fun than I had imagined it would be."

"I hope your flight is delayed," I said to the reflection of the car in my rearview mirror. Just over a year ago, Josh had returned to the driver's seat of his car parked at a cruise ship terminal, anger tingeing his final words to me after I had all but given up on our relationship. What was it about us and transportation hubs in late winter?

At the time, I had given him no warning before unleashing months of frustration on him. I can laugh now at the irony of failing to communicate with him about how challenging I found it to be unable to communicate with him while at sea. I'd learned my lesson. Hadn't he?

At least I had made the effort to explain to him how I no longer wanted to participate in our relationship through a cell phone I could use for only a few hours each week. He ditched me today without providing even a hint as to why he was upset. I wanted to believe his mood shift stemmed from having to face the reality of going back on tour, but deep down, I knew that wasn't the case. Josh had a superpower he relied on when performance anxieties mounted. He grew bolder with each challenge, more eager to embrace it. I was right to take his sullenness personally.

Did he have second thoughts about marrying me? I dug through my memory files, flinging useless bits of information aside in my search for something more helpful. Each image of him since the night he proposed to me reminded me of his love, his enthusiasm to plan our wedding, and his commitment to our future. Replaying today's adventures, I couldn't pinpoint any moment when I had said or done anything to hurt him. I had to have overlooked an offense, but what could it have been?

It felt like someone had stuffed my skull full of cotton batting that blocked my access to rational thoughts. My chest itched, and my fingertips buzzed. From my ribcage down, I was devoid of sensation. Contrary to its usual tendency, my stomach didn't flit about with nerves. My feet, unconnected to the drama, eavesdropped on my brain. Upon hearing the news, they offered to hit the gas pedal and whisk me off to Denver. Drawing a breath deep into my lungs, I used the air to mix the hyperactivity of my upper body with the calm of my lower half.

I channeled my inner Mags, admitting I would gain nothing by expecting Josh to behave as I wanted him to behave. If I didn't know why Josh was upset, I couldn't control the situation. He had introduced the mayhem; it was his to rein in. Even though my future depended on a specific outcome, the best thing I could do for my sanity was not to let the current state of things impact how I lived my life until we spoke again. Hmm. This maturity thing might actually be working for me.

When Chloe and I met in college, I was mature when it came to being a harpist. I excelled at setting musical goals, and I had the discipline to achieve them. When it came to being a human being, well... I was eighteen. Chloe's self-discipline extended beyond the practice room. She oozed confidence and maturity. I worshipped her. Over time, my worship for her became love.

For the past year, an unnamed demon had tortured her, drawing her ever more inward. Not knowing the source of her despair didn't make me feel less close to her. Love required empathy. I didn't need to experience or understand her pain. That she ached was cause enough for me to ache with her.

Since I'd been able to adapt to her dark mood and her reticence for explaining it, I was sure I would be able to endure waiting for Josh to inform me about whatever plagued him. I had to find the inner strength. I vowed to continue to love him, to ache with him despite not knowing why he ached.

Yeah, right. I ached over the next few hours, to be sure, but it was an ache born from rejection, not from empathy for my fiancé. As powerful as a black hole, the mystery behind the rejection sucked me into it, demanding obsessive behavior from me to energize it. Throughout the evening, when I wasn't inventing a narrative to fill in the gaps in Josh's story, I followed his flight to Denver online. After he landed at ten forty-four, I transitioned from monitoring the position of the little plane icon every ten minutes to staring down my message app, willing it to prove Josh had not forgotten me.

I tore myself away from my nest on the couch an hour after he landed to prepare for bed. There was no point in driving myself nuts as I waited for a call or text that might not come. I committed myself so thoroughly to a round of teeth-brushing sure to make my dentist proud, I forgot about the phone resting on the toilet seat cover. The violin solo from *Scheherazade* — Josh's ringtone — sprang forth from my phone's speaker, startling a spray of foamy toothpaste out of me. With half the toothpaste still in my mouth and the other half decorating the mirror, I couldn't decide which to do first: Answer the phone? Spit and rinse? Wipe away the minty-fresh splatter from the mirror before it dried into a mess guaranteed to piss off Chloe?

I opted for an amalgam, answering the phone mid-spit. Wiping a dribble from my chin with the back of my hand, I offered Josh a greeting garbled by a not-yet-empty mouth and running water. At least the noises camouflaged the hurt in my voice.

His voice came through clearly. "I shouldn't have left you like that. I spent the entire plane ride wishing I had explained to you why I was mad at you."

"Well?" I spritzed the mirror with bathroom cleaner. With a swipe of my washcloth, I turned the foamy white blobs into cloudy streaks. All the better to hide the haggard expression I wore.

"I don't even know if I have the right to be mad at you. I can't figure out what is true anymore."

"Look. I can't think of a single thing I've done to deserve you treating me like you did. And since when are you the muddled, dramatic sort? You know you can talk to me about everything, right? So, just tell me already!"

"Let me forward you the email Sam sent me while you were in the bathroom at the restaurant. You'll understand why I've been upset once you've read it."

I padded into my bedroom and opened my laptop.

> Hey, Sam,
> I have to stop what's going on between us.
> Josh and I were about to break up I was
> hoping to rekindle something between you
> and me. We're very much in love
> Reconnecting with you was lots of fun.
> maybe our paths will cross in the future
> All my best,
> Ellen

"You still there?" Josh asked.

"Yeah, I'm here. I'm sorry, but I'm having a really hard time accepting that you took this email to be the truth without even confronting me about it first. This email is BS. I didn't write it. I mean, yeah, it looks like it's from me. And I did send him an email the same day. Hold on a second. I'm going to forward you the original." The swoosh of justice winging its way to Denver punctuated my last sentence. "Do you really believe I'd send an email with bad punctuation and capitalization issues?" A tense burst of laughter bit at the inside of my nose.

Josh didn't laugh with me. "Here it is. Give me a second to read it." I held my breath while I waited.

> Hey, Sam,
> I have to step in and stop whatever
> misconception you have about what's
> going on or could go on between us. If I
> led you to believe Josh and I were about to
> break up or that I was hoping to rekindle
> something between you and me, I do
> apologize. That wasn't my intention.
> We're very much in love (I mean Josh and
> me), and I can't wait to marry him.

Reconnecting with you was lots of fun,
though. Who knows: maybe our paths will
cross in the future on our next visit to the
Harrington Estate?
All my best,
Ellen

"The schmuck! He edited out half your email to trick me into thinking you guys had been having an affair! When you were in the bathroom, he told me the reason your relationship ended was because you had cheated on him. I know you have promised me before that you had never cheated on anyone, but here was this guy telling me differently. And when he forwarded me this piece of garbage. I totally fell for it. Will you forgive me?"

"I still don't get why you were so quick to assume I was cheating on you. It's totally unfair that you believed him — a stranger — over me. I'm your fiancée. If you don't trust me, we have a problem."

"I do trust you. I screwed up."

"Yeah, you did. You've made me miserable. You know how hard it is for us to be apart for a long time. Why would you go and make it worse? And with the wedding coming up, I couldn't help but wonder if the way you acted today meant you don't want to marry me."

"Ellen, you know how much I love you. I want nothing more than to marry you."

"How was I supposed to believe that after the way you behaved?"

"I suck. I totally suck. I don't know what to say. I was in a vulnerable place, really nervous about this tour. And I felt so guilty for leaving you at the spur of the moment. Freud would have had a field day with me. It's like I wanted to find a place outside of myself to focus my negative energy. Like, I didn't want to be responsible for making myself feel bad. Sam gave me a reason to be mad at someone else. You. God, I'm such a jerk!"

"You're not a jerk. To be honest, I didn't even recognize you today. I don't know where that dude came from, but I seriously hope we've seen the last of him. You have to cut yourself some slack. If heading out on tour made you nervous, you should have talked to me about it. You're such a badass, we could have found a way for you to power through the nerves. And as far as feeling guilty about leaving, I mean, of course, I don't want you to be gone all month, but it would be selfish of me to hold you back from pursuing your career."

"You're right. And way too patient with me. How stupid was I to let Sam distract me? I shouldn't have listened to a word he said or given him my email address. I'm such a horrible fiancé. I let him ruin our last couple of hours together. How can I make it up to you?"

"For starters, you have to promise me that in the future, you'll talk to me about whatever has you in a funk before you let it make you all crazy."

"I promise."

"And you'll never, ever, ever let one of our exes ruin things between us."

"I promise, promise, promise," he said with a laugh.

"Well, I suppose I forgive you now. Do you want to move our conversation to a video chat? I could help you, um, adjust your antenna?"

"If you're saying what I think you're saying, yes. Yes, please. Damn, I wish I had my mother's magician's assistant costume. I'd wear it as my penance."

"You know, it might take a while for my sense of forgiveness to sink in. You'd better watch your step, or I'll make you wear it to our wedding instead of a tux."

I DIDN'T RELY on email to lay into Sam. The next morning, I enjoyed the satisfaction of rolling the words of condemnation around in my mouth before casting them into the phone. Equally delicious was hearing him bleat his sheepish apologies. I would have preferred to have had this conversation with him at the bistro in Princeton. To have seen his face! And to have avoided going through this nonsense with Josh in the first place.

I wished I could fly to Denver to make up with Josh like I had done with the Dayton trip last year. Thanks to the turn of events at the Vista, I did have a day off on Sunday, but I had to play a wedding on Saturday and teach on Monday. As desperate as I was to have Josh's reassuring touch solidify the end of our temporary estrangement, I had to concede how ridiculous it would be to make the trip in a single day. Stuck at home, I resumed my role of playing Penelope to his Odysseus. In addition to finishing the scarf I had begun knitting aboard the Orpheus, I devoted myself to our wedding.

I would have had enough time before my gig on Saturday to join Nathan, Derrick, and the other men when they picked out their suits for the wedding. Derrick banned me from the trip, though, employing some twisted logic that if Josh couldn't see my dress before the wedding, I couldn't see what the men were wearing. My consolation prize was a text describing the gray suits with black neckties he had chosen for the groomsmaids — his preferred term for Josh's side of the wedding party. He did reveal that he had picked out a black tux and bow tie for Josh. *Ooh, big surprise.* I wasn't sure whether he had been joking about him and Nathan wearing suits in a gray windowpane fabric. And he had to have been teasing me when he talked about pairing lavender ties with the suits.

I had debated postponing our cake tasting appointment until Josh returned, but, well, cake. Wisely, he put his trust in my taste buds. I was sure I could handle the responsibility. He also knew better than to suggest I sample any flavor that didn't begin with *choco* and end with *late*. I had invited Chloe to go in Josh's place after he had received the news about the tour, but she wouldn't commit to coming along with me.

The day of the appointment, I prepared to do solo battle with the anticipated onslaught of calories by nibbling on a salad for lunch. A commotion from Chloe's room interrupted my dreams of ooey-gooey chocolate frosting. I rushed into the hallway in front of her room. "You OK in there?"

The padding of her bare feet on the wood floor grew louder as she approached the door. She opened it, holding on to the knob. Her face had an incandescent glow, one it had been missing in recent months. "Sorry. I got a little carried away when I read an email. Everything's good. Really good!" She hugged me.

"And they lived happily ever after? The only problem with your story is you forgot to tell it to me."

Chloe took my hands in hers. "I know I've been a giant ball of mystery and misery for a while now. And I'm so sorry for keeping the reason behind my mood a secret. Sometimes I have to deal with things on my own. You know that about me, of course."

"This ain't my first rodeo where you're concerned."

With a laugh, she said, "The thing is, even though I received the best possible news, I can't tell you about it just yet. Soon, though. I promise!"

"To think I was going to share my cake tasting appointment with you," I said with mock indignation.

"That's today? I know I hadn't given you an answer, but if the invitation's still good, I'd love to come with you."

"How much is it going to cost me?"

"Come again?"

"The wedding jar. How much money do I need to deposit into it in order to earn an afternoon of incessant prattling about my wedding?"

"Have I made you that nervous about talking about your wedding? I thought it might have been a bad idea to implement the wedding jar system. You've paid in plenty. And, especially since you've had to slash your budget because of the new car, it wouldn't be fair for me to continue to extract money from you. Consider your account settled from here on out."

Picturing the jar, now stuffed nearly to capacity with wads of my hard-earned cash, I asked, "Will you be reimbursing me the funds I've already deposited?"

"I have a reputation to preserve. I can't go all generous on you now, can I?" The only answer I had for her was an exaggerated roll of my eyes. It was just for show.

Save for the two years she had been in San Francisco pursuing her master's degree, Chloe and I had been inseparable since we met each other almost twelve years ago. Technically, I was a few months older than her, but I'd always regarded her as my big sister.

From advice on trivial issues like boys and fashion to bigger, emotional hurdles I needed to overcome, she had provided the foundation for my maturation. Her confidence and willingness to bulldoze my problems with or without my permission had been my lifeline since we first had met. While she was quick to loan me her clothes and keep our wine rack full, it was how invested she was in helping me to live my best life that proved how truly generous a friend she was. She did have an acidic side, but the longer I'd known her, the more I'd come to understand that this side of her generally reflected her current state of mind rather than her readiness to pass withering judgment on whatever nonsense I'd gotten myself tangled up in.

The past year had been a momentous one for me. While Chloe had been with me for all of it, she had played a subordinate role. Had I really taken the lead in conquering my problems? If so, was it because she hadn't been emotionally available to me, or was it because I had grown independent? Chicken, egg, it didn't matter which came first. Chloe was back!

Amber's favorite wedding cake bakery was in Montclair, not far from our apartment. Chloe and I walked to the bakery together, conversing with the energy of reunited lovers. My spat with Josh had been so short, so inexplicable, the memory of it was fleeting in comparison to Chloe's return to the land of the cheerful after so many months away.

"What are we talking about, cake-wise?" she asked.

"Definitely chocolate. And I'm leaning toward buttercream frosting rather than fondant icing."

"Are you sure?" The arch in Chloe's eyebrows expressed she held a different opinion. I'd missed that arch.

"When I dream of cake, it's of the birthday cake variety. Cake shouldn't be pretentious. It needs to be rich and flavorful. In other words, chocolate. Wedding cakes are like models. Their job is to look good in the pictures. When it comes to eating them, meh. Cakes, I mean. Not models. Especially when they're entombed by fondant. That stuff is inedible. Again, I'm talking about eating cake, not people."

"I'm glad you clarified that. You had me worried for a second. You really should consider getting a formal wedding cake, though. Given the setting of your reception, a traditional wedding cake is the way to go. I was thinking lemon with a raspberry filling. Three tiers. Wrap each cake in white fondant and decorate them with silver bands. If you want a chocolate cake, get a groom's cake."

"Where are we, North Carolina? I had never even heard of a groom's cake until I began to research wedding cakes. And silver decorations? What flavor is silver? I would never expect lemon cake with raspberries inside a white and silver cake."

Chloe smiled at me. "You're right. I've described my ideal wedding cake, not yours. So long as the frosting is not lavender, I support whatever you choose."

"Maybe I'll order a cupcake just for you. Lemon with frosting in a vibrant hue of purple. And rainbow sprinkles."

"We'll see about that. Have I told you what an amazing job you've done planning your wedding? Once you got into gear, you showed it who was the boss. I love your venue and your flowers. And our dresses, of course. Yours especially. I am so excited for you guys!" She wrapped me in an enthusiastic hug.

"Thanks! Me too!"

"So, what else have you planned? Are you tossing a bouquet? And if so, will you be aiming for Gwen?"

We entered the shop with the energy of two best friends already hopped up on sugar. I basked in the warm, sweet scent of oven-baked love wafting throughout the space. Our heels pierced the silence, clicking against the tiled floor in the sliver of a storefront. Walls the color of buttercream icing held blackboards listing the available treats in a swooping script.

"Ellen?" A middle-aged woman wiped her hands on her apron.

"Yes, I am. And this is Chloe, my designated cake sampler."

"I'm Sally. Well, I hope you're in the mood for a bit of cake sampling, too. Per your request, I've baked a variety of chocolate cakes for you to try."

If I could be a professional cake tester, I surely would. Creating a soundtrack better suited to a porno, I sighed, groaned, and swooned my way through devil's food cake with raspberry filling, a cocoa cake with a fudgy filling, and the winner, a dark chocolate cake with coffee mousse filling. Sally promised she could create a swirled pattern in white buttercream icing to mimic the bodice of my dress. I wished Josh could have joined us, but on the other hand, I wouldn't have traded my afternoon with Chloe for anything. Except for maybe a bigger stomach.

"GWEN! All is right with the world!" I wrapped my arms around Gwen, not daring to let go. It seemed like it had been forever since she had last been in our apartment. In an instant, everything felt normal. Spending time at home, just Gwen, Chloe, and me, took me back to the four years we had spent living together in college. With Gwen and Matt cohabiting in New York and me two months away from getting married, we no longer lived like the close-knit trio we had always been. It wasn't so much our bonds had broken. For other reasons, good reasons, the bonds had stretched a bit. I couldn't wait to savor our evening of bouncing back together.

Because I had to dip into my wedding savings to buy Guinevere, one of the items I had to forgo for the wedding was professional hair and makeup. It wouldn't exactly have been a luxury expenditure. My hair could star in its own sitcom. A pile of unruly, coarse, and mousy curls, I'd cast it in the role of the heroine who compensated for her insecurity by spewing endless sassy quips and behaving defiantly. In the ultimate punch line, I was bereft of the skill set needed to be its director.

Chloe had volunteered to do my hair and makeup for the wedding. She had wrestled my hair into submission before, but never when the stakes were this high. According to Amber's timeline, now was the perfect time to have a test run of my hairstyle and makeup. Chloe covered the dining table with her massive stockpile of hair-corralling devices and enough cosmetics to paint a mural the length of a city block. I poured the three of us glasses of sparkling wine.

I explained my vision to Chloe. "So what I'm thinking is I want to harness my hair's inner Pre-Raphaelite tendencies. I don't want to straighten it or tame its volume. Pull it back but leave a bit of poof on the top and sides. Ooh, and leave a couple of tendrils to frame my face. Then you can arrange the ends in a loose bun ending just below the nape of my neck. But don't make it neat by hiding the ends. The loose curls can span the back of my head. I have a rhinestone and pearl comb for you to stick in somewhere. Here: check out this photo. I want something like her hairdo."

Chloe and Gwen admired the image on my tablet's screen. "So pretty. I can totally create a version of the hairstyle for you. How about your makeup? Smokey eye or a strong lip?"

"I want to keep the look simple and natural. Play up my eyes without it being obvious you used tons of makeup. I want to keep my face pale with just a hint of a pink on my cheeks, but let's have my skin shimmer in some super hydrated, radiant sort of way. For my lips, I want to go with a red, but not a bold shade. More of a sweet red."

"You got it. A blushing bride you shall be!" Chloe led me to a chair in front of the table. Gwen pushed aside an eyeshadow box with six shades of blue in it, making room for her glass. I would have preferred for her to chuck the eyeshadows in the garbage. I hoped Chloe didn't plan to turn me into a nineteen-seventies-era disco queen.

I needed to distract myself from the painful tugs of Chloe's comb evicting knots and squirrel homes from my hair. "How's the whole 'living in sin' thing going, Gwen?"

"You sound like my dad. My mom is all for it, of course. To her, nothing says strong, modern woman better than a woman eschewing convention in favor of pursuing her own desires. I'll let her believe what she wants to believe. It just makes my life easier, that's all. Most of the musicians who hire me to be their accompanists live in the City. Speaking of which, did I tell you I'm accompanying one of the semi-finalists in the Metropolitan Opera National Council Auditions next week? I'm this close to realizing my dream! Maybe someone at the Met will take notice of me and add my name to their roster of accompanists!"

"How awesome! You totally deserve to work at the Met!" I said to my lap. Chloe held my head still, preventing me from looking up at Gwen.

"I'll keep my fingers crossed. But more important, what goes on at home? We need the juicy details, my friend!" Chloe grabbed a fistful of my hair, tugging it with enough force to encourage another inch of it to spring forth from my scalp.

"We're still in the honeymoon phase if that's what you're asking." I recognized a tone in Gwen's voice, the one she used to prevent us from prying secrets out of her.

"Ah, crap!" I sat erect in my seat. Chloe dropped the chunk of hair she had been twisting behind my ear.

"Did I hurt you?"

"No. This conversation reminds me that Josh and I had pledged by the end of April we would decide where we were going to live."

"You still have over two weeks before your deadline. I bet the solution will turn out to be simpler than you have imagined, anyhow."

"You know my housing dilemma involves you, too? We're probably not going to be roommates after the wedding." I swiveled on my seat to face her.

"Now's as good a time as any to tell you guys something." Chloe pushed me to face forward in my chair, her hands moving more gently through my hair. "It's kind of a long story. Maybe we need a refill." Gwen topped off each of our glasses.

"I had been suffering a bit of a midlife crisis a couple of decades too early. I began to question my life before we agreed to take the gig on the Orpheus. At the time, I thought all I needed was a change of scenery. After the first month aboard the ship, I realized I had a bigger problem. You actually helped me to begin to identify what had been nagging me."

"I did?" I gulped my wine and widened my eyes.

"Yeah. When you embraced the Sheldon of it all, when you chose to dedicate yourself to becoming a kickass lounge harpist, I recognized the absence of a similar goal in my life. I had lost my way as a flutist and teacher. The bulk of my students were beginners or people who weren't going to go far with their studies. I desperately craved the opportunity to expand my teaching experience to include working with advanced students. My performance career had stagnated, too. The gigs I've played with other strong musicians usually involved lesser pieces of music. On the rare occasions I've gotten to dig into some meaty repertoire, it was with amateur ensembles. I've missed the challenge of playing tough and satisfying pieces with musicians who brought out the best in me."

"I hear you. I often reflect on how different my career is from the one I had prepared for in college."

"But you have found fulfillment in your career. I haven't."

"Wow, Chloe. That's heavy. I wish you had shared your thoughts with me. I could have helped you to brainstorm alternatives like taking auditions or maybe reaching out to some of Josh's New York contacts."

"You're sweet. It wasn't something I wanted to say out loud. I floundered on my own for a while. I definitely reached a point where I knew being on the ship wasn't helping me. Speaking of which, have I told you recently how sorry I am for roping you into my early disembarkation scheme aboard the Orpheus?" Chloe leaned forward from behind my chair, embracing me across my chest.

"I'm glad you've finally admitted it had been your plan to give them a reason to fire you. But no worries. Coming home early provided me with the opportunity to fix things with Josh. You're forgiven." I patted her hands.

"You may have forgiven her, but you guys coming home ruined my living situation," Gwen chuckled. Being our apartment sitter while we were on the ship gave her the perfect alibi for hiding her relationship with Matt from her parents.

"Get over it already! Everything worked out for the two of you, didn't it?"

"True." Gwen tipped her glass toward Chloe in a toast.

"I stewed over how to address my issues last summer, but nothing came to me. In September, I called my old flute professor from the San Francisco Conservatory. She had won the principal flute chair in LA a couple of years ago and is now on the faculty at UCLA, too. She suggested I apply to be a doctoral candidate. Now you know why

I've been practicing like a fiend for months. While I was in San Francisco over the holidays, she offered to help me prepare for the audition. I flew to LA for the coachings, which is why I came home later than planned. The closer it drew to my audition, the more nervous I became. And after auditioning in LA in February, waiting for the results was no less stressful."

Gwen gave her a playful shove. "Way to keep a secret, Chloe! How did the audition go?"

"They started to send out acceptances at the end of February, but mine didn't come until the third week of March. I knew I'd have an answer, good or bad, by the end of March, but the waiting nearly did me in. It was good news: they've accepted me!"

Gwen and I jumped up to celebrate with Chloe. My happy dance lost some of its bounce when her news hit me. "Won't it be a long commute from Montclair to LA? With all the online classes available these days, I suppose you can do it remotely?"

"No. The whole point of applying to UCLA was for me to take lessons and to benefit from my teacher's connections in LA. I might even have the opportunity to sub in her orchestra. I'll be a teaching assistant, which means I'll teach college-level students. Pursuing my doctorate will provide every opportunity and experience I have been missing."

An aching sensation in response to what Chloe had experienced and had kept to herself flowed through my heart even though I knew joy had replaced her sadness. My hurt originated from a different source. It was impossible for the three of us to continue to cling to our history of living our lives in lockstep. My two best friends meant the world to me. I hated that moving on, whether it be by falling in love or by pursuing a new career path, meant letting go of our togetherness. "The band's breaking up!"

"Don't say that! We will be leading independent lives, but I'll never stop loving the two of you." A fluttering of bobby pins falling from her fingers landed in my lap. My fingertips, damp with the tears I had wiped away, chased after the pins. "Now do you understand how me going to LA solves your housing crisis? I've already talked to our landlord. He'll put you and Josh on the new lease. It should work out for all of us. You'll be away for one week on your honeymoon, so you'll only have to shuttle between your two apartments for a short time after the wedding. I'll move out sometime in mid-July, and I'd be happy to pay my share of the rent until the end of the month. See? Everything's settled." She sniffled, a wry smile on her lips. "Your hair's done, but you can't see it until I finish your makeup."

Chloe turned my chair away from the table, preventing me from keeping track of which pots and potions she selected. The coolness of the lotion she blended into my face relaxed me. The second product she applied dragged against my skin under the sweeps of her thumb and pointer finger. I tried to guess each shade she brushed on my eyelids.

"I know you're going to object, but I've decided we need to boost your eyelashes with some falsies. Not full-on drag queen, mind you. They'll be subtle. Unclench your face and let me get to work." The liquid glue she applied to the edges of my eyelid began to burn. I squirmed. "Hold still. There. Now the other eye." I tried to blink. My right eye moved in slow motion under the weight of the fur coat she had draped on it. "I'm not kidding. Don't move."

"Give me a mirror! Everything is blurry because I'm staring through a hairy black curtain. Take them off!"

"I won't. And I'm not going to let you see it yet. But I promise you, it's perfect. Right, Gwen?"

Gwen had been watching the process with dubious fascination. "Um, yeah, I see what you're going for."

A lip liner tugged on the perimeter of my lips. Chloe held a lipstick just out of sight, gathering its pigment in the bristles of a brush. With careful strokes, she painted my lips. She cocked her head, regarding her work. Satisfied, she returned the lipstick and brush to the table. My face tickled from the flurry of dabs she made across it with a powder-puff. "Done! Gwen, hand me the mirror."

The weight of the mirror caused it to slip sideways within my grip on its handle. I held it with both hands, bringing in front of me. I was speechless. I didn't know where to focus first. The millipedes crawling around my eyes, masquerading as eyelashes? The brownish-red lipstick ringed by dark brown liner? The streaks of hot pink blush darting across my cheekbones? Or should I conduct a thorough investigation of the hairstyle? A thin row of tendrils dripped below rolls of hair from the beginning of the part atop my forehead to the nape of my neck. The hair above the rolls puffed away from my head, caught in mid-escape. I couldn't blame it for trying to flee.

I moved the show into the bathroom to examine the mad collection of curls dancing across the back of my head. They had taken over my scalp like poison ivy, obliterating the pearl and rhinestone floral comb cowering below their mass.

Chloe's eyes had a sparkle to them. Her taste level had sunk below her typical high standards. She couldn't possibly be proud of the mess she had made of my hair and makeup. "Let me snap a few photos. I know what I want to do differently next time. We'll go with more subtle eyelashes. A lighter pink for your cheeks and a different lipstick. You and I can choose the colors. My hairstyle experiment didn't turn out the way I expected, either. I'll rethink how I need to do it. This is why we did a trial run. I promise you I will make you gorgeous in June."

Hideous as the outcome was, I didn't have a choice. I needed her help. "I'm sitting in front of a mirror on my wedding day and giving myself veto power every step of the way. And I'm cutting you off from alcohol and discussing emotional subjects during the process."

"Whatever works for you. But, since I'm free to drink tonight, let's open the second bottle of wine."

"Give me a minute. I'm going to restore things to normal in the hair and face department. You'd better save me some wine. I'll need more than a washcloth and comb to obliterate the memory of what you've done to my face and hair!"

IT WAS NICE of my mother to change her plans for Mother's Day in order to spend the day with her daughter. What her preexisting plans were, I did not know. Having not made them with either of her children, how could she even call them Mother's Day plans?

Admittedly, I had played gigs on the holiday in previous years rather than take the time to celebrate with my mother. Lulled into complacency when I had a steady brunch gig at the beginning of the year, I had turned down the one Mother's Day gig offer I had received. With a glaring hole in my calendar and a box of wedding invitations, response cards, and directions to our venue I needed to stuff into envelopes, I offered to spend the day with my mother doing wedding things together. Best gift ever, right? She fussed about having to cancel her plans, but in the end, she agreed it would be lovely to have me to come for a visit. Like she was doing me a favor.

I cleared away the remains of our feast of bagels, lox, and mimosas from the table, replacing the plates with stacks of invitations and their accompanying pieces. My mom plucked the top invitation from its stack. She pinched the cream-colored card between her fingers, waving it back and forth. It emitted a low rattle in response. "These are very contemporary. Why did you print them with only lower-case letters and no last names? You didn't even choose the traditional text where your parents invite the guests to celebrate the marriage of their daughter. Hmm."

I framed a large, square invitation with my fingertips. Graphite ink spelled out "ellen & josh" on the top left corner. The contrast between the heavy, formal stock and the casual text suited my taste, but I had anticipated my mother not sharing my opinion. "I wanted the invitation to come from you. I hate that Daddy... I tried several versions of the wording, but I couldn't stand not seeing his name beside yours."

My mother reached for my hand. "Of course. Now it makes sense why you did it this way. Are guests mailing the responses to you or to me?"

"To you, just as you requested. The RSVP envelopes are addressed and stamped. I didn't have a chance to bring a completed invitation to the post office to ask about the postage. I'm pretty sure the weight exceeds regular first-class mail. I sort of remember reading something on the website where I ordered them mentioning they may require additional postage because of the size and shape, too. I'll have to ask a postal clerk about it."

"Leave it to me. I'll be able to swing by the post office tomorrow to buy the stamps. You'll want pretty wedding or love-themed stamps for them, right?"

"You'd take care of the postage for us? Thanks, Mom! And if they have wedding stamps, we'd prefer them."

She and I developed a method for gathering the three items to stuff into the large envelope. Dancing around each other to reach the next stack, we fell into an easy conversation.

"I still can't believe our Chloe is leaving us! It won't be the same without her. I hope she'll fly back east once in a while to visit us."

"She promises she will. So many changes for all of us! Speaking of which, what's the latest on Nathan, Derrick, and the baby?"

"Nathan tells me everything is going according to plan. Laurel is in her third trimester. Thirty years later, I remember it clear as day. The constant trips to the bathroom, the heartburn…"

I dropped an envelope onto the completed pile. "I'm really glad you suffered through pregnancy and childbirth for my sake!"

My mom tucked a section of hair behind her ear. "I'm not asking for appreciation. The sacrifice was worth it. Not that I want to go through the sleepless nights of caring for a newborn again. Your brother and Derrick will have their hands full if the little sweetie is anything like his or her father. I do wish they would let Laurel tell them whether they're having a boy or a girl!"

"Defining people by gender isn't such a big thing anymore. I totally support their decision not to prescribe stereotypical gender traits onto the little nugget before it's born. Or even after."

"I can't say I understand any of it, but they're the parents, not me." My phone rang, but I let it go to voicemail without checking to see who was calling me. "Aren't you going to answer your phone?" my mother asked.

"It can wait. If I were playing a gig today, I wouldn't be able to take it, anyway."

My mother reached for another invitation. "It really is a shame about your brunch gig. Have you done anything about trying to find a replacement?"

"I'm waiting until after the wedding. It will be a whole research project, finding popular restaurants with Sunday brunches and without live music. I'll put together a mailing offering my services to send to restaurants sometime during the summer."

As we worked, I turned over each filled envelope to examine the names and addresses printed on them. Over the course of the afternoon, I watched our guest list materialize on the stack of completed invitations. We were closing in on our wedding day. By the end of the month, Josh and I would apply for a marriage license. Amber would come home next Sunday. She'd tackle any last-minute details that come up. Quakes of excitement shuddered through my chest.

I had recognized most of the names on the envelopes. The unfamiliar guests usually lived in Pennsylvania. They would be Josh's relatives or friends of his parents. I held the envelope I had just stuffed in my hand. This guest, Douglas Thompson, lived in Piscataway, New Jersey. "Mom, how did the guy who sold me my car wind up on our guest list? Did I make a mistake and copy his address onto my list?"

"No. His name being on the list is not a mistake. I've invited him." She took the envelope from me to place on the completed stack.

"It's kind of odd to invite some random guy you met on vacation to our wedding."

"He's my friend. Aren't I allowed to invite my friends to your wedding? Last I checked, I am paying for most of it." I peeked at my watch. I had arrived two and a half hours ago. I may well have set a record for the length of time I had spent with my mother before she gave me that *look*, the one that guaranteed my inner pugilist would emerge, gloves laced up. Three deep breaths did the trick, helping me to stuff my little warrior back inside.

"I'm not denying you the right to invite your friends. I just didn't know you had kept in touch with him or that he was a close enough friend, you'd want to invite him."

She inserted another trio of cards into an envelope. I had slacked off in my work once I had added Douglas's envelope to the finished stack. "Well, he is a close friend. Now you know."

What exactly did I know? Were he and my mom...? "You're not dating him, are you?" A bitter taste filled my mouth.

"Dating is a funny word for someone my age to use. We spend time together, and we have grown quite fond of each other."

"In a romantic way?" I gave my head a subtle shake, hoping to manipulate her into answering in the negative.

"Yes. We have romantic feelings for each other."

I held a breath until my lungs began to hurt. "Does Nathan know?"

"I haven't mentioned it to him, either."

"Why keep Douglas from us?"

"Falling in love is different for people my age than it is for younger folks. We come with a lot of baggage. Children, previous marriages—"

"So Nathan and I are baggage? Daddy is baggage?"

My mother pressed her fingers against her mouth and looked upward in consternation. "I'm sorry. Baggage was the wrong word to use. When I met your father, I had my life in front of me. The two of you and your father were my world for many years. He had his first stroke at fifty-four; I was fifty-three. While we had discussed retirement prior to his stroke, we hadn't made concrete plans. We had talked about going on safari, taking a cruise to the Antarctic. These were dreams for a distant future. Now I'm sixty-one, and retirement is on the horizon. I'm not ready to resign myself to a quiet, solitary life because he is gone. With Douglas, I can share my future with someone. But it is difficult to separate what has been from what is to come. I have to bring my husband into my new relationship."

I turned to stone at the thought of my mother being unfaithful to my father. It wasn't rational. He was gone. I couldn't force her to honor her marriage vows. A separate part of me wanted my mother to find her happiness. I wasn't a monster. I simply was not ready to embrace this particular path toward her finding her joy. With my voice lacking conviction and warmth, I said, "I'm glad you've found a friend in Douglas."

"So am I. He's a good man. But I understand how you may need to take your time to grow accustomed to the idea of me having a new man in my life. When you're ready, we'll get together with Douglas and his daughters for a meal. You remember Erica and Lisa?"

"So they know?"

"They have known since last summer. Since Douglas and his ex had previously agreed that her serious boyfriend could spend time with their girls, he lobbied for me to have the same rights. I celebrated Thanksgiving with their family. We had planned to spend time together today. In retrospect, I should have been honest with the two of you long ago. But the situation is different for me than for him. He's divorced; I'm widowed. I didn't choose to part from my husband. I know your loyalty will always be to your father, as it should be. I never could find the right time to talk to you about Douglas. With all of the life changes you and Nathan are undergoing, I didn't want to overwhelm you."

I pursed my lips. "I appreciate why you hesitated to tell us. I'm sure whenever you told me your news, I would have found it to be a bit upsetting. But your having kept your secret life from me complicates everything. It makes your romance harder to accept."

"I'm sorry I handled things badly. I don't for a second want you to feel betrayed or for you to think I've betrayed your father. I'm in a tricky place: the source of my happiness was something I knew would be painful to share with my family. I may have waited too long to tell you, but I exercised caution because I love you." She rested her chin in her palm, her eyes unblinking.

"And I don't want to be selfish by denying you your happiness. I'm not going to tell you that you can't continue to see Douglas. I won't hide his invitation or refuse to talk to him at the wedding. I'm just not ready to consider him a part of our family if that's OK with you."

"I fully understand. When you're ready." She removed another invitation from the stack, ready to rejoin the assembly line.

Knowing I had prevented her from spending the day with Douglas made her appear lonely, isolated from her happiness. The weight of being true to both her devotion to my father and to her own heart must be unfathomably heavy. I wrapped my arms around her, resting my head on her shoulder. "Thanks for telling me, Mom. I love you, you know."

"I love you too, Dandelion!"

I couldn't remember the last time my mother had called me by the childhood nickname I had earned by my ever-present nimbus of fluffy curls.

We returned to our task in silence. My over-active brain flitted after random thoughts. I stumbled over one of them. "Now it makes sense why Douglas gave me such a good deal on Guinevere! He was trying to win me over."

"I told him to treat you like a random customer. He assured me the price was fair for both of you."

The stacks of invitations and response cards finally disappeared, replaced by wobbly piles of thick, sealed envelopes. We shifted them into an empty cardboard box.

"This was a lovely day, Ellen. I'm glad the two of us could spend time working on your wedding together. I promise I won't rush you into embracing Douglas's place in my life. I hope in time you'll understand how I can both love your father and care about another man."

"Maybe the summer will be the right time for me to get to know him better. You sure you're fine with me leaving you to take care of the postage for the invitations?"

"It won't be a bit of trouble."

AS A KID, I loved it when my parents held hands. With their fingers bunched into a single fist, they would swing their arms between them and smile at each other each time they turned their heads inward. Before they went out to celebrate a special occasion, I would sneak into their room to watch them primp. My father would select his cufflinks from a flat wooden box with rounded edges. He'd let me hold it. I'd run my fingers along its smooth surface, a hypnotic gesture befitting the mesmerizing effect of witnessing my parents' transformations. My reaction never equaled theirs at the moment when they would inspect the other before going out for the night. Decked out in their finery, they held their breath and their gazes, their eyes sparkling. We don't often give our parents credit for possessing a romantic love for each other, but these telltale moments reminded me my parents dug each other in a different way than the love I felt for them.

On the ship, seconds before I knew Douglas existed, I had detected a hint of such spark in my mother. He had already changed her. The truth was the alteration didn't herald something new in her. She had recovered a part of her she had lost after my dad had fallen ill. With Douglas, she let herself enjoy the moment. She was at ease. She felt beautiful. She and Douglas had become to each other what she and my dad had been, what Josh and I were to each other.

My mother and I had sparred far less often over the last year than had been typical. Could it be Douglas deserved the credit for mellowing her out? I wished I could call Nathan to discuss the events of the afternoon with him. I would have to wait until I knew my mother had spoken to him.

In the muddle of processing my mother's news, I had forgotten to check my messages. I played back the voicemail I had received during our envelope stuffing party.

"Hello, my favorite harpist! It's Helena from the Vista. We've had a bit of a situation today. A guest requested a song Tiffany didn't know or didn't want to play. I'm still not entirely clear what happened. Anyhow, they got into a bit of an altercation. Tiffany used some colorful language, as I'm sure you can imagine. Lily and Claude witnessed the whole thing. They've had enough of her and have asked me to invite you to return. In the event some other restaurant hasn't snatched you up, I hope you'll be able to resume playing at the Vista, starting next Sunday. Give me a call when you get this message."

Yes! I shot my hands skyward in a victorious salute. I returned Helena's call, assuring her I couldn't wait to reclaim my brunch gig. I'd have to send in a sub on my wedding day and the Sunday after, but me having to miss two days of work wasn't a deterrent to them rehiring me.

Ricocheting from my mother's news to Helena's left me dazed and exhausted. Fitting five additional gigs into my schedule with only six weeks until the wedding awakened the dozing herd of butterflies in my gut.

Having Amber back home, ready to help me starting next week would mean I wouldn't face any last-minute wedding snafus alone. Even without her help these last four months, I had knocked off one item after another from her checklist. As I had predicted months ago, planning a wedding had turned out to be easier than how people often described it, at least once I conquered my phobia of the word *perfect*.

I had made Gwen and Chloe promise me they wouldn't throw me a bridal shower. I had no desire to wear a paper plate decorated with curling ribbon on my head or to open boxes filled with scanty little nothings in front of my mother. I hoped my friends took my advice because if they had planned to throw a shower on one of the remaining Sundays, well, what could I say? I had told them not to. Knowing we should enjoy a pre-wedding bonding event, I'd booked mani/pedi appointments for my half of the wedding party the day before the wedding.

The week flew by. By the time Nathan and I had a chance to talk after my mother had broken the news to him, Derrick had coaxed him away from the ledge. Like Chloe, Derrick could not have been happier to know my mother was dating. Neither my brother nor I had reached such a state. Nathan and I basically mumbled words of support for our mother to each other. We meant what we said, but the sentiments sprang from our brains, not our hearts. "Does this mean we're inheriting a pair of teenaged stepsisters?" he asked. "It was hard enough having to cope with you as a teen. I'm too old to go through that nonsense again."

"Lisa's a senior. I bet she's OK. Erica's the younger sister. She's a sophomore. Things get better after you turn sixteen or seventeen. How often are we going to have to see them, anyway? Besides, you might find yourself parenting a teenaged daughter of your own in a few years. Don't judge."

"Our child will be a shining light of well-adjusted youth. If it isn't, I can count on Derrick to take control of the situation."

I could hear Derrick cackling in the background. I said, "You're going to have to buy your husband lots of gifts if that's how you think parenting is going to go down. But seriously, since I'm five and a half weeks from my wedding day, that means you guys are seven weeks away from being daddies. I can't stand it!"

"Neither can we. We just spent the weekend in Chicago with Laurel and Stuart. She has hit the stage where being pregnant is no longer sunshine and lollipops. I thought we would have had way more fun hanging out with her and the baby bump, but Derrick decided to start reading the complete works of Shakespeare to the kid. Laurel slept through the first act of Henry VI, Part II. I wish I had." Derrick's muffled response bled through the phone.

"What did he say?"

"He called me an uncultured cretin. I'm used to it. We're raring to go here, Shakespeare aside. The nursery is done, and we're fully stocked with diapers, bottles, and way too much advice from everyone we know who has raised a child. All we ask is for Laurel to continue to incubate the kid until we're done with school on June seventeenth."

"You mean until after my wedding."

"Oh, yes. Of course. I didn't mean we want her to deliver early. Everything is still on course for July second."

Chloe had to confront her own deadline. In eight weeks, she would be moving to California. She began to prepare for her departure by taking inventory of her belongings. We had bought our couch, coffee table, and dining set together, all of which she would leave behind with me. While she examined the contents of the kitchen cabinets, I reminded her to start saving boxes and newspapers for the packing process. The groaning cupboards and cluttered countertops housed a significant stock of cookware and dishes, all of which belonged to her. Well, almost all. I had added a pair of green ceramic mugs and a wok to our shelves when we moved in. Oh, and a potholder.

Chloe gaped at the quantity of kitchenware our cabinets housed. "The first step toward recovery is to admit you have a problem, so they say. I've never been strong enough to resist a home goods sale. Do you want me to leave you anything?"

"You'll need to set yourself up in a new apartment. You should take everything. Josh and I have registered for everyday china, a new set of pots and pans, all the usual suspects. Once our guests receive their invitations and start to buy gifts from our registry, I'll have a better idea of what we'll still need to fill the shelves. We'll be fine starting from scratch."

"Mmm. Shopping for new kitchen gear. No. Must resist." She closed the last cabinet. "Do you think I'm crazy to rent a van and drive to California by myself?"

"Crazy? No way! I'm jealous! That's what I wanted to do for our honeymoon, drive cross-country in a van." I stretched out my arm, my hand mimicking the action of pouring out a forty-ounce bottle of beer onto the ground. "RIP Minerva. Even without a van, we couldn't spare the time to take a long trip. A week in New Orleans should be fun, too."

"Of course it will be. Let's go tackle my closet. I'm not sure whether it will be me you miss when I'm gone or easy access to a second wardrobe. If you play your cards right, I might leave behind a pair of shoes or three to spend the rest of their days here in New Jersey."

On Sunday, I strode through the Vista with my harp like I owned the joint. It didn't hurt to have Helena, Julio, and company greet me like a conquering hero. The Orpheus swayed in her berth across the river from my harp. Amber had disembarked this morning. Part of me wanted to rush into the City to shove my wedding binder into her hands the second I finished my gig and say, *Tag! You're it.* Another part of me remembered how disorienting it had been to return home after only three months at sea. I'd give her a day. I shot her a quick *welcome home* text on a break. She answered me right away, promising we would touch base tomorrow.

Even though it seemed like an eternity since she had joined up in January, time was slipping away faster than I could fathom. That's the thing with making detailed plans: you're keeping track of everything, counting down days, and checking things off of your to-do list. The effort embodied forward motion, a desire to bring the future into being. I'd been waiting for our wedding day since the day Josh proposed, and now it was only one month away.

We weren't the only people reaching for their future. One by one, my closest peeps had set goals of their own. Gwen had moved in with her boyfriend, Chloe had planned a future in LA, my mother fell in love, and Nathan and Derrick, now married, were weeks away from becoming new parents. I thought I was bringing Josh into my well-populated world, but in the time it had taken us to plan our wedding, everyone close to me had moved in a different direction, solidifying relationships of their own.

Despite the confidence I experienced from reclaiming the Vista brunch as a permanent, steady gig, I couldn't help but wrestle with insecurities raised by all the changes in our lives. I woke up the next morning with them limbering up for what I gathered would be a marathon through the folds of my brain. Amber saved me from firing the starter's pistol when she called me after breakfast. "Everything's coming together! Sid and Maxwell have their final inspection today. It's the big kahuna, the one that will grant them occupancy rights."

"Are we worried?"

"Of course not. Their contractor is as by-the-book as they come. Never a permit out of place. The guys tell me the renovations are flawless."

"How about the finial that kept coming loose?"

"Funny you should mention the finial. The contractor fixed that sucker but good last week. Sid took it hard. He had named it Edgar. He swears once they've passed the inspection, he's going to bust it again. Now about your dress. Are you going to invite me to come see it?"

SITTING ACROSS FROM ME at my dining table the next day, Amber tapped her pen against the page of my binder opened in front of her. No matter how hard she tried, she couldn't find a hole in the wedding checklist. "You've gotten your dress altered?"

"Yup."

"So have I. How about the other women?"

"They have, too. The tux rental place is bringing the guys' suits to the hotel the day before."

She opened to the next section of my binder. "Where are we with the payments?"

"Every vendor except for the band has a deposit. The caterer requested an additional payment before the balance is due. My mother mailed it out yesterday." I reached for the binder, remembering I hadn't marked the updated info on the contract.

"Harry and I checked and double-checked every item on your rental list after the mishap with the wrong size tables. It is a good thing you caught the error. I apologize for any stress it caused."

An image of Josh jigging around a tiny table materialized in my mind. With a giggle, I said, "Man, if we hadn't gone to Sid and Maxwell's house right before their party, we might have been up the creek."

"Not to brag, but I'm sure I would have caught it today while we were going over the contracts. Your wedding plans are airtight, Ellen. We're down to the small details. We still need photos to display of the two of you and your families. I have a collection of frames I'll loan you. Are you doing a candle lighting or smashing of the glass during the ceremony? I'm putting together a list of all the items we'll need to bring to the venue."

"Josh and I met with Mags last week to work on our service. I'll forward you a copy. We won't need a candle. Despite neither of us being Jewish, Josh insists on ending the ceremony by stomping on a glass."

"A light bulb wrapped in a napkin will do the trick. I've made a note. I still need to send you my list of which vendors you should tip with recommendations for the amounts. According to the checklist, we're good to go. How about you? Are you stoked?"

"I am! The nonstop flutters in my stomach remind me how close I am to our wedding day, kind of like they do before a big performance. I know I'm prepared. I'm not really nervous. The sensation is more about anticipating the day and hoping everything goes perfectly. No, I've picked the wrong word. I hope everything is beautiful." My hands, like cicadas, swished a rhythmic pattern when I rubbed them together.

Amber closed the binder decisively. "And it will be!"

"Speaking of checklists, did you hear how the inspection went yesterday?"

"I'm still waiting to hear from Sid and Maxwell. I assume the fact I haven't heard from them is a good sign.

They warned me beforehand it's not uncommon for small issues to arise during a final inspection. They're convinced that building inspectors believe if they don't find anything wrong, they've done a bad job inspecting. With a contractor like theirs, if they need to make any tweaks, they will be the sorts of things the contractor can fix right away while the inspector is on site. The process was bound to be painless for Sid and Maxwell. We don't have any reason to fret. I'll let you know the second I hear they passed the inspection." She checked the time. "I have a half hour before I have to leave to catch the train. Let's go through your photos to find good shots for you to print up."

I couldn't pull myself away from my laptop after Amber left. I didn't need to find many more photos. The seduction of reliving the past through the photo collection was too strong to resist, though. I dove in deep, revisiting vacations with my family, birthday parties, school concerts.

The family photos revealed my mother hadn't changed her hairstyle in decades. Little differences, like how much volume she puffed into it, were all that distinguished one phase of my childhood from the next. My father's hair appeared to deflate over the years. Where my mother had her trusty hairdresser to help her to maintain her preferred shade of auburn, my father's hair transitioned from a deep brown to a speckled mix of light brown and gray.

I landed on the picture I had sought. I didn't know when or where it was taken. Using the hair equivalent of carbon dating, I figured it must have been from the late eighties. My father had lifted my mother off the ground, his arms squeezing her around her waist from behind. He leaned back. Her legs stuck straight out in front of them, and she held her arms away from her sides. His face was barely visible, blurred in the background. She squinted her eyes, her mouth wide open, mid-laugh. I knew exactly how she felt. This could be my expression on any day I had spent with Josh. I copied the photo into the wedding folder on my desktop.

My phone's ring interpreted my reveries. "Hey Mom, I was just going through some photos of you and Dad."

"What a pleasant way to spend an afternoon. I'm afraid I'm going to have to spoil the mood, though." A furrow engraved new lines on my forehead as I waited for her to explain herself. "I've just come home from work to find the mailbox stuffed to the gills. The post office returned over twenty of your invitations to me."

My heart missed a beat. "How is that possible? Did I screw up the addresses?"

"No. It seems to be an issue of insufficient postage. I don't see how, though. I used the scale at my office. I'm quite good with the scale, you know. Everyone in the office comes to me with their packages. I could tell just by holding one of your invitations in my hand it weighed more than an ounce. Sure enough, the scale agreed with me. I went to the post office on my lunch break last Monday to buy seventy-cent stamps."

Waiting for a chance to speak, my mouth opened and closed like that of a fish who had flopped onto the dresser next to his tank after taking a heroic leap out of the water. "But did you show the clerk the envelopes? I told you because of their size and shape, they might require an additional fee. Don't you remember?"

"I'm sorry, but I don't recall you telling me any such thing. We talked about how they may cost more, but I thought it was only because of their weight."

I screwed my eyes shut and lifted my head heavenward. "I knew I should have taken them home with me! The post office is going to return all of them to you. What are we going to do?" I sprang from my chair, desperately needing to pace the room to calm myself.

"We could invite the guests by phone."

"Then why did I bother buying invitations? This isn't some last-minute picnic we're throwing for a few people! We need formal invitations. I don't even know when I'll have the time or the patience to call everyone. I can't handle this!" My feet began kicking at imaginary targets.

"If I made the mistake, I am truly sorry. You should have left explicit instructions for me. But have some perspective. We're only talking about pieces of paper. Maybe we can use one of those internet invitation sites. Do you know what I'm talking about? I've received some very attractive invitations via email."

My pacing pattern reduced to smaller and smaller circles. "I can't deal with invitations right now. Every solution sounds wrong to me."

"I'm only trying to help. We can't wait forever to solve your problem, you know."

"Well, yeah. Let me ask Amber for suggestions."

"Yes, you should ask her. She'll know how to handle the situation. Everything will be fine." Did she even hear herself? "Let me know what your decision is. Have a good night!" Like that was possible.

I blinked my eyes hard in an attempt to wring tears from my tear ducts. My eyes remained as dry as my mouth. I had screwed this whole thing up. Amber's checklist informed me I should have mailed my invitations six to eight weeks before the wedding. I waited until the last minute to tackle the process of stuffing the envelopes. I should have put the box on the coffee table the day it arrived from the printer. Chloe and I could have taken a leisurely approach, stuffing envelopes in our free time. I would have made sure the postal clerk calculated the proper postage. But now, four and a half weeks before my wedding, I had to start over.

I didn't give Chloe even a minute to decompress after she came home from teaching. "It's a flippin' disaster!"

"What is?" She threw her bag on the table.

With a rasp in my voice, I explained the situation.

"Bummer! I loved your invitations. But it's not the end of the world. I mean, you're not the Queen of England." Way to kick a gal when she's down, Chloe! "Well, you're not. No one will be offended if you opt for a less formal means of inviting them to your wedding."

"It offends me! And sending them any other way besides through the mail will be a pain in the ass. My master list only has people's home addresses. I'm going to have to start from scratch to build a list of phone numbers or emails. We'll have to figure out how to include the directions with the invitations, too. Can you imagine dictating them to every guest over the phone?"

"It sounds like electronic invitations would be the way to ensure everyone receives the information they need. I wasn't going to mention it because it was moot, but Gwen and I had been in the early stages of planning a little Ellen the bride celebration on a Sunday early in June before you started working at the Vista again."

"I told you I don't want a party."

"Hear me out. Why don't I ask Gwen, Amber, Sheila, your mom, even your brother and Derrick, to come over this weekend? We can make calls, gather emails, do whatever it takes to rebuild your mailing list for Invitations 2.0. We'll knock it out in no time flat."

"No, thanks. Honestly, it will be easier for me to start filling in the addresses I know on my own and ask for help from my mom, Josh, and his parents when I need it. Thanks for offering to help, but this doesn't call for more bodies. Just more time. Of which I have none."

AMBER'S REPLY to my desperate text last night said only that she would call me soon to help sort out the invitation mess. If my wedding planner wasn't stressing, I shouldn't be, right? I huffed my way through each set on the weight machines at the Y. The meditative act of counting reps lasted only until the end of a set. Each rest period stretched beyond a useful length. I'd lose myself in visions of worst-case scenarios while I sat slumped over in the machines. We hadn't sent our guests *save the date* cards. By the time they heard from me, they'd all have made other plans. Sure, the people closest to us knew the pertinent information about our wedding. But how about the people we didn't stay in touch with? I pictured empty tables dotting the ballroom, an unpopulated dance floor in its center. I would be hosting the world's saddest wedding. With clenched teeth, I forced the weight machine handles away from my chest.

I toiled on the list after lunch. Hunched over my laptop, I typed each name on my list into the *to* field of an empty email, coaxing the computer to fill in the address. Because I have a bad habit of creating unnecessary work for myself, I had decided each guest, rather than each household, would receive a new invitation. My list ballooned from eighty-four street addresses to one hundred thirty-two names.

Before my first student of the afternoon arrived for her lesson, I had populated my new list with only twenty-eight email addresses. I portioned off the remaining names into three segments to foist off onto my mother, Josh, and his mother for their input. My dream of sending the invitations tonight drowned in a sea of frustrated tears.

Amber called while I was teaching my last student. I screened her, dedicating myself to helping the student conquer a particularly thorny passage in her sonata. Erecting a fortress around the two of us and the harp, I shut out my wedding crisis. Long before I had met Josh or began to plan our wedding, I had built my career. I wouldn't be worth my reputation if I prioritized my personal life over my student.

I let the lesson extend beyond five o'clock. The student's mother shifted on the couch, putting her paperback face down in her lap. Her subliminal message reminded me time was up. I couldn't avoid the real world at the expense of their schedule. Sending the two of them home, I returned Amber's phone call.

She didn't even say *hello*. "So you got my message?"

"I haven't listened to it yet. I might have solved my problem, though. I've decided to email the new invitations."

"You haven't sent them out yet, have you?"

I twisted my hair around my pointer finger. "Not yet. We still have a lot of work to do gathering the addresses. It could take another day or two."

"It might be a blessing in disguise for you to have to resend your invitations."

I dropped into the easy chair by the couch, a familiar panic coursing through my chest. "What are you saying? What don't I know?"

"Maybe you should pour yourself a glass of wine before I tell you. And drop in a Xanax or two, for good measure."

I scooted forward in the seat. "You're scaring me, Amber! What's going on? Did the manor burn down?"

"No. They failed the inspection."

I expelled the air I had trapped in my chest, and my butt sank deeper into the seat cushion. "You mentioned failing the inspection was a possibility, but you promised me the contractor would be able to fix any problems at the inspection."

"I wish the issue had been so simple. A former owner did some work on an upstairs bathroom without the proper permits. They moved an outlet when they put in a jetted tub. The way they did it is definitely not up to code."

"I don't understand how an upstairs bathroom has anything to do with the first floor. Sid and Maxwell had the necessary permits for the work they were doing downstairs. We're not using the upper floors. Why would the inspector have gone upstairs?"

"Who knows? He called his office to have someone search for a permit regarding the bathroom renovation, which they couldn't find. Without it, he wouldn't sign off on the inspection." I narrowed my eyes, contemplating a bizarre possible explanation for the failed inspection. "Hey, you still there?" Amber asked.

"Yeah. Just out of curiosity, who was the inspector?"

"I don't know. Why do you ask?"

"I have a hunch. Could you call your friends right now to find out?" Proving my suspicion to be true wouldn't change her news, but I couldn't help but fixate on confirming my theory.

"Sure. I'll talk to you in a second."

While I waited for Amber to call back, I resumed my favorite circular path for pacing, adding a mantra to my worried steps. "He wouldn't have. No, he wouldn't have."

I answered the phone the second I heard it ring. "It's me again. Maxwell said his name is Samuel Pettyman."

I kicked one of the chairs in the dining area. It wobbled backward but righted itself without falling over. I rewarded the chair's impressive sense of balance by collapsing into it. "The prick!"

"Who? Maxwell?"

"No. Sam. You know, my ex-boyfriend, the guy we ran into at the bistro."

"Him? I thought he would be our ally in the Building Department."

"I told you about how he tried to break us up? The failed inspection is him getting his revenge on us."

"Crazy exes. Even when we ditch them, they stick with us like a case of food poisoning. We could report him."

"Sure. But if he found a legitimate violation, what good would reporting him do? Sid and Maxwell still would have to make the repairs. Forget about Sam. Tell me about the manor. They can take care of the issues in the bathroom in less than a month, right?"

"Well, the quick fix for the bathroom involves bringing in plumbers and electricians to move the plumbing and the outlet. Probably a day or two's work, tops. But we're at the height of renovation season. None of their contractor's usual guys are available right away. It will be at least early July before they can complete the work. And then they'll have to schedule another inspection. Rough estimate, we're looking at the house being ready for occupancy no earlier than the third week of July."

While I had focused my energy on being mad at Sam, my knuckles had turned white from my death grip on the phone. Amber's update on the renovation schedule short-circuited the flow of energy. My hand loosened its grasp on my phone, letting it slip away. In a spastic reflex, I trapped it between my elbow and my waist. "So I don't have a place to get married?"

"Let's examine it from a different angle. You do have a place to get married. You just need to pick a new date."

"We've already booked our honeymoon. We've changed our schedules and turned down gigs. Chloe is moving to California in mid-July. No, we're definitely doing it on June twenty-second."

"Then let me work on a new plan. I'm going to scour the state to find you a replacement venue. Don't do a thing. Hold off on the invitations. Don't call any vendors. I'm going to fix everything for you."

Touring the venue last summer, I had a mini panic attack. Revisiting the memory, my body replayed its clenching and sweating routine. "I should have listened to my gut the day we visited the site. I knew that first day they wouldn't have it ready in time for our wedding."

"It was the perfect place. We couldn't have predicted things how things would turn out. Sid, Maxwell, and their contractor did everything right. They're standup guys."

I didn't correct her. I had predicted it. But I let Josh and Amber talk me into booking it. "Whatever. It doesn't change the fact that I still don't have a wedding venue."

"I'm going to make your problems vanish. Go tell that handsome fiancé of yours to take you out to dinner. Use the time to remember why you went through the trouble to plan a wedding in the first place. It was about preparing to spend the rest of your life with the man you love. Leave me to work my magic."

Josh responded to my SOS like a superhero. After letting himself into the apartment, he hunted for me. I couldn't muster the energy to call out my bedroom to aid his search. Using his superpowers, he located my lair and confronted the blotchy-faced ball of defeat I had become.

Sitting on the side of my bed, he twisted himself to lower his chest on top of me to gather me in his arms. "There is nothing he can do to stop us from getting married. He's just daring us to double down on our plans. We're going to get married so hard, he'll have bruises!"

I sniffled, unconvinced. "But we can't get married! Not without a place to do it."

"Can't we pitch a tent in the backyard of the manor? They have enough space out back."

The swishing of my hair brushing against his chin answered for me when I shook my head. "The backyard is still a mess. They've only worked on the landscaping in the front of the house. And we still wouldn't have access to the kitchen or bathrooms."

"Amber will be able to scrounge up an alternate venue. She knows everybody in the industry."

"But it's wedding season. Every place has probably been booked for over a year. We're screwed!"

"And hungry. Let me take you out to dinner."

"I don't want to go out. Look at me! I'm a mess!" I wriggled out from the cocoon formed by his chest and arms.

"Not the way I see it. While you talk yourself into spending a romantic evening with me, I'll think about where we'll eat, and I'll raid Chloe's wine rack for a bottle to take with us. If she notices her wine collection has shrunk, tell her I wanted to help her to improve the gas mileage on her rental van when she drives to California. You know, by lightening the load."

I unfolded myself from my sulking position, throwing my legs over the side of the bed. With shuffling steps, I made my way to the bathroom. I snuck up on my reflection in hopes it wouldn't do the same to me. It was no use. I let out a wounded shriek. My hair appeared to be flipping me the bird. It bent up and away from my shoulders at a harsh angle. My eyes hid behind swollen lids. Streaks of red slashed across my pale cheeks. Dried snot clung to the inside of my nostrils.

Gripping the edge of the door, I poked my head into the hallway. "You're going to have to wait a bit longer. I need a shower. Stat."

The gushing water in the shower drowned out my sighs and moans. I let the warm water beat against my face, unwilling to turn around to lather shampoo into my hair. How could months of planning all wash down the drain in two days? I swore I would never leave the bathroom. What was the point? The last two days proved I shouldn't bother trying to make anything work. The future of our wedding was as clear as my reflection in the fogged-up mirror. Only the gurgling of my stomach persuaded me to emerge from the bathroom.

Josh kissed the top of my damp head. In my room, I fought with myself over the need to swap my cozy robe for street attire. I slung clothes on without considering the finished product. A shimmery black ballet sweater hid the T-shirt I had received for pledging money to a local radio station during a fundraiser. I chose to wear jeans, a visual hint for Josh not to go overboard in his efforts to make our evening special.

I joined him in the living room. He watched a cop show on TV, his legs stretched out on the coffee table. I sat next to him. "Couldn't we just order pizza?"

He clicked the remote, silencing the TV. "Nope. We're going on a date."

JOSH'S HAND was warm against mine, a contrast to the cool evening air. Despite my overwhelming urge to cower alone in my bedroom, I took comfort in the steadfast security of his grip. Mastering any instrument requires strong, relaxed hands. His thick fingers interlaced with mine to spread them apart. He constrained my energy without force. I let him lead us to dinner. We walked in silence until he guided us to turn onto Church Street.

"I was thinking we'd head to Il Giardino dell'Uliveto. We haven't eaten there since I proposed to you."

"It feels a little fancy. I'd be OK with a burger."

"Too late. I have my heart set on their chicken Francese."

Assuming the social responsibilities for the two of us, Josh approached the hostess with more animation than was necessary to complete the transaction.

"Well, hi, there! Remember us? I proposed to this amazing woman last year at a table in the back corner."

"I remember you! Have you gotten married yet?"

"No. Everything fell apart." I gloomed up the conversation, meeting her face with my hound dog eyes for a fleeting second. A sea of white pulled my attention over her shoulder. "Since when do you have a piano? I don't remember it."

She turned to look behind her, perhaps having forgotten a shiny white baby grand piano now occupied the space in front of the picture window where a table used to dwell. "The owner's mother moved out of her house into a small apartment a couple of weeks ago and had to get rid of it. She insisted he take it. Lacking the room in his home, he dumped it here. We lost a four-top to accommodate it. But there it sits."

Josh pulled out a card. "If you ever need a pianist to play it, I'd be happy to make a recommendation. We're both musicians. But not pianists."

"Thanks. I'll let the owner know. Would you like to sit upstairs?"

Josh and I shrugged our shoulders. "Sure. We've never sat upstairs before," he said.

We followed the hostess up a wide staircase with open, dark stained wooden treads. The metal orbs of the chandeliers hung below us once we passed the midpoint on the stairs. At the top, we were closer to the ribs of the curved ceiling than to the white cloth-covered tables below us. The room appeared more expansive from this height than it did from the first floor.

Two other couples, their faces illuminated by candles, occupied tables on the upper level. The hostess motioned to a table on the far side of the balcony. I stood a chance of wallowing unnoticed in this semi-private room. I still would have preferred to have stayed home, but the scent of fried calamari wafting toward me went a long way toward making the case for eating out.

Once the server had taken our orders and poured our wine, Josh held his wineglass above the center of the table. I pinched the stem of my glass between two fingers and my thumb but didn't raise it. He said, "To my phenomenal fiancée for reminding me every day why I want to spend the rest of my life with her."

I touched my glass to his with an anemic clink. "Not so phenomenal. How the hell could someone with a ton of wedding expertise, someone who had the assistance of a seasoned wedding planner foul things up on such an epic scale?"

"What exactly are you trying to take responsibility for? A failed building inspection? Sam acting like a tool? In my opinion, you did the most important thing I could ask for from someone to whom I'm about to pledge undying fidelity: you shut him down when he tried to break us apart. Defending our relationship might have put our plans in jeopardy, but it was well worth the risk if you ask me." He reached for my hands. I chugged a mouthful of wine before sliding my hands between his waiting palms.

"But I didn't have to be so harsh with him. If my language had been diplomatic, or if I had been on top of it the second he started to flirt with me, or—"

Josh cut me off. "He would have done the same thing no matter how it played out. From the day you ran into him, he wasn't in a rational frame of mind. How could you have changed anything?"

"It was a big mistake to have told him where our wedding was."

"How would you have known he would intervene with our plans? Besides, didn't you tell me Amber mentioned the property first? She thought he'd be an asset."

"Well, she was wrong."

"She couldn't have anticipated his actions. And it proves you haven't done anything to harm our plans. Blaming yourself is pointless. And it pisses me off, to be honest." I pulled my hands away from his, giving him the stink eye in the process. "I'm always going to protect you against people who try to harm you. What should I do if you're the one beating yourself up?"

"Sell tickets and call the play-by-play?"

He chuckled and lifted his hands away from the table to allow the server to put our appetizer in the center of it. "Well, unlace those boxing gloves. It will be awfully tricky eating the fried calamari with them on your hands."

Keeping my mouth filled with the magical cornmeal-battered rings gave me an excuse to avoid conversation. Mid-chew, I turned my head toward the stairs. Heavy footfalls tapped a steady beat on the wooden treads. A gentleman in a suit rested his hand on top of the balcony wall. He nodded at the guests at the other two tables on our level before walking toward our corner.

"I'm John, the owner. Melanie told me you had come back to see us! What are you celebrating today?"

I lowered an uneaten forkful of calamari onto my plate. "Nothing. Our wedding plans have fallen through."

Josh corrected me. "Not our plans to marry. Just where we'll get married."

"What a shame. Did you know we rent the restaurant for private events?"

I surveyed the room. With only ten small tables upstairs and not many more below us, I couldn't entertain thoughts about considering the restaurant to be a viable option.

"Did you hear that, Ellen? Wouldn't this be a perfect place for our wedding? How romantic to tie the knot in the same spot where I proposed to you!" Lit from within, he glowed with optimism.

"I doubt we can fit one hundred twenty guests in here." I nodded at John, setting him up to confirm the fault behind his idea.

"We can accommodate fifty-six people downstairs. Up here, the fire department limits us to only forty-three guests."

Josh wasn't ready to let go of the idea. "How many people are coming to our rehearsal dinner?"

I tapped my finger on my lips, my head tilted upward. "Either forty-one or forty-two."

"Should we do it?"

My brow collapsed onto my eyelids. "Should we do what?"

"If no one has received an invitation, people won't know they've been uninvited. We could cut our list down to only those whom we've invited to the rehearsal dinner."

Would it be horrible to eliminate two-thirds of our guests from the list? Our closest family members and best friends would make the cut. It's not that we don't care about the other guests, but do they have to come to our wedding? "Well, it wouldn't even matter if it turns out the restaurant isn't available on our wedding date."

"Would you like me to check?" John waited for our answer.

With the same lack of commitment I had shown when the hostess asked us if we wanted to sit upstairs, I nodded at Josh. "Sure. It wouldn't hurt to find out. Our date is Sunday, June twenty-second during the day."

"You might be in luck. We don't serve lunch on Sundays. The room could be yours until four or five in the afternoon depending on when our first reservation is. I'll be right back with an answer."

Josh couldn't contain his enthusiasm. "How awesome would this be? We wanted the event to be a personal reflection of our love. Amber won't be able to find a better venue. Remember how much you loved your brother's wedding? You asked me if I thought we should scale ours back, host a celebration more like theirs. Here's the opportunity to have a wedding like theirs."

He was right. Nathan and Derrick had conceived and executed their wedding day without stress and drama. The planning didn't consume them. The meaning of the day didn't become defused by a three-ring circus of a wedding. The guests remained connected to the grooms throughout the event.

I thought of the floor plan for our not-to-be wedding. Like royalty, Josh and I would have sat at a table for two overlooking the dance floor opposite the band. The dance floor itself would have cleaved our guest list in two, assigning them to the six large tables spread out on each side of it. The guests wouldn't have been within shouting distance of us. To compensate for our isolation, we would have had to spend half of the reception walking from table to table to greet our guests. Amber warned me the bride and groom usually went hungry during the reception, save for a scant few stolen bites of room temperature food. No way was I going to miss the food at my wedding!

My hands braced on the balcony railing, I peered over its edge. The restaurant was long enough to provide a decent aisle. We could create an altar in front of the piano. Light would stream in through the window early in the day. Our string quartet could play from up in the balcony. I didn't hate the idea of holding a wedding here.

I heard the shuffle of John's feet on the stairs. We trained our eyes on the opening of the staircase. He ascended the last step and walked swiftly toward us with papers in his hands. "We're in business! Were you looking for a reception space only, or will you need it for the ceremony, too?"

"The whole shebang. Originally, our ceremony would have started at eleven thirty in the morning. Cocktails were from noon until one, and the reception would have lasted until five o'clock."

"Would it be OK with you to have a three-hour dinner reception, ending the event a little earlier, maybe around four, four-thirty?"

"It shouldn't be a problem. I wouldn't expect the guests on our short list to turn the venue into a disco. They'll be ready to head home once we've served the cake. The band! There isn't room for a band or dancing!"

"Since we still haven't even chosen our first dance, I don't see what we have to lose. The band will be easy to fire. They wouldn't take a deposit when I booked them. Don't let the absence of a dance floor stop you from considering this venue." Josh opened the brochure John had handed to him. "Since they offer fried calamari for the cocktails, and chicken Francese is an option for the main course, I can't come up with a single reason this can't our venue."

I perused the catering brochure, doing a little math in my head. Subtracting the deposits we would lose from canceling the caterer and the rentals, my reception budget would be half what it had been when we began to make our plans. The cost per person here was lower than the price per head for our caterer. Multiplying it by forty-two, we would come in a few hundred dollars under budget. My body released its hoarded tension.

"I'm not ready to make a decision tonight. I have to run it by my mother. She wanted a big wedding. I'll have to ask the florist and the photographer if they will have a problem coming to Montclair. I have a lot of issues to address before I'll know if having our wedding here is a viable option. But your proposal is worth considering. Can I call you tomorrow with my answer?"

"Not a problem. Take my card. Don't hesitate to call with any questions."

When Josh and I were left alone again, I said, "Isn't it funny? The day we started to date, we had to right a wedding that had gone wrong. And here we are, working as a team to fix our own wedding."

"If I recall correctly, you did all the heavy lifting on that job."

"But you put together the band. With the same ease, you've come up with a possible solution for our wedding."

"It's only because I'm plotting my next chance to eat their chicken Francese."

I wasn't ready to admit to Josh how the glob of dread in my stomach had dissolved, replaced by butterflies doing a happy dance. I took another peek at the room below. The white lid of the piano drew my attention to it. "Sheldon!"

Josh stood to scan the tables below us. "He's here?"

"No. Let's hire Sheldon to play the reception!"

"WOULD YOU HELP me choose a color, Derrick?" My mother and Derrick stood in front of a display of nail polish bottles as large and colorful as a stained-glass window in a cathedral.

With a decisive tilt to his head, he said, "Something dark and winey."

"I'd like something winey. I'm thirsty." Chloe reached for a bottle of sage green polish.

"I'm always whiney. I can't find the right shade of blue for my toes," I said, adding a nasal quality to my voice for emphasis. I was treating my bridal babes and my mother to a mani/pedi day at the salon near the hotel where we would be having our rehearsal dinner tonight.

"Ooh, how about this one? It's called 'Currant Affair.' Scandalous, Mrs. Blum!" Derrick handed the bottle to my mother.

Pressing the purple fabric swatch whose frayed edges were hairier than a tarantula to her hip, she held the bottle against it. "You have such a wonderful eye, dear. And please, after all this time, it's Lorraine. Left to my own devices, I would have picked a polish to match my dress exactly. I like your choice much better."

"Thanks, um, Lorraine. Sometimes matchy-matchy works, sometimes it doesn't. I'm going to push my luck with matching and choose lavender for my toes." Derrick held a bottle against the back of his hand. "Too blue." He picked another bottle from the shelf. "Hmm, Nathan, is this the same shade as our ties and socks?"

"I thought you were kidding about wearing lavender!" I snatched the bottle from his hand, replacing it on the shelf.

Derrick reclaimed the bottle. "All right, you guys! I have an announcement. Ellen wants us all to wear lavender polish on our fingers and toes."

"It isn't nice to torture the bride." I made a grab for the bottle, but he held it above his head, out of reach.

"But darling, this shade pairs beautifully with the gray and the flowers. What color do you think we should wear?"

"I'm getting a French manicure." Derrick faked a yawn. I ignored his implications. "I figured I'd go with a light blue on my toes for my 'something blue.'"

"So daring. Please tell me you're not going to cover your feet with those ghastly, slouchy boots you always wear."

"I thought about wearing a white pair. But they'd be too hot. You'll be pleased: I'm wearing sandals. White satin with a thin strap across the toe, a covered back, and a strap around my ankle."

"And the heel?"

"Ridiculously high. I doubt I'll be able to climb the stairs up to the cocktail hour."

"That's the best kind of heel: ridiculous. I'm jealous. No one will be able to see my pretty lavender toes under my shoes. But they'll be the reason I have a Mona Lisa smile on my lips throughout the wedding."

"Chloe, what do you think of Derrick's color choice?" my mother asked.

Taking the bottle from him, Chloe held it in her palm, her arm outstretched as if she were about to begin reciting Hamlet's speech to Yorick's skull. "This may surprise all of you, Mrs. Blum especially. I think we all should wear lavender on our fingers and toes. Gwen, Sheila, Amber?"

"I'll wear whatever you suggest, Chloe." Gwen had given the rainbow hues a wide berth.

Sheila turned Chloe's hand to examine the bottle. "I'm OK with it."

Amber wobbled her head. "Lavender is not exactly my color. I'm a red gal, but red would be the wrong color for Ellen's color scheme. Maybe I'll get a French manicure, too, and save the lavender for my toes. I'm wearing pumps, but I'll have my toes painted lavender in solidarity."

"Betrayed by my own wedding party!" I harrumphed.

Derrick laughed at my theatrics. "There's no arguing with good taste. Our gorgeousness will speak for itself tomorrow."

My mother, Nathan, Derrick and I settled into the spa chairs for our pedicures while Chloe, Gwen, Amber, and Sheila sat at the manicure stations across from us. Derrick purred along with the massage program he chose for his chair.

"Who is taking care of what tomorrow?" My mother gingerly dunked her feet into the steaming foot spa bath.

"Chloe will be helping me turn into a bride. Amber's riding on the party bus with everyone. She should arrive at Il Giardino dell'Uliveto by ten-thirty. Trust me, once she's in wedding mode, it's best to stay out of her way and let her do her thing. Are you staying down here tonight?"

"No. I've decided I'll head home tonight after the dinner. Will I see you before the ceremony? Do you even want to see your mother beforehand?"

"Of course I want to see you! Once I arrive at the restaurant, I'll be hiding out in the back, by the bathrooms. Chloe can let you know when we arrive."

"Because I wasn't sure if I would be able to spend time with you before the wedding, I brought you a necklace for tomorrow. But only if you want to wear it." She fumbled inside her pocketbook, extracting a flat, square blue velvet box. "They're only crystals, but your father gave them to me to wear on our wedding day."

The hinge on the box squeaked. Its contents transported me to my mother's bedroom. In my mind, I stood in front of a portrait positioned on top of her dresser. In the photo of her on her wedding day, a single strand of glittering jewels spanned her neck, capturing the same sparkle flickering in her eyes. I ran my finger over the top edge of the arc of the necklace. "They are so beautiful, Mom! They'll be perfect with the earrings Josh gave me for my birthday. How thoughtful of you to loan them to me. And wearing them will be the perfect way to keep Dad with me."

She dabbed at the corner of her eye with the tip of her middle finger. "I didn't know whether you needed something old or borrowed."

"I need both. I guess I can get married now!" I snapped the box closed.

"Will this truly be the wedding you want? You're not going to miss having a big party?"

"This is exactly the wedding we want. I can't wait!"

I sat on the edge of the bed in Josh's hotel room, wiggling my blue toenails to watch the reflected light shimmer and dance at the end of my toes. "I was sorry your mom couldn't join us at the salon. Was their trip OK?"

"Yeah. They just got a late start. She went straight to meet with the banquet manager once they pulled in."

"I know we promised not to give each other gifts, that we would wait until we knew what we still needed from our registry, but I have a small gift for you." I pulled a squishy gift barely constrained by silver wrapping paper from a bag.

Josh tore the paper away, freeing a blue and brown scarf from the wreckage. "Not quite seasonally appropriate, but I love the colors." He wrapped it around his neck, sending the loose end behind him with a flourish.

"I knit the scarf, you know."

"You know how to knit?"

"Amber taught me. On the ship. I started it before you and I met up in Florida. I didn't get around to finishing it until you went on tour in March."

"I love it!" He unwrapped it from his neck, binding us together with it before kissing me.

I twisted my torso toward the clock on the bedside table. "It's almost time to go downstairs. Or… do you want to elope?"

Josh checked my expression to determine if I was kidding. "Not a chance! I'm ready to party!" Dropping the scarf and holding his fists in front of his chest, he swiveled his body back and forth from knees to hips. It was clear I hadn't chosen my future husband for his dance skills. In the event a musical accompaniment would improve matters, his phone sounded the title song from *Jazz Hands*. "Yo, Frank! What's up?"

Leave it to the contractor for the Broadway shows Josh plays to call the night before our wedding. He probably needs a new concertmaster to join a tour tomorrow. Fat chance! I gave Josh his privacy, staying in the bathroom until I could no longer hear the muffled sound of his voice.

When I reentered the room, I found him collapsed in the armchair by the window, dazed. I rested on the arm of the chair, draping my arm around his shoulders. "Good news or bad?"

He shook his head. "I can't even say it out loud. I'm dumbfounded. You're never going to believe what Frank asked me."

"Tell me already! You know you can't ditch our wedding for a gig, right?"

"I wouldn't dream of it. No, they don't need me until early October. For a new show." He held his hand to his lips and stared into space. With a burst, he broke his pose. "They're freaking giving me a show!"

I answered in slow motion. "Like, you'll be a regular musician in a Broadway pit?"

"Exactly. I'll be the concertmaster. My dream job!"

I leaned toward him to hug him but tumbled into his lap instead. My legs dangled from his right shoulder, and my head became wedged under his left armpit. Righting myself onto his lap, I said, "No way! I'm beyond proud of you! We should go celebrate."

"Hey, I know a party we can go crash. Wanna blow this popsicle stand?"

Five round tables dotted a section of a hotel ballroom they had portioned off with beige, sliding walls. My Uncle Leonard and Aunt Sherry acted like long lost friends of

Josh's aunts and uncles. His brother, Brian, was in danger of his girlfriend Samantha pitching a fit if he continued to flirt with Chloe. I bet his sister-in-law Jane was glad she and Josh's other brother, Erik, were on the opposite side of the table, talking to Gwen and Matt.

Josh and I sat at a table with his parents, my mom, and Douglas. Inventorying the room, I listened to the whir of the conversations around me. Except for the part about us exchanging vows, this was our wedding. This same group of people would gather tomorrow. How could the day not be a success? We had people who loved us, delicious food to eat, and lots of booze. I grinned to myself, squeezing Josh's hand. He planted a kiss on my lips. A clinking of silverware on glasses buzzed in the background.

I broke away from his kiss. "No. Wait until tomorrow. You make the couple kiss *after* the wedding, not before."

A softer but steady clinking continued. Josh was tapping his knife on his wine glass. "So, you're probably wondering why I gathered you here today." He welcomed the expected laugh with a knowing nod. "Once upon a time, there was a beautiful princess who played the harp. A clueless prince who had fallen under the spell of a mean witch forgot about being cast out of the viola section, so smitten with the princess was he when he first gazed upon her beauty. He, aw hell, I can't keep this up. Life is not a fairy tale. We've experienced loss since we first met. I never knew Mr. Blum. As robbed as I feel for missing out on knowing him, I can't imagine the hole he left in the lives of all who loved him."

Tears welled in my eyes. The rasp of a collective sniff ran through the room. "He's here today. Ellen is the woman we know her to be because she is his daughter. If he hadn't helped her to develop a sense of humor, she wouldn't have laughed at my viola joke the day we met. I hear he was a calm, rational man. Maybe the calm part didn't rub off on Ellen." Too many people in the room laughed in recognition of the truth of his observation. I gave Josh a warning glare.

"But she has style when it comes to solving problems. Her determination to rush headfirst toward a solution comes from her mother. That and an undying love for the color purple. Just kidding, sweetie. Who else could change the plans for a wedding in one single, frenzied day a month before the wedding? Or would drive to Toledo to make up with me and start her plea with the words, *jazz hands*?" Josh and I wiggled our wrists in tandem, our mouths open in laughter.

"When Ellen decides to go for it, it's a done deal. And I'm the luckiest man in the world because, once upon a time, she set her eye on me and went for it. To Ellen!" I blushed, my face hurting from the strength of my smile.

Josh motioned with his hands. "I'm not done. Dad, sit down. And what's with the hat?"

Mr. Yates, a guilty expression on his face, returned a top hat and wand to their spot below the table. "I know how popular my magic act is with this crowd."

A roar from a dozen of the guests erupted. "No!"

Josh said, "Once upon a time… I have to stop doing that. The night Ellen and I fell in love with each other, I tricked her into telling me an embarrassing story. Ironically, it involved the man who tried to ruin our wedding."

"You're not going to repeat it, are you?" I pulled his suit jacket sleeve, urging him to abandon his trajectory.

"I wouldn't dare. But, if you're keeping track, which I know you are, I never reciprocated. My gift to you tonight is to tell you my embarrassing story." I rubbed my hands together. "My story dates back to the first concert I played with a professional orchestra right out of college. Before the concert, I introduced myself to the conductor. My nerves had me a little manic. You've made fun of how toothy my smile becomes and how I over-enunciate my words when I'm in a hyper mood. Here I was, talking his ear off to thank him for giving me a chance, blah, blah, blah. I had a few minutes following our conversation to hit the bathroom before the show. Out of habit, I gave myself a quick smile check in the mirror. A spinach leaf obliterated my front tooth. I had been grinning at the conductor like the village idiot, totally oblivious to how I must have looked like a gapped-tooth imbecile."

Josh raised his eyebrows at me, asking me to confirm whether he had evened the score between us. I bobbled my head like a pendulum while I weighed his story against mine. His brother, Brian, called out, "How about the goat? The goat incident is the better story!"

"Thanks for letting the goat out of the bag, Bri!" Josh lowered himself into his seat. "Alright. I'll tell it, but only to my bride." Cupping his hand over my ear, he whispered, "I had a string quartet gig once for an Easter brunch. They had set up a little petting zoo out on the patio. During a break, with my violin still in my hand, I wandered over to the enclosures to see the little critters. I leaned over the pen with the lambs in it, unaware that one of the goats had gotten loose. While I pet a lamb, I felt something yanking at the cuff of my pants. I shrieked and dropped my violin. Gazing up at me was this tiny goat with these huge brown eyes. The violin suffered a bit of damage from the fall. I had to explain to the other musicians I couldn't play the rest of the gig because I was scared by a baby goat. Satisfied?" He inhaled sharply through his nose, his back ramrod straight.

I paused long enough for his eyes to widen with concern. Breaking into a smile, I said, "Yes. Now we're even!"

"GO SPEND some quality time with your hair dryer. I want your hair to be bone dry by eight forty-five. Gwen or I can take over holding dryer if you need a break."

The droplets of water my wet hair released slithered under the collar of my robe and down my back. I saluted Chloe. Having doubted the functionality of my alarm clock plus the alarm apps on my phone and on Chloe's, I had awakened repeatedly overnight to make sure I didn't oversleep for my wedding. By six-thirty, I had given up on falling back to sleep. Chloe advised me not to drink coffee, given my nervousness. It was highly unlikely, despite my shortened beauty rest, I would grow sleepy today without caffeine. But when I crashed, I'd crash hard. Hopefully, it wouldn't hit until I was on the airplane tomorrow.

"You guys, I'm getting married today!" We had our fifth squeal fest and group hug of the morning. Before we had moved the event from Princeton to Montclair, I had reserved a room at the hotel where we held our dinner last night. I was glad I had canceled the reservation. Choosing to wake up in my own apartment instead of a hotel room went a long way toward keeping me centered and relatively calm. It saved me the stress of having to pack my wedding dress and all the necessary effluvia to bring with me to Princeton. I was likely to have brought the wrong shoes, the wrong bra, and would have spent my wedding day melting everyone's faces with my morning breath because I had forgotten to pack a toothbrush and toothpaste.

"Get thee under the dryer." Chloe pointed toward the bathroom, her brow arranged in stern, straight line.

"I'm going, I'm going!"

Thirty-five minutes later, Chloe buried her fingers into the roots of my hair to monitor my progress. Our intercom sounded. "Gwen, buzz them in. I'm going to finish drying Ellen's hair."

I shouted above the dryer's motor, "The photographer is a little early. I thought she wasn't coming until nine."

"She has to prepare her lenses and take measurements with her light meter." Chloe pressed the crown of my head forward, forcing me to lower my head.

Once my hair had passed Chloe's second inspection, I padded into the living room. A woman with rosy cheeks and straight, fire engine red hair opened a silver case on our dining table. I whispered to Chloe, "She's not my photographer. I don't want some assistant I don't know doing the shots of me getting ready." I scowled at the stranger behind Chloe's back.

"I have a surprise for you. This is Nancy. She's going to do your hair and makeup."

"But—"

"All along I, I mean, *we* had planned to use the money from the wedding jar to buy you something for today that you wouldn't have spent the money on yourself but wouldn't have let us treat you to. It took us the longest time to decide what it was you would have wanted. Your decision to forgo hiring someone to get you all gussied up today gave me the idea to hire a pro to do your hair and makeup. Once you had put aside enough to cover Nancy's fee, we no longer needed the wedding jar."

"Then why did we have the trial run back in April? And why did you do such a hideous job?"

"Because it was fun!" Chloe smirked.

"Gwen, did you know about Chloe's scheme?"

She clamped her hands together under her chin, her eyes and nose crinkling. "We had thought about it right from the beginning. You told us we couldn't contribute to your wedding fund, so we had to come up with a way for you to set money aside without knowing you were doing it. I suggested going about it in a, oh, how should I say it?"

I helped her to find the words. "Nicer way?"

"Um, well, yeah. I didn't like how Chloe tricked you into thinking you couldn't talk about the wedding without paying for the right, but we couldn't think of another way. It was impossible to keep a straight face while Chloe did your hair and makeup. Your expression when you saw it was priceless!"

"I can't believe you did this for me! Nice to meet you, Nancy. You've probably figured out it's going to be your job to whip this mane of mine into shape. I have a photo of how I want my hair. Let me find it."

"No need. Chloe forwarded it to me. Now let's turn you into a bride!"

Like out of season trick-or-treaters, Chloe, Gwen, and I paraded in our wedding finery up Fullerton in the decidedly un-Halloweenlike seventy-five-degree air. The back door to the restaurant was only two and a half blocks away. I stood less of a chance of destroying my dress while walking than I did by folding myself into a car to make the short trip.

Each clad in her silvery gray dress with bags filled with shoes, hairspray, bobby pins, deodorant, and lipsticks over their shoulders, Chloe and Gwen stretched the hem of my dress away from my feet and the dirty sidewalk like children playing with a parachute. My gym shoes fully on display beneath the gown, we drew smiles and well wishes from the trickle of pedestrians headed into the library. I stiffly focused on preserving the integrity of my hair and dress while we walked.

The party bus occupied the far corner of the lot behind Il Giardino dell'Uliveto. One detail I didn't need to fret over: our guests had arrived. Gwen spread her hands farther apart on the hem of my skirt, taking sole responsibility for the task of holding my dress. Chloe popped into the restaurant to make sure Josh was out of sight before I entered. "All clear!" she cried.

My mother, Amber, and Sheila were in the rear lobby of the restaurant, a nervous, excited trio. Beyond them, a black and red lacquered folding screen stood like a sentry at the entrance to the dining room. My mother walked a circle around me. "My little girl! You look beautiful!" Amber handed her a tissue. Dabbing her eyes with surgical precision, she drew her lips inward in a wistful smile. "I wish your father were here to see you get married."

"Mom! You're not allowed to make me cry yet!" Armed with a second tissue, Amber pursued a tear threatening to escape from the corner of my eye.

"You know he predicted you would marry Josh? Even though you didn't start dating until after your father was gone, he suspected as much the first night you talked about him. Was it over Easter dinner? And a month later, when you were upset about having left a message for Josh on the wrong voicemail, he knew for sure. It didn't trouble him that it was taking some time for you to discover what you meant to each other. 'All in good time,' he had said. You and your brother both found your soul mates. I'd like to believe your father and I were good role models."

"You were. And lightning has struck twice for you. I could see last night how much Douglas cares for you. I hope he continues to make you as happy as Daddy did."

Approaching my dress like it was a puzzle to solve, she gave me a delicate hug. A heady mix of her lily perfume, hairspray, and the powder on her face enveloped me in their familiar scent, a memory from the times I had watched her prepare to go out years ago. "He does, Dandelion. He does."

I peered through the slit between the screen and the wall. My Uncle Leonard and Aunt Sherry helped themselves to coffee from an urn on the table where Josh had proposed to me. Strains of Mozart from the string quartet mingled with sounds of people talking. Atop the piano, a vase held a small tree limb with tons of thin branches spreading upward and out. Clusters of white orchids clung to it like leaves. Hanging from the top of the window, a curtain of orchids strung like popcorn garlands. It turned the view onto the sidewalk hazy.

"Amber, those aren't the arrangements I picked. Are the flowers at the altar your doing?"

"When I called the florist to tell him we needed fewer and smaller centerpieces, he wouldn't agree to us changing the fee on the contract. You know what happens if I have money to spend on a wedding!"

Forming a heart between the fingertips of my hands, I drew it to my chest. "It's breathtaking!"

"Why thank you!" Derrick said, straightening the folding screen behind him. "You were talking about me, I presume?"

"No, she saw me first." Nathan planted a light kiss my cheek. "You sure clean up nice, Kiddo!"

"Thanks! And you guys look like Tweedle Dee and Twee—"

"Don't say it!" Nathan gave me some side eye. He and Derrick held each other's waists, dressed like twins in their gray windowpane suits.

"You made it! I was so worried when I heard you had missed the bus. Please tell me you didn't oversleep." My mother gripped each of Nathan's shoulders.

"One of us insisted the bus wasn't leaving until ten o'clock." His head tipped in Derrick's direction. "So we drove. We're here with time to spare. You can stop worrying. Driving makes it easier for us, anyway, since we can head straight home this evening."

I studied them. "I don't hate the lavender ties. You guys might even be dressed too hip for my wedding!"

Derrick gestured alongside his face, voguing. "Like you said, we're breathtaking! Oh, I nearly forgot. Amber, John sent me back here to collect your headsets."

Hands on my hips, I said, "I knew you couldn't run a wedding without those. Are we set with someone to cue the quartet to play our processionals?"

"Don't even think about running your wedding. I have everything under control. You need to hide in the bathroom so John and I can line up the men. Josh will be back here in a minute, and we don't want him to see you."

"Are you keeping an eye on the time? We have to start and end the ceremony on time."

"Ellen, I got this! I promise I will run the show with the precision of a Swiss watch. Sheldon will finish in time to catch the four forty-five bus to Manhattan. We'll clear out of the restaurant before they need to get ready for their dinner service. If you don't get your butt into the bathroom this instant, you'll be the reason we don't keep to the schedule!"

The bathroom couldn't accommodate anyone beyond Chloe, my dress, and me. I stood in front of the mirror, turning to each side to triple check the state of my hair and makeup. I swept my fingertips across the row of crystal beads under my clavicle. "I'm really doing this, aren't I?"

"Are you having second thoughts?" Chloe corralled a curl on my head that had taken a wrong turn.

"If by second thoughts you mean do I think today is the best day of my life, and have I thought the same thing every single second since I woke up, then yes."

"I can't believe today is your wedding day! It sure took a lot to get here. And I don't just mean having to plan a totally new wedding. Remember the six months you spent obsessing over Josh before you started to date? And how messed up everything got when he was on tour and you were on the ship? Based on your devotion to him, I'm starting to believe true love exists."

"Of course it exists! You'll find someone. Who wouldn't fall in love with you?"

"Attracting men is not my concern. I'm in the same place you were in at the end of college. Boys are a distraction. I finally know what I want from my life. I will not allow a man to detour me away from achieving my goals. If I happen to meet someone who embellishes rather than detracts from my life, fine. But I'm not going to bother to look for him. Not for a long time."

"It's finally hitting me that you're going away. This last year, or maybe even after my father's death, has been about letting go. I have to let go of living my life entwined with yours and Gwen's. And I had to say goodbye to Minerva. Now my mother has fallen in love. I can't continue to bind her to my dad for eternity. How weird is it we each have undergone major life changes in the same period of time? I'm not ready to say goodbye to you!"

"Don't you dare start to cry! I don't have time to fix both our faces. Quick: tell me a dirty joke!" Chloe fanned her fingers rapidly in front of her eyes.

"Um, a pig fell in the mud? I can't think of a joke."

The door opened. Puccini's *O Mio Babbino Caro* drifted into the bathroom along with Amber. The processional had begun. "Josh and half the groomsmen are at the altar. It's safe for you to come out now."

One by one, men in gray suits and women in silver-mist dresses walked solemnly down the aisle. John folded the screen, placing it against the wall. He gave the cue through his headset to the manager stationed in the balcony to have the string quartet switch music. I closed my eyes, savoring the swelling melody of the Intermezzo from *Cavalleria Rusticana.* John, stepping to the side, gave me a gentle push on my shoulder. My stomach performed a frontside corkscrew seven-twenty like a snowboarder on a halfpipe.

Sheldon beamed at me from the aisle seat in the last row. I meant to find Josh and keep my eyes fixed on him the whole way down the aisle. But sitting between the two of us, everyone we loved — and who loved us — had turned their heads to watch me process. Each smile beamed at me, swaddling me with a palpable sense of love and security. I had to tear my gaze away from them to focus on Josh.

He stood stock-still, somber in his black tux. Pent-up energy pinged within him. His hands clasped in front of his thighs, Josh stared at me, oblivious to everyone in the room. His smile guided my heart toward him. I couldn't believe he would soon be my husband.

WITH HEIGHTENED SENSORY ACUITY, I took my first step. I made sure to position my bouquet in front of my belly button exactly as per Amber's instructions. Who knew flowers could be so heavy? I couldn't ignore the way a tiny edge of the plastic heel stop on my left shoe snagged fibers on the carpet with each step. Part of me floated above the aisle. I moved as if I were walking atop a giant mound of whipped cream. I arrived at the altar in no time flat, yet it could have been a million years since I had started to walk down the aisle. Everything was how I had imagined it. But none of it seemed real.

Chloe relieved me of my bouquet. My hands, devoid of their ballast, floated aimlessly at my hips. Although she stood only a couple of feet away from me, Mags' voice faded into the background. I had no control over the smile camped out across my face. My eyes locked onto Josh's.

Smiling through closed lips, he moved his head in subtle gestures from side to side. I knew he could see only me. The slick of his gelled hair took on a dull sheen from the light filtering through the orchids swaying in front of the window. His rented tux fit him better than his work tuxes. The shoulders were less boxy, and the pant legs skimmed his calves with little fabric to spare. A simple boutonniere of lavender and eucalyptus pinned to his lapel was tantalizingly far from my nose. I craved the chance to hug him so I could inhale the commingled fragrance of the boutonniere and the piney scent of his soap.

The part of me still grounded in reality reminded the floaty part I could not stand like a simpering fool throughout the service. Reaching for Josh's hand, I pivoted toward Mags. She greeted the late arrival of our attention with a chuckle inserted into her homily.

"Love is a subversive act. Humans are born to be selfish. Infants demand everything but offer little beyond smiles and gurgles to those who care for them. As children, we crave our independence. In our teen years, we master the art of shutting out those who love us." My mother laughed far more loudly than I would consider to be polite for the mother of the bride. "And yet we desire to unite ourselves with another. We fall in love. We do it even when we know heartbreak could be around the corner. We do it even when we don't love ourselves. We break the rules when we fall in love. We trust when caution would be the prudent decision. We go all in.

"And what of marrying for love? Throughout most of history, it was unheard of. Love was a sign of insanity. Marriage was meant to be a practical endeavor. It enhanced power and pooled resources for the two families. It enlarged the workforce through sanctioned procreation. Marrying for love? Such a useless, deranged conceit! It took a revolution to change the course not only of history but also of love. People in the United States and France fought for the right to be happy. Personal happiness. Think about it. The right to be happy. Can you imagine living without it? And with the belief that people had the right to be happy, the pursuit of love as a source of happiness gained acceptance.

"Marriage can be a subversive act. My husband James and I honored our ancestors with a ritual enslaved people brought with them from Africa. We jumped over a broomstick at our wedding. For people who had been enslaved, who had no legal right to marry, jumping the broom signified the forging of their union and connected our people to their past.

"The presciently, magnificently named case, *Loving v. Virginia*, evolved from the subversive act of two people of different races falling in love and wishing to marry each other." Douglas tightened the grip he had on my mother's hand. "Ellen, your own brother and his husband stand on the shoulders of those who were subversive enough to fight for the right to fall in love and marry someone of the same gender." I craned my neck to peer beyond Chloe and Gwen, catching Nathan and Derrick mid-kiss.

"We live in a time when no societal impediments prevent two consenting adults from falling in love and marrying, which is where your story begins. With the simple act of co-narrating a joke, you forged your bond. You wrote your destiny. Nothing should have stopped you from falling in love. But we know the two of you. Simple isn't your style. You chose, instead, to erect a line of hurdles on your path to true love." Cue the laughter. With it, I earned the moniker of blushing bride.

"In a couple of minutes, you will recite your marriage vows to each other. If you'll allow me to be so bold, I'd like to offer suggestions for what they should include. Josh, I hope you vow to Ellen your commitment to be courageous and to believe you deserve everything you desire. On any occasion when stating your wishes becomes too great a challenge, ask her to help you start the conversation. She'll never shy away from offering her views." Wrinkling my nose, I nodded.

"And Ellen, promise this handsome man you will never let any disruptions in the communications between you become a reason to give up on him. Words are not all that comprise a conversation. Look into his eyes and remember them as they appear today. His eyes hold the velvety depth of the night sky. They shine with the light of the sun and all the stars because he sees the universe when he looks at you. If words ever fail him, ask his eyes how he feels about you. They will never be silent.

"And both of you: vow to commit the subversive act of falling in love anew each day. While the freedom to marry brings with it the freedom to split up, defy the statistics. Let each disagreement lead you to strengthen your bond. Conflicts shouldn't tear couples apart. They present you with an opportunity to grow closer to each other as you conquer your problems together. Be revolutionaries in your marriage. Always strive to form not a perfect union but a better one. And do it with love."

Mags wrapped Josh in her arms. My hair, dress, and makeup again warned a loved one to exercise caution with me. With the delicacy of a hummingbird, she pecked my cheek.

Mags whispered to Josh, reminding him he would say his vows first. He slipped his hand inside his jacket, extracting a folded square of white lined paper from a pocket. Adjusting his glasses, he said, "I'm going to start with the vows I will not make. I will not vow never to take a gig on the road. I will not promise never to steal food from your plate. I will not vow to wear matching socks." He lifted the cuff of his right leg, revealing a black sock. Under his left pant leg, a lavender sock mocked me.

I mouthed to Derrick, "Is this your doing?" He shrugged, an exaggerated expression of feigned innocence spreading across his face.

"The list of things I will not promise to do pales in comparison to everything I will vow to do as your husband." He pressed his lips together, a fortifying breath through his nose failing to prevent tears from glistening in his eyes. "I, Josh, do solemnly vow to be your husband. I vow never to choose another person to be my confidant, my lover, my most trusted companion. I vow to welcome your love and devotion to me like a life-giving elixir. And I do solemnly vow to love you as I love no other until the last breath leaves my body." Chloe pulled two tissues from her pocket, one for her and one for me. Josh, dabbing his lavender pocket square against his tear ducts, whispered to me, "You're up!"

"My dress is missing a crucial design element: pockets. For want of a place to stow either tissues or a written speech, Ima gonna have to wing it." I wiggled my fingers in front of me, beckoning Josh to hold my hands lest mine betray the nervousness infecting me. "Here goes. The day I met you, I had determined I was ready to be a mature human being. I was certain that falling in love would go a long way toward helping me to achieve my goal. What I learned was trying to fall in love or trying to be mature was as effective a plan as trying to separate mud from water by shaking the glass containing both.

"You have to leave the glass untouched in order for the mud to settle. It is only when I stand still that my mind settles. And you alone have the power to make me stand still. Still doesn't imply we don't move forward or set goals. Still is the starting point to our lives. Still is where we define our goals and make our plans. But still is also where we savor the warmth of the other's body during an embrace. Still is where I see the entire universe in your eyes — thanks for the poetic imagery, Mags!

"I vow to stand still with you, to view not only the world I want to conquer but the world I have found in you from which I shall never stray. I cannot promise I won't indulge my habit of muddying the waters when my brain ODs on caffeine and anxieties. But I pledge to remember to stand still with you again whenever I need clarity.

"I vow to learn how to become the tidy one in our relationship. I vow to learn each appropriate dance move with which to properly identify the many Broadway shows you will play during your career. By the way, jazz hands!" We untangled our sweaty fingers. I channeled Liza Minnelli to match his Bob Fosse. I was quite sure it was our best effort to date. It was a good thing I had hired a videographer to capture each moment of the ceremony.

With clogged nose and eyes hazed over with tears, I finished my vows. "I vow to love you, to honor you, to cherish you all the days of my life." Not daring to break my gaze on him, I fumbled behind me to reclaim the tissue Chloe held out to me.

The vows were the hardest part. Exchanging rings encouraged smiles, not tears. Our wedding ceremony raced toward its end. With the shattering of glass still echoing in my ears, Josh and I sealed our vows with a kiss. The fragility of my hairdo and dress did not scare him into avoiding a proper embrace. Hugging me so tightly we melded together, I had no urge to respond to the exit music meant to play us out.

Josh whispered in my ear, "What song are we dancing to?" With the hostess stand cleared away for the afternoon, the front entrance provided enough space for Josh and me to share our first dance.

Peeling my cheek from his boutonniere, I said, "*Two for the Road* by Mancini. Sheldon insists he knows no better song for a first dance."

"I'm not familiar with it, but I approve."

"I made the mistake of telling him this song wasn't in my repertoire. I'd like to say I had missed him berating me, but I'd be lying. I promised him I would learn it soon."

"Do you think everyone is imagining us sharing sweet, romantic words with each other right now?"

"Talking shop is our pillow talk."

Josh pulsed his eyebrows. "Gigs, gigs, gigs."

"Ooh, honey, I'm so hot for you right now!"

"Even if I'm wearing unmatched socks?"

"Speaking of those, I haven't seen Derrick or Nathan since we finished the photos."

Josh twirled us around to get a better view of the room. "I think that's them in the back, by the bathrooms."

I rewarded Sheldon with a kiss on his cheek at the end of our dance. My rumbling stomach insisted I follow Josh to our table rather than continue to talk with Sheldon. Nathan and Derrick intercepted me before I reached the table. "What happened to Tweedle Dee and Tweedle Dum?" Nathan wore a hunter green polo shirt with khakis. Derrick had tucked one side of his crisp white shirt into a pair of dark jeans.

"We can't stay." Nathan held onto Derrick's hand like it was a balloon in a windstorm.

"I beg your pardon. It's my wedding. I forbid you from leaving. You haven't even eaten your salads."

"Laurel is in labor!" Nathan exclaimed.

"Likely excuse. No, really? Mom! Come here! Does she know? Holy cow, I'm so thrilled for you!" Hopping like a toad on Adderall, I squealed through the fingers I had spread across my mouth.

"Nathan, your outfit is not appropriate for a wedding. And you, too, Derrick? If the suits were so uncomfortable, you should have picked a different style."

Nathan ignored her harangue. "We have to go, Mom. We're having a baby!"

My mother grabbed the napkin from the place setting on the table nearest to her, blowing her nose into it with a trumpeting blast. "My little grandbaby is coming? You have to leave this minute. Don't miss a moment of your baby's birthday!"

"We are on our way to Chicago. We have tickets for a nine o'clock flight out of Philly and have booked a room at a hotel a block from the hospital. I promise we'll update you every step of the way. Provided everything goes well, when the pediatrician gives us the go-ahead, the three of us will rent a car for the return trip. We should be home about the same time you guys return from your honeymoon. Rest up, because our little tax deduction will want to meet its Auntie, Uncle, and Granny as soon as possible!" Nathan hugged us, squirming in his excitement.

Derrick waited for his turn to embrace us. "Tell whichever one of Josh's brothers is taking care of the suits, he'll find ours hanging on the coat rack. Now, go have fun at your wedding!"

Four o'clock arrived in an instant. Despite my plan to avoid all dishes involving tomato sauce, an orange blotch the shape and size of Florida stained my skirt near my right knee. I was sure I had more shades of lipstick on my cheeks than I will ever wear on my lips over the course of my lifetime. But I didn't care.

Josh and I stood together in the nearly empty restaurant, watching Chloe and Amber collect our personal items and gifts. "Well, we did it. Like I said when we got engaged, all we needed were two people in love and someone to make it legal. The rest wasn't important."

"I wouldn't have done anything differently. I loved everything about today. The first glimpse I had of you this morning took my breath away." His pointer finger shimmied across the back of my right hand, clasped in his. "I can't imagine not sharing our happiness with our friends and families. Today was worth the angst of each and every problem we had faced along the way."

"I agree. But being your wife is worth even more." My left thumb spun my engagement ring above the shiny gold band resting on the webbing between my fingers.

Josh scooped me into his arms. "So, how's married life treating you?"

"Perfectly!"

Thank you for reading *Ellen the Bride,* the third and final book in the Ellen the Harpist series. If you enjoyed my novel, please share a review on your favorite website or social media platform. Your review may be just the inspiration another reader needs to choose my novel.

acknowledgements

I'm finding it hard to believe I've come to the end of the Ellen the Harpist series, which I began writing in 2013. I may have begun my journey in solitude, but I wouldn't have reached this point without a host of amazing people.

From the authors, who introduced me to the ins and outs of indie publishing before I published my first book to the vast network of authors I have met online along the way, I am so grateful for how generous you have been with your knowledge.

Kirsty McManus and Phyllis Hirsh continue to be the best beta readers an author could wish for.

The many, many couples who chose to hire me to provide harp music at their weddings helped to fire up my imagination about what unplanned surprises could creep into otherwise beautiful, meaningful days. I assure you the worst scenarios I have documented in this series are fictional.

Families are always a great source of inspiration for a writer. Thankfully, my parents and sister taught me about the importance of family in the most loving way.

And finally, my own wedding day was pure bliss if only because I got to marry the most wonderful man. I love you, Kevin!

Novels
The Inked Together Series
Inked Together
Found Together
Back Together
The Empire State of Mind Series
Splitting Heirs
Last Resort
Home Cooking
Keyed Up
Date Bloomer
The Ellen the Harpist Series
Ellen the Harpist
Ellen at Sea
Ellen the Bride
Standalones
A Christmas Rescue
Pet Peeves

Novellas
King & Queen of the Bouncy Castle
King & Queen of the Roller Derby
King & Queen of the Bowling Alley
King & Queen of the Poker Game
King & Queen of the Carnival

Short Stories
Watching the Grass Grow

Wedding Ceremony Music Guide
From Here Comes the Bride to There Go the Grooms

Visit dianemichaelsbooksandharp.com to view her sheet music for harp.

Diane Michaels is a harpist and author. She balances her fondness for ice cream with her enjoyment of working out and walking through the woods. When she is not spying on the world from behind her harp to collect ideas for her next book, she and her husband make up stories and songs about and for their miniature poodle, Lola. Visit dianemichaelsbooksandharp.com to receive a free book.